SURRENDER

A.K. EVANS

Copyright 2019 by A.K. Evans
All rights reserved.

ISBN: 978-1-951441-01-2

No part of this book may be reproduced, distributer, or transmitted in any form or by any means including photocopying, recording, or other electronic or mechanical methods, without the prior written permission of the author except in the case of brief quotations in a book review.

This is a work of fiction. Names, characters, places, and incidents are the product of the author's imagination or are used fictitiously. Any resemblance to actual events, locales, or persons, living or dead, is coincidental.

Cover Artist
cover artwork © Sarah Hansen, Okay Creations
www.okaycreations.com

Editing & Proofreading
Ellie McLove, My Brother's Editor
www.grayinkonline.com

Formatting
Stacey Blake at Champagne Book Design
www.champagnebookdesign.com

SURRENDER

PROLOGUE

Leni

"SO, I'M JUST NOT SURE WHAT I SHOULD DO. I MEAN, WE HAD such a great time last weekend, and he said he'd call, but I haven't heard from him. And now it's Friday," Toni rambled on. She continued fretting over the guy she'd apparently met and hooked up with last weekend who had yet to call her, but I couldn't pay attention to much of what she was saying.

The truth is, Toni and I weren't exactly friends. We both simply worked at the same place and had become acquaintances. I had no problem with Toni's outgoing nature. In fact, I actually enjoyed being around her most days.

But today was not one of those days.

Today, I was merely going through the motions hoping I'd make it out alright.

Because today was the day I was going to be quitting my job.

This job wasn't just any job, though. It was the stepping stone for what was supposed to be my career. My career chosen by my parents. One that meant I was going to end up becoming the CEO of one of the world's largest tech companies one day.

To most, this might have been a dream come true. I guess, in a way, it had been for me, too. I was about a month away from graduating from college with my business degree. An education that had been paid for in full by my parents.

When I first enrolled, I had taken the business classes because that was just the next step. I'd always done what I was told. I didn't necessarily mind it. I mean, I had lived a life most people could only dream about.

My parents were extremely wealthy, and I never wanted for anything. Or, I shouldn't have.

But I did.

I just didn't know what it was until just before I entered my freshman year at college. And by that point, there was no turning back. I was too afraid of how my parents would react to do anything about it.

So, I'd done what was expected of me and worked hard in school. I got good grades, made a handful of friends, and had a paid internship at my parents' company between each semester and over every summer.

Once I entered the spring semester of my senior year, my parents began grooming me for the role they assumed I'd fill the minute I graduated. For the last several weeks I'd been working here as part of a program my school offered to students who were preparing to enter the workforce.

I was fortunate to have a position lined up, which was why I had agonized over this decision for several weeks now. Part of me wondered if I was throwing away a golden opportunity.

Maybe I was. Maybe I'd regret it down the road. But I had a feeling I'd regret not taking a chance on myself even more.

So, today was going to be my last day. The timing would work out perfectly. The program for school was ending. I'd have another month to prepare for finals without the added pressure of work. And then I'd graduate.

But I wouldn't walk into a nice, cushy job.

Nope.

I was going to take a risk.

I was going to go against everything I'd ever done in my life and dive into my true passion.

Yoga.

I'd found it not quite four years ago, and it became a crucial part of my life. It was something I'd needed for a long time that I hadn't realized until I tried it.

At the beginning of my senior year in high school, I started noticing myself grow more anxious. I couldn't pinpoint what was causing my anxiety, and I didn't want to burden my hard-working parents with something that seemed so ridiculous. As the year went on, I did my best to ignore the nerves I was constantly feeling, but it was hard.

Over the summer following my graduation from high school—after I'd already been accepted to college—I discovered a way to cope with what I was feeling.

Yoga had become a saving grace for me. Every day that went by, I found myself craving the movement and needing to practice. So, I did.

And I grew stronger, happier, and calmer. I knew then that I'd found my calling; I just didn't know turning it into a career was an option. And I struggled with disappointing my parents.

But as time went on and I learned and practiced more, I realized I could make a career out of it. I could do something that would make me feel happy and fulfilled all while keeping a roof over my head. I also knew precisely how I'd accomplish it, too.

So, every dollar I made each summer and semester break, I stashed away. In my spare time, I practiced and honed my craft. And I developed a large social media following.

Now, I knew I had the means to make something of myself

in a world I believed I belonged. I just hoped I'd be able to convince my parents of the same.

"Leni?" Toni's voice broke into my thoughts.

I blinked my eyes and shook my head as if physically trying to rid myself of my worries.

"Yeah?"

"So, what do you think I should do?" she asked.

My shoulders fell. I'd missed most of what she'd been talking about, but I had a pretty good idea what she was asking.

I stood, walked toward her, and placed my hand on her shoulder. "Toni, if he doesn't call, he's not worth your time. Forget about him and move on."

"But I like him," she said.

"I understand that, but do you really want to be with someone who doesn't like you back? If he doesn't call you, he's not someone who deserves your time."

"I guess you're right," she murmured.

"Yeah," I replied. "Listen, I'm sorry, but I've got to go. I'll keep my fingers crossed for you, but don't pine over this guy. You deserve better."

"Thanks, Leni."

I smiled at her and gave her a nod. Then, I took in a deep breath and walked through the office down the long narrow hall to where my mother and father had their offices. No sooner did I step into the room outside their private offices when I heard, "Hey, Leni!"

Turning to my left, I saw Connor. He was my father's assistant and had been ever since my father's former assistant retired two years ago. Connor was only three years older than me. He'd graduated from college and started working at my parents' company immediately afterward. Then, when the position was posted within the company for a replacement assistant for my father, Connor applied and got the job.

"Hi, Connor," I returned.

"Excited this is your last day until you graduate?" he asked.

He had no idea how much excitement I felt about not having to come and work here anymore. Of course, as much as I was excited, I was also terrified.

"Yeah," I confirmed. "I actually need to talk to my dad about something. Is he in his office?"

"He was on a call earlier, but he should be free by now. Let me check," Connor started, lifting the phone from the receiver and holding it to his ear. He pressed a button, waited, and finally said, "Hi, Mr. Ford. I've got Leni out here. She's looking to speak with you."

There was silence a moment while my father answered. Connor smiled and ended, "I'll send her in."

Connor hung up, jerked his head toward the door, and declared, "He's all yours."

"Thanks."

With that, I opened the door and walked into my father's office.

The moment I was inside, he stood and rounded his desk to meet me. He gave me a kiss on the cheek. "Hi, princess," he greeted me.

"Hi, Daddy," I returned.

"Everything okay?" he wondered. "Or are you coming in to spend some time with me before you drown yourself in your books for the next month and nobody sees you? I can't believe I almost have a college graduate on my hands. The time just flew by."

"Yeah, it did," I agreed. I failed to make any additional conversation.

As my father walked back around his desk to his chair, he urged, "Have a seat."

I didn't know if it was wise to sit, but since it distracted me for a few seconds, I did.

Once we were both seated across from each other, my father asked, "So, to what do I owe for the pleasure of a meeting from my daughter this afternoon?"

I took in a deep breath, let it out slowly, and stated, "Today is my last day."

My father smiled. "I know. Like I said, I can't believe how fast the time has gone. We're only a month away from your graduation."

This was so incredibly nerve-wracking. "No, Dad. I mean today is my last day ever."

Confusion washed over my father's face. "What are you talking about?"

I nervously bit my lip, contemplating how to tell him. A few seconds later, I blurted, "I've decided I do not want a career at Ford Communications."

His eyes rounded in surprise. "Excuse me?"

Before I had the chance to respond, the door to my father's office opened and in walked my mother.

"Colette, I'm so glad you're here. Leni has some news she wants to share with us," my father stated. I could tell from the tone in his voice he wasn't happy.

My mother didn't miss his mood either, and her eyes shot to mine. "What's going on?" she wondered.

I swallowed hard and explained, "I just told Dad that I've made the choice to not work at Ford Communications following my graduation."

Mom stared at me in shock. "What? What do you mean?"

"I've thought about it for a long time, and it's just not for me," I said.

She took a few steps toward me, sat in the chair next to mine, and reasoned, "But we've got a whole new division set up to launch shortly after you graduate. It'll be your baby, your project. You'll be in charge of the entire platform."

"I know, I know," I assured her. "I'm truly grateful for the opportunities you've both given me. I understand just how lucky I am to have the chance to oversee such a project. But I can't do it. On the bright side, since Connor and I worked together on the project, I know he'll be more than capable of overseeing it."

My father took the opportunity to chime in. "What do you plan to do for work, Leni? I really don't understand where this is coming from," he clipped.

I'd always been a rule follower, so it was no surprise this was coming as a shock to them. I expected they'd have questions, but I hadn't prepared myself for the anger I was currently seeing from my father. Disappointment? Yes. Anger? Not at all.

Even still, I pushed forward. This was my time to stand up for myself and what I wanted to do with my life. If I showed the slightest bit of weakness now, I didn't know what that would say about my ability to make it on my own. And right now, I had something to prove.

"I'm in the process of becoming a certified yoga instructor, and I'm going to open my own studio," I finally stated.

"Oh, not this again," my mother sighed.

My eyes went to her. My parents knew about my love for yoga. When I'd be home on the semester or summer break, I'd practice. They'd see it. Sadly, they didn't share the same joy and excitement over it as I did.

"Leni, yoga is not going to provide you with the life you're accustomed to. If you want to do yoga to stay in shape, that's great. But to think you can have a lucrative career from it is crazy."

Yoga wasn't just about staying in shape. It was so much more than that. Unfortunately, no matter how many times I tried to explain that to my parents, they never really cared to listen.

Trying to explain that to them once again now would have been a foolish waste of time.

"It's not about the money," I insisted.

"Everything is," my father scoffed. "I can't believe you're willing to throw away the opportunity of a lifetime for something so ridiculous."

"Doesn't my happiness matter?" I asked, hoping I could get them to see it from my side.

"Why can't you be happy here?" my mother asked.

"She can," my father insisted. "She'll be far happier here knowing she's got the security of this job. Stretching on a piece of rubber isn't going to make her happy. It's going to make her broke."

I let out a sigh and felt my shoulders fall. I came into my father's office worried that I'd be a disappointment to him. I had no doubt that he was currently seeing me as just that. But I never expected I find myself feeling this disappointed with him.

"So, everything we've done to ensure you have a successful future here was for nothing?" my mother asked.

"I am truly grateful for everything you've both done for me, but I can't move forward in a place where I don't feel fulfilled. I won't be able to do this for the rest of my life. Like I said, I know it's a great opportunity, and I'm thankful. But you'd both be doing yourselves a big disservice by putting me in a position that I don't have the desire to fulfill. Connor does, and I know how hard he'll work at it. That project has huge potential, especially if you have someone who's as passionate about it as I am about yoga leading it."

"You're not coming home to live on my couch after graduation," my father stated. "If you want to change your mind and sign the official papers for the position here before your graduation, we're happy to have you at home with us. But if you choose to pursue this yoga nonsense, you'll need to find other living arrangements."

"Paul," my mother gasped.

"It's not up for debate, Colette," my father clipped.

Wow.

The fact that he put it like that was a bit funny. My parents lived in a mansion. There were more bedrooms in the place than they knew what to do with. Yet, my father acting like me living there, on the couch no less, would be such a huge inconvenience.

Coming into today, I hadn't expected he was going to take things to this level, but I was still prepared for the worst.

Apparently, this situation was the worst thing I could do.

"I understand," I replied, keeping my voice firm. It was a struggle because inside I was dying. And because I knew I wasn't going to last much longer without breaking down, I stood from the chair.

"You have thirty days to change your mind, Leni," my father warned. "Don't make the wrong choice."

I turned and walked to the door. When I got there, I looked back at him and assured him, "I don't need the thirty days. This isn't the place for me."

"Leni—" my mother got out, but I cut her off.

"I am who I am," I told my parents. "You can either love

me and accept me the way I am or not. I know this isn't what you wanted, and I really do appreciate everything you've done, but I need to do what's best for me. I hope you'll find a way to accept my choice."

With that, I opened the door and stepped out. When I closed it behind me, I dropped my head and took a few settling breaths.

"Leni?" Connor's voice interrupted my attempts to calm myself.

I looked at him with tears filling my eyes.

He was instantly bewildered at the sight of my sad face. "Are you okay?" he asked.

As one tear rolled down my cheek, I shook my head. But I didn't answer with words. Instead, I propelled myself forward and out of the office.

It was time for me to start my life.

One month later

"Lennox Ford."

I climbed the stairs at the sound of my name and walked over to the podium. I took my diploma in one hand and shook the college president's hand with the other. When I stood at the middle of the platform just before the stairs, I looked out at the crowd.

It was filled with hundreds of smiling, supportive families.

Not one of those faces belonged to a member of mine.

Even still, I was proud of myself for not surrendering to my parents' threats. In the end, they would be the ones missing out.

CHAPTER 1

Leni

DEEP BREATH IN. HOLD. SIGH IT OUT.
Repeat.

I continued with my ujjayi pranayama, a breathing technique that when translated means to conquer. While it is considered one of the most basic breathing techniques in the yoga world, I almost always worked it into my daily practice. Perhaps it was my need to feel like I was victorious.

An uncertain amount of time passed when I finally opened my eyes, ending my morning meditation.

Feeling refreshed and ready to start my movement practice, which consisted of a series of poses known as asana, I shifted my body from my seated position to standing. I'd barely just gotten myself upright and in tadasana, known as mountain pose, when I heard a loud crash at the front of my yoga studio.

My body jolted at the unwelcome sound and snapped me out of my focused mental state. Feeling the nerves build up inside my belly, I hustled out of the back room and down to the front of my studio. And as I did, I heard the crackling sound. Instinct told me I knew what that sound was, but my fear had me telling myself I was wrong.

My feet carried me those last few steps, and suddenly, I was assaulted by the sight, sound, and smell of my studio being consumed by flames.

I couldn't go out the front door, unless I was prepared to walk through fire.

Unfortunately, there was no other way out. There was a door located at the back of the studio, but I wouldn't be able to get out that way. The space I rented was in an old building. From the day I moved in a few years ago until now, I'd never been able to get the back door unlocked. Talking to my landlord about it had been on my list of things to do at one point, but I had forgotten about it until this very moment.

I backed away from the fire, the heat becoming too intense and the flames engulfing more of the space. I couldn't die in here. I couldn't *burn* to death.

Oh God.

The sound of the fire. I'd never forget the sound.

My nerves had thrown me right into full-blown panic mode.

Breathe.

I had to breathe.

Breathe and move.

That was the only way I'd survive this.

I took in a deep breath, cleared my head, and focused. There was one option to get myself out of here alive. I ran over to the shelf behind my desk and grabbed the largest crystal I had in the bunch. Without any other choice, I hurled the crystal at the large picture window opposite the front door. The fire hadn't quite filled that space, but I knew I didn't have much time.

The heavy crystal connected with the glass, shattering it. Seconds later, not caring that I was barefoot and in only a pair of tiny yoga shorts and a sports bra, I heaved my body out the open space. Pain seared through one of my feet as the shards of glass sliced into the flesh on the ball of my foot.

I ignored the pain as I ran next door to Harvey's Tool Box. Flinging the door open, I shouted, "Harvey!"

Harvey was an older man, easily in his mid-sixties, but he still got around really well. Within seconds of me yelling for him, he appeared in front of me. Before he had the chance to say anything, I yelled, "The building is on fire! You have to get out!"

Urging me out ahead of him, Harvey and I left his store. With the exception of Harvey and me, the only other business open this early was Tasha's Café all the way at the opposite end of the block. The café was just one of two free-standing structures on the block. The other was Petals, the flower shop owned by my friend, Zara.

"Yeah, I'm calling to report a fire." Harvey's voice broke into my thoughts. I looked over to see him on his cell phone.

As he gave specifics of the location of the fire, I stood there and stared as my livelihood went up in flames. Even though I knew the Windsor Fire Department would be here within minutes, I had no doubt there'd be nothing left of my studio. There was already too much damage.

This couldn't be happening.

What was I going to do? Where would I teach?

Though it felt like hours had passed, I knew it hadn't been more than a couple minutes when I heard the sirens. And it wasn't more than a few seconds later when I saw the fleet of trucks race down the street.

From that moment on, a bunch of activity swirled around me. But I couldn't pay attention to any of it because my insides were shaking. Part of it was because it was early in the morning. It might have been late August, but we lived in the mountains. Early morning temperatures were cold and my current outfit was not exactly practical.

But the shaking was mostly due to my panic and anxiety. I could feel it building inside me and knew it was only a matter of time before I completely lost it.

As the firefighters battled the blaze, I stood there and watched, feeling the fear and uncertainty wash over me. My vision grew blurry as tears welled in my eyes.

It was gone.

My studio was gone.

And with it went my safe place.

One of only two constants I had in my life.

I was just barely hanging on to my emotions when the last of the flames had been extinguished. While I stared at the open hole in the space where my studio used to be, I could no longer hold back what I was feeling. The tears flowed from my eyes, and it became harder and harder to breathe.

I couldn't believe it. No matter that it nearly killed me or that I'd watched it all happen, I was still in disbelief.

There was nothing left.

Something washed over me as the reality began to settle in. I had no way to escape it. The thought filled me with dread and panic gripped me.

No longer able to hold myself upright, sobs poured out of me and my legs began to buckle. Before I hit the ground, I felt a pair of strong hands catch me under my arms, lift me to standing again, and pull me into a hug.

I didn't look up. I had no idea who was holding me. All I knew was that I needed the comfort being offered. My body trembled, but within seconds, I felt a warm sweatshirt being draped over my shoulders.

"Shh, you're okay now," a gentle, masculine voice stated.

The voice was so soothing I couldn't help but tilt my head back. My eyes met the scrutiny of the most breathtaking man I'd ever seen. I swallowed hard, still gazing up at him, and saw the warmth in his eyes.

"Are you alright?" he asked.

No.

No, I wasn't.

Not at all.

I couldn't speak, so I simply shook my head.

His arms got a little tighter around me.

"What's your name, sweetheart?" he pressed, asking a question that would force me to speak.

"Lennox. Lennox Ford. But everyone calls me Leni," I managed to get out.

"I'm Holden."

I gave him a nod and remained quiet. Maybe I should have been freaked out by how comforting it felt to be in the arms of a man I didn't know, but for some reason, I wasn't.

"Detective Baines told me you were inside when it happened," he stated.

I didn't know who Detective Baines was, nor did I know how he knew I was inside considering I hadn't spoken with anyone about it.

The confusion must have been written all over my face because Holden explained, "Harvey told him you ran into his place to get him out."

"Can you tell me what happened?" he asked.

I nervously bit my lip, relatively certain I wasn't going to be able to handle recounting this.

"I come in early to get my morning yoga practice in before my classes start," I began. "I'd just finished my meditation and was about to start the movement part of my practice when I heard a loud crash at the front of the studio. Being at the back of the studio, I walked toward the front and found the entire area in front of the door was engulfed in flames. I panicked because that was the only way out."

I stopped and closed my eyes, the sound of the fire flooding my mind.

Shaking my head in an effort to rid myself of the horrible thoughts of what could have happened, I looked back at Holden and continued, "I ran over behind my desk and got my largest, heaviest crystal to throw at the picture window. I didn't have much time or space left because the fire was spreading so quickly, so I ran out the small opening."

Holden glanced over at the sidewalk in front of the where the window used to be before he took a step back from me and looked down. "You're barefoot," he pointed out.

I looked down at my feet and back up at him. "Yeah."

"Are your feet okay?" he asked. There was an edge of concern and worry in his tone.

I had my weight on my right foot, my left barely touching the ground. To answer Holden's question, I simply shook my head.

He shifted his body, slid an arm around my waist at the front of me, and lowered to the ground behind me. In the next second, the fingers of his opposite hand curled around my left ankle and lifted it.

The next thing I knew, I was no longer standing. I was lifted in Holden's arms and he was carrying me out into the street.

Slightly panicked, I looked up at him for an explanation as to what he was doing, but he never looked down at me. The look on his face was one of concentration and determination.

"Her foot's been cut on the glass from the window," he finally declared.

I turned my attention in the direction he was looking and saw he had stopped at the back of an ambulance and was speaking to a medic. After the medic opened the door, Holden immediately stepped inside and settled me on the gurney. I expected him to take off, but he stood there by my side as the paramedic began assessing the state of my foot.

As I sat there, I tried to take some settling breaths. The last thing I needed was to have a complete meltdown right now. I managed to hold it together until, after some time passed, the medic stated, "You're bandaged up right now, but you need to be seen by a doctor to make sure you don't need any stitches. With the location of the cut, you might need to be off it for a few days."

My body tensed.

Oh God.

Oh no.

I couldn't be still.

There was no way.

Holden seemed to have sensed I was struggling because he asked the medic, "Can you give us a minute?"

The paramedic nodded and stepped out.

Holden took my hand in his, crouched down beside me, and wondered, "Is there something I can do to help you?"

Other than his name, I didn't even know who he was.

"Why?" I asked.

"Why what?"

"I don't even know you," I stated the obvious.

He took in a deep breath. "My name is Holden Locke, and I work for a private investigation and security firm called Cunningham Security. I'm part of a team that's helping the Windsor Police Department to investigate the countless fires that have hit the town over the last couple of months. If there's something I can do for you, I will."

He had no idea how what he was offering made me feel. He was the kind of man that would step up and do something for a woman he didn't know when the people who should have been here for me at a time like this wouldn't ever give me a second glance. "That's really kind of you. Thank you."

Holden flashed me a smile. "You didn't answer my question."

Before I could respond, I heard a familiar female voice shout, "Leni!"

My head snapped to the side where I saw Zara standing at the entrance to the back of the ambulance. She was out of breath and looked as devastated as I felt. Wasting no time, she climbed up into the ambulance and pulled me into her arms. Holden slipped his hand out of mine. I missed the connection but embraced my friend instead.

While Zara comforted me, I felt Holden's movement beside us. He placed his hand on the top of my head, held it there a moment, and moved out of the ambulance.

"What happened?" Zara asked once we were alone. "Are you okay?"

Just as I was about to tell her the story, Tasha—the owner of Tasha's Café—had hopped in. She sat down with us, and I told them how my morning had gone. Right when I was in the middle of giving them the details about what happened, Zara's boyfriend stuck his head inside and asked for the keys to her flower shop. She handed them off. Once he was gone, I gave the girls the rest of the story.

Then, I met Detective Baines. He asked me about what happened, and I recounted everything that I'd relayed to Holden already.

"How about I take you to get your foot checked out?" Zara suggested after Detective Baines left the ambulance.

"You don't mind?" I asked.

She shook her head. "Let's just go into the shop first so I can let Pierce know what's happening."

Pierce was Zara's boyfriend. The two of them had gotten together shortly after the fires had started.

"I'll get some food made up for when you two get back," Tasha announced.

"That's perfect. Thanks, Tash."

The girls helped me out of the ambulance so I could hobble over to Zara's shop. Once inside, we found that Pierce was there with Holden and another guy they worked with. My friend explained that she was going to be taking me to have my foot checked out. I did my best to avoid everyone's gaze because I knew if I saw sympathetic looks, I'd lose it.

"Did you find anything on the cameras?" Zara asked.

Pierce answered, "Yeah. We were able to see how it happened. And we've got a lead now that we can follow up on, too. We might have a possible suspect."

"That's great news," Zara exclaimed. "Do you think it's going to amount to anything? Will you find this guy?"

The menacing tone of Holden's voice filled the room. "Oh, we're going to find him," he promised. "And we're getting started on it right now."

I closed my eyes and let out a breath.

Pierce and Zara continued to talk, but I wasn't paying attention. It wasn't until I heard Holden's voice calling my name that I looked up.

"Do you need anything, sweetheart?" His voice was so gentle and full of concern. I was a bit thrown by how he'd gone from being so angry to so sweet in a matter of seconds.

Tears filled my eyes as I stared at him. "I need a place to work," I told him.

I'm sure it came across as urgency because I truly did need to work, but the truth was that I was feeling so overwhelmed by him and everything I'd been through over the last couple hours.

"We'll get you up and running again. It's just going to take a little bit of time," he assured me.

I wasn't sure what he meant when he said 'we'. Even still, I gave him a nod.

At that, Zara took off upstairs. I was still in incredibly tiny shorts, a bra, and Holden's hoodie, so she was going to loan me a pair of sandals and a t-shirt.

Pierce and the other guy walked toward the front door and out of the shop. Holden stayed with me.

I shrugged his sweatshirt off and held it out to him. "Thank you for letting me borrow this," I said.

He put his hand to my wrist and urged it away from him. "Keep it for now. It's cold out. I can grab it from you later."

Later? I thought. *Am I going to see him later?*

"What about you?" I asked.

His eyes roamed briefly over my body. "Leni, I'll be fine. Keep the hoodie."

The sound of his voice saying my name was something I liked a whole lot. And for that reason, I slipped my arms back through the sleeves of the sweatshirt.

Moments later, Zara returned.

When she did, Holden lifted me up in his arms and carried me out to her car. After he closed my door, Zara and I took off.

CHAPTER 2

Leni

"I CAN'T BELIEVE I HAVE TO BE ON CRUTCHES FOR THREE DAYS *and* I have no place to work."

Zara and I returned to her loft a couple hours ago. My landlord had arrived while I was getting my foot checked out. When we got back, I had the chance to chat with him and discuss what the plan was moving forward. If nothing else, I was grateful that he was such a good man. He assured me that he had every intention of getting to work immediately and would do whatever he could to see to it that I wasn't down a long time.

As promised, Tasha had joined us not long afterward with food. The girls couldn't help but notice my despondency.

"It's only three days," Tasha reasoned. "Enjoy the time off to relax."

Easier said than done.

I knew most people might welcome doctor's orders for stillness, but I wasn't one of them. I had to move. I craved it.

It was as crucial to my well-being as eating or breathing.

Not wanting to get my mind swirling with a million other dreadful thoughts, I did my best to perk up. It was mostly useless, though. Zara and Tasha did their best to help distract me from my thoughts but also listened when I felt the need to talk. I didn't share any deep, dark secrets, but I did give them a hint about how bad I was handling the situation. Luckily, Zara's cat, Callie, sensed my mood and offered up some cuddles to comfort me.

"Would it help to stay here with me tonight?" Zara asked.

"No. Thank you, though. I think I need to get back home and try to sort some things out. I have to try to see if I can find a place to work out of in the meantime," I returned. "Thanks for being here for me today."

"If you need anything, don't hesitate to call me," she insisted.

I gave her a nod and moved toward the door when it suddenly hit me. My body froze.

"Is something wrong?" Zara asked.

I dropped my head. "I just realized that my car keys were in the studio. I can't even drive myself home now," I told her.

Before Zara could reply, her phone rang.

She answered and listened to whoever was on the other end.

"We're okay; however, Leni has an issue," she began. "She was going to head home, but she just realized that her car keys were in the studio."

Zara listened for the response I assumed had to be coming from Pierce.

"Really?" she asked.

Silence again.

"Okay. Are you on your way here or are you still working?" she wondered.

A pause before she disconnected.

"If you want me to take you home, I can," she started. "Or if you'd prefer, Holden and Pierce are on their way here now. Holden won't mind giving you a ride either. If you aren't comfortable with that, though, I'm happy to take you."

I couldn't help but smile. It was the first I could remember doing it all day.

"And there's the silver lining," I declared. "My studio burns down, but there's a great-looking guy standing by to help me through my nightmare."

Zara grinned and joked, "He is pretty handsome, isn't he?"

Handsome didn't even come close to it. I let out a little laugh and rolled my eyes.

A few minutes later, Pierce and Holden arrived. They came inside, and Holden quickly noted, using only his eyes and the expression on his face, that I was still wearing his hoodie.

"Are you ready?" he asked.

I gave him a nod, thanked Zara, and said goodbye to both her and Pierce.

After Holden and I were in his truck, I gave him directions to my place. We had been driving in silence for several minutes before he broke it. "What did the doctor say about your foot?"

"I have two stitches in it and need to stay off it for three days."

"That's not too bad," he reasoned.

See?

It was likely that nobody but me would believe it was anything but bad. Instead of refuting his statement, I quietly agreed, "Yeah."

I was staring out the window when Holden asked, "Have you called anyone? Family? Friends? A boyfriend?"

I rolled my head along the headrest to look at him. There was no way I was going to dump that on him. "No. Except for a few people that live close by, most of the friends I have meaningful connections with don't live anywhere near here. And there is no boyfriend."

"Family?" he repeated.

It seemed I wasn't going to get away with not commenting on that.

"There's only one person I can call who'd be interested in hearing what happened to me today, but I'd rather not burden my eighty-seven-year-old grandmother with this right now. Especially because she's probably in the middle of bingo night at the assisted living facility."

I watched as Holden's jaw clenched.

Mere moments passed when I saw his arm reach out toward me and felt his fingers curl around mine to give me a squeeze.

We arrived at my home a few minutes later. Holden came around and helped me out, making sure I was steady on my crutches. Then, he walked beside me to my door.

I lived in a small house. It was a cute cabin on a tiny piece of land, but I loved it. Since I lived alone, I didn't need anything too big.

Simplicity was what I needed, and a small home forced me to have that. It was later in my life when I learned the lesson; however, I was happy I did.

Once we made it to the door, I looked at Holden and sighed, "My keys for my house were on the keyring with my car keys."

"Do you have a spare key anywhere?" he asked.

"Inside."

He jerked his chin down in understanding and instructed, "Hang tight. I'll be right back."

I watched as Holden jogged over to the passenger side of

his truck. He leaned in, grabbed something, and made his way back to me. Then, with expert-like ease, he picked my lock.

My eyes widened as he pushed the door open.

"Wow," I whispered.

Holden put his hand to the small of my back and guided me inside. I hobbled in, flipped on the lights, and turned toward him.

"Thank you for bringing me home. Can I get you anything?"

He shook his head. "It wasn't a problem at all. Unfortunately, as much as I'd love to, I can't stay. I've got to go back to work. But is there anything else I can help you with before I leave?"

Wow. He had to go back to work and I'd already taken up plenty of his time.

"Oh, gosh. No, I'm so sorry."

"Why are you apologizing?" he asked.

"It's just...well, you've been really kind to me. And I feel awful that you've got to go back to work."

He raised his brows in question. "Did you ask to have your business torched today?"

I winced, dropping my head and closing my eyes as I recalled feeling utterly terrified that I wouldn't make it out of there alive.

"Leni..." He trailed off as he took steps closer to me. His hand curled behind my neck, squeezed, and tugged me toward him. My forehead landed on his chest. "I'm sorry. I shouldn't have said it like that," Holden lamented.

I took in a few deep breaths, settled myself, and lifted my gaze to his. "It's okay. I'm okay now."

"Are you sure?"

I nodded.

"Your offer, though," he started. "I can't do it tonight, but maybe after I solve this case we can get together."

Butterflies took flight in my belly. "I'd like that."

"Do you have someone that'll be able to give you a ride if you need one tomorrow?"

"Yeah," I insisted. "I'm good."

Satisfied with my answer, Holden turned and walked back to the door. Once there, he turned and looked back at me. "Take care of yourself, sweetheart."

I didn't have to force the smile I gave him when I replied, "Thanks, Holden."

"Lock up behind me," he ordered.

With that, he left.

After I locked up behind him, I moved through my house on my crutches doing things I needed to do and wanting to keep myself busy. The doctor recommended keeping my foot elevated and I knew the reason why when it started throbbing. I decided to call it a night and climb into bed.

And when I was curled up there, I realized the reason I felt so calm for someone who had experienced what I did that day.

I never gave Holden his sweatshirt back.

His scent was still bringing me comfort.

Holden

Three days had passed since I held her in my arms.

Three days since she nearly lost her life.

And in those three days, I had trouble thinking about anything other than her.

If it weren't for the fact that I needed to focus on the case and find the guy responsible for the fires, I knew that the only thing I would have had on my mind was Leni.

And that worried me.

From the moment I first saw her standing outside her studio, I knew there was something about her. Initially, I thought it was just in my nature to have empathy for someone in a situation like that. But once I got close, I knew it was something so much more. I felt such anger over the case we'd be working on for months. With each new fire that was set, we all grew more and more frustrated, but it was when I saw Leni devastated, injured, trembling, and on the verge of a breakdown when I finally felt myself getting personally involved.

Since that day, I couldn't get the images of her out of my head. Physically, she was beyond beautiful. She wore those tiny shorts that just barely covered her gorgeous ass and showed off her tanned, sculpted legs. Never in my life had I seen such a perfect set of legs on any woman. Her midsection was toned and tight. Her arms were slender with defined, compact muscles that showed her physical strength. Leni's breasts weren't large, but there was still plenty to have fun with.

And for three days all I thought about was having fun with her. Having her golden, sun-kissed body underneath mine. I had no doubts she'd feel fantastic there because the moment I had her in my arms that morning, I realized just how perfect she fit and felt against me.

Add to her beautiful body the sound of her voice and her pretty face and I was finding it difficult to concentrate.

Part of my concern was not only for her physical well-being, but also her emotional state. Seeing her reaction to the fire, knowing she was struggling with not having a place to work, I knew I needed to do something to help her. There was also the fact of her saying she had no family, other than her grandmother, that would care to hear that she'd nearly died. I couldn't even begin to imagine what the story was there. While I had every intention of figuring out what that was, I needed to start with what I knew was going to be the easiest thing to fix for her.

That was precisely the reason I was on my way now to see my brother, Reece. I pulled up outside the gym he owned—a place I'd spent a lot of my time—and parked my truck.

Walking in, I immediately spotted my brother sitting in his office. A familiar face, the staff knew who I was and didn't stop me when I walked right past the check-in desk to Reece's office.

The moment I walked in, he ended the call he was on.

"What's going on, bro? Haven't seen you in here much the last week," he greeted me.

I sat down in the chair opposite his desk and explained, "This fucking case is killing me. We finally have a lead and are following our suspect. I'm just hoping we can wrap it up soon."

Reece gave me a nod. "I heard about the fire from earlier this week on the news. They were saying a couple of businesses were affected."

"Yeah. Three of them. That fire is actually the reason I'm here."

His expression grew curious.

"I need your help."

Reece's brows shot up. "My help? What do you need?" he asked.

Taking in a deep breath, I prepared myself for what I knew was going to come once I explained it. "Of the three businesses, one of them was completely decimated. It was a yoga studio and the owner no longer has any place to work out of until the rebuild is complete. My guess is that it's going to be a few months before she's back up and running there. I was wondering if you'd be able to help her out and give her a place to hold her classes until then."

Reece smirked and asked, "Her?"

"Yes."

"You said she did yoga?"

I felt myself growing impatient. I loved my brother, knew he'd never cross a line like that, but also didn't want to hear him thinking about Leni that way. He hadn't seen her yet. Once he did, it would only get worse.

"Yeah," I answered.

"Is she single?" he pressed.

My eyes narrowed on him. "Don't go there," I warned him.

Reece grinned, sat back in his chair, and clasped his hands in front of him. "This is the best news ever."

"Stop," I ordered.

He shook his head. "No way. For a long time, I wasn't sure you were ever going to go there. Then, you finally did, and I was happy for you. But when she did what she did... well, I've been worried ever since if you would bounce back from it. That one did a number on you."

Reece was talking about my ex-fiancée. Kristen and I were together for two-and-a-half years before I ended things between us. It was an ugly break up, but I was glad it happened when it did. I had fallen for her and was at a point where I thought she was the one. Thankfully, I didn't get tied to her any more than I already had.

Ever since things ended with Kristen, though, I'd been very hesitant to get into another meaningful relationship.

Instead, I went out on dates and hooked up knowing I wasn't interested in making anything serious with anyone.

"This coming from the guy who has yet to settle down," I shot back.

"Yeah, but I've never been interested in settling down. You are… or at least, you were."

Before I could respond, there was a knock at the door. Reece and I turned our attention to the entrance as the door opened. A second later, a woman popped her head in. "Reece," she called before she stepped fully into his office.

"What can I do for you, Tanya?" Reece clipped.

Tanya's eyes darted back and forth between the two of us. "Hi, Holden," she acknowledged me.

"Tanya," I returned.

Her gaze lingered on me a moment, but she snapped her head in my brother's direction when he interjected, "We're in the middle of something, Tanya. Did you have a question?"

"I'm sorry," she started. "I need a spotter and was wondering if you'd be able to give me one."

"I've got a gym full of qualified staff that are paid to do things like that," he noted.

She shifted uncomfortably and pressed, "I know. But you gave me a spot last week. Not only did you do that, but you gave me a few tips. I figured you might be able to help me again."

Reece rolled his eyes. "I helped you last week when I was seriously short-staffed due to one person being on vacation and another being sick. In that case, I pick up the slack. Today, I'm not short-staffed."

Tanya slid her eyes back to mine. Either she didn't make the attempt, or she just wasn't very good at hiding the fact that she was taking me in… again. "Maybe when you're finished in here, you could offer me a spot," she suggested.

"Sorry, Tanya. I don't have much time today."

Disappointment flickered in her face. She gave me a curt nod and moved back to the door. "Right. Thanks anyway."

With that, she left. Once the door closed behind her, I turned my attention back to Reece to find him still staring at the door, shaking his head.

"What was I thinking?" he asked.

I let out a chuckle. "I have no idea."

The truth was, Tanya's interruption that morning was typical. She always found a different reason to do it, but she never missed the opportunity. Any chance she had to put herself in the presence of my brother and me, she did. For years, she made it clear she was interested in me. And while there was no denying that Tanya was a pretty woman, she wasn't my type.

Unfortunately, she refused to accept this. So, when her advances went unacknowledged, she took it to the next level. Tanya set her sights on Reece. My brother wasn't looking for a relationship, but also wasn't going to turn down a willing participant. They hooked up. Reece did it for the fun; Tanya's motives ran much deeper. She was hoping to catch my eye that way.

I'm not sure why she believed sleeping with my brother was the way to get me to notice her, but things certainly didn't work out the way she had hoped. Even still, her failed attempt didn't stop her from continuing to try. I wondered how much longer she'd keep up the charade. Not only were things never going to change for me with regard to her, but Reece was now constantly reminded of how bad of a decision he'd made.

I sighed.

"Okay, moving on from that," I started, pulling his attention back to me. "Do you think you'll be able to help Leni out and give her a place to work from for a few months?"

Reece grinned at me. "Leni," he repeated her name before he dipped his chin and insisted, "Yeah. Just bring her in so I can meet her, and we'll figure out what she needs for time and space."

"Thanks, man. I appreciate it."

"No problem."

I stood from the chair and said, "I'm going to go talk to her about it after I get in a workout. Once I know that she's interested, I'll reach out to you and let you know when I'll be bringing her by. Does that work?"

Reece gave me a nod just as his phone rang.

"I'm out of here," I declared. "Catch you later, Reece."

"Talk to you soon, Holden."

I left my brother's office, got in a quick workout, and went home to shower. Two hours after I'd had my conversation with Reece, I was knocking on Leni's front door.

The second the door opened, I noticed two things. First, Leni was still wearing my sweatshirt. I liked seeing that.

A lot.

Unfortunately, I couldn't focus on that because one look at her face told me something wasn't right. As much relief as I felt finally seeing her again, I was more concerned about why she was so upset.

"Holden," she stated, clearly shocked I was there.

"What's wrong?"

She shook her head. "It's nothing. Really. Please, come on in." After I stepped inside, Leni closed the door behind me and continued, "Is everything okay?"

"Yeah, I wanted to stop by and check on you."

She blinked up at me in surprise. "Oh."

We moved farther into the house and sat down next to each other on the couch.

"How's your foot?" I asked.

"Getting better. Today is the first day I can start putting weight on it, so I'm taking full advantage of that."

"That's good. I'm happy to hear you're on the mend."

We sat in silence for a moment before she snapped herself out of her thoughts and apologized, "I'm so sorry. I'm being rude. Can I offer you something to drink?"

I put my hand on her bare leg. She was wearing a pair of those incredibly small shorts again, only a different color this time. With my hand resting just above her knee, I assured her, "It's fine. I'm not here for that. I actually wanted to see if you had managed to get anything figured out yet with work."

Leni's mood instantly changed. Her body went rigid and her face turned sad. "Not yet. I'm supposed to meet with my landlord tomorrow to get a better idea on when things should be back up and running again, but I know it's going to take a couple months. For the last few days, I've been researching other locations. I've contacted some of them and explained my situation hoping to find a temporary spot to work out of, but I haven't had any luck."

Seeing the sadness in her eyes and hearing the despondency in her voice, I couldn't hold back. I blurted, "I've got a place for you."

Her eyes widened. "What?"

"My younger brother owns a gym," I started. "I went over there this morning and talked to him about your situation. He is more than willing to help you out."

I noticed Leni's breathing pick up. "Are you serious?"

My eyes were locked on the rapid rising and falling of her chest. "Leni?" I called. "Sweetheart, are you okay?"

I directed my gaze to hers and saw the tears welling in her eyes. She rasped, "I could kiss you right now."

That was not the response I was expecting, but it was certainly one I was happy to hear. "I won't stop you if you do," I assured her.

Leni snapped her lips together and seemed to be contemplating whether she really wanted to kiss me. Sadly, she didn't. Instead, she broke down into tears. I wasted no time moving closer to her and pulling her into my arms. As much as I liked having her there, I hated the reason for it.

Leni quickly pulled herself together. Once she did, she lifted her head from my chest and lamented, "I'm sorry. It's just that... well, I've been trying so hard to locate a place that would allow me to work there temporarily. Over the past few days, I've been doing a lot of searching. I found a couple studios and gyms, but when I called them, I didn't have any luck. Even when I explained my situation, nobody was willing to help me out. They either didn't have any available time that I could come in and teach or they wanted someone who was looking for a permanent position."

"Then this will be perfect for you. Reece's gym isn't far from here, and he's more than willing to help you out regardless of what your schedule is."

Leni smiled at me and said, "Thank you, Holden. I don't know why you'd do this for me, but I'm so grateful."

"You're welcome."

A moment of silence stretched between us, our eyes never leaving one another, before I stated, "I have to get going. I need to get to work. But one day, hopefully soon, I'll be able to show you that I'm just the kind of guy who will always help someone in need."

The look in Leni's eyes heated, and it killed me to see that and not do anything about it. Doing my best to ignore that look and the fact that my cock had been hard the minute she opened the door and I saw her wearing those little shorts and my sweatshirt, I stood from the couch and held my hand out to her.

Once Leni placed her hand in mine, she stood and walked with me to the front door. I stopped there and turned around to face her again. "If Monday morning works for you, I'll come by and pick you up to take you over to meet Reece."

She didn't hesitate to respond. "Monday morning is perfect. Thanks again, Holden."

I gave her a nod. "Later, Leni."

With that, I turned and left.

And now that I'd checked on her, confirmed she was okay, and done something to help her get up and running again, I was hoping I could set aside my personal thoughts about her long enough to close this case.

CHAPTER 3

Leni

I WALKED THROUGH THE DOOR OF PETALS AND WAS INSTANTLY assaulted by the beautiful floral scents.

"Hey, Leni," Zara greeted me. "How's it going?"

"It's going," I started. "I just met with my landlord about the studio."

Zara moved out from behind the counter to put the arrangement she'd just finished on the display. "Oh, what did he say? Does he know how long it'll be until it's all rebuilt, and you can start working here again?" she asked.

I shook my head. "Not exactly. He's been doing what he can on his end to have everything ready to go, but he needs to get the approval from the police and fire department first. They need to let him know once they've completed the investigation since it's technically a crime scene. Once he has that, though, he believes it should be three to four months."

Zara frowned. "I feel awful about this, Leni. What are you going to do?"

I felt a smile tugging at my lips just thinking about Holden. Every time I thought about this whole situation, the nerves would start to take over. But then my mind would drift to Holden, and I'd feel just a touch calmer.

"Holden is helping me," I shared.

Zara's eyes narrowed, but a sneaky grin spread on her face at the same time. "What's going on between the two of you?"

I shrugged because I really didn't know. "I'm not sure. He's just been really, really kind to me." I went on and explained how Holden had shown up at my place yesterday with news about his brother's willingness to lend me some space in his gym.

"He likes you," she stated.

I blinked in surprise. "What?"

"I think he likes you," she semi-repeated.

"Do you really believe that?" I asked excitedly. The truth was that I hadn't stopped thinking about Holden since the day of the fire. And thinking of him was the only thing, aside from yoga, that brought me peace over the whole situation I was facing. "Because I can't stop thinking about him."

"Obviously, I can't say for sure, but I think so. Between the way he looked at you the day of the fire and now the fact that he's trying to help you find a place to work, I'd have to say that he's definitely interested."

I let out a sigh of relief. "How well do you know him?" I wondered.

Zara shook her head. "I don't. I probably know less about him than you do. But he works with Pierce. I've met a few of Pierce's co-workers, and they all seem like really great guys. That leads me to believe Holden's a decent guy, too."

"I hope so."

I stayed at the shop and chatted with Zara for another few minutes and promised to let her know once I was set up and teaching again. She had started taking classes a few months ago and was improving with each class.

Before I left, Zara insisted I let her know once everything

was ready to go with the studio because she wanted to help me get it all set up again. I appreciated that a lot and thanked her again for everything she'd done for me already.

On my way home, I thought about all the things I needed to get done. Over the last few days, I put out the word on my social media accounts and my website about the fire. My plan for today was to send out another update and let everyone know that I had a temporary solution in the works and to expect a follow up from me within the next few days. Thankfully, I had very loyal students who I knew would follow me no matter where I was teaching.

So, once I got home, I got to work on sending out that update. Afterward, I got in a workout. As long as I continued to keep my mind occupied and my body moving, I knew I'd get through this. But I wasn't too proud to admit that the one thing I had lurking at the back of my mind was the fact that even though I knew I could do it on my own, I was hoping Holden was going to be there to help me through it.

I was upside down on my mat when a knock came at my door. Carefully, I lowered myself out of my handstand.

Opening the door, I was surprised to see the man I hadn't been able to get out of my head for days staring back at me. "Holden," I began, my surprise and excitement undeniable. As I stepped back and allowed him to come in, I continued, "How are you? Is everything okay?"

Holden stepped inside and replied, "I'm good. Are you busy?"

I closed the door behind him.

"I was just in the middle of a workout. I thought you were coming by on Monday morning. Did I get the day wrong?"

His eyes roamed over my body. I was currently wearing another pair of tiny yoga shorts and sports bra. Holden's voice was husky when he answered, "No, we agreed on Monday. I wanted to come by because I'd like to take you out to lunch to celebrate."

"Celebrate?" I repeated. "Celebrate what?"

A grin formed on his face before he shared, "We found the guy responsible for the fires."

My eyes widened in surprise. "You did?"

He returned a nod.

Relief spread through me. Perhaps I lost everything, including my studio, as a result of what this guy did, but I was relieved to know that he wouldn't be able to ruin someone else's livelihood. To top it off, I was comforted by the fact that he'd be held responsible for what he did to all the businesses in town.

I was so overwhelmed by how I felt hearing the news that my instincts sent me right to Holden. Stepping close, I threw my arms around his shoulders and pressed my body tight to his. "That's such good news," I sighed.

Holden hesitated briefly, but ultimately wrapped his arms around me and returned the hug.

Part of me wondered if I shouldn't have hugged him, but the truth was I'd learned a long time ago that I needed to trust my instincts. I'd had a rough few days since the fire, and the comfort of Holden's embrace was something I needed. Actually, it had been my nights that were the problem. Every time I closed my eyes, I ended up seeing myself back in the studio, feeling trapped. I was having such a hard time falling asleep every night as a result. For that reason, I started doing whatever I could to exhaust myself during the day. When it was time for bed I'd curl up with a journal or a book so I could do something to distract myself from the negative thoughts threatening to send me into a panic.

Holden's arms loosened around me as his hands came to my hips and he took a step back. "We got him last night. So, yeah, it's really good news that we can finally put this case to bed."

I smiled at him and asked, "And now you want to take me out to lunch to celebrate?"

Nodding, he gave my hips a squeeze. "Yeah."

There was no doubt in my mind that I wanted to go with him. I hadn't been able to stop thinking about him since he dropped me off that day. He was incredibly handsome and clearly a very good guy, so I absolutely wanted to get to know him better.

"I'd love to go out with you," I finally replied. "Can you give me some time to get myself ready, though? I need to hop in the shower quick and change my clothes."

"Sure."

"Perfect. Make yourself comfortable. If you want anything to drink, you can raid the fridge. And I've got Netflix if you want some entertainment while you wait. I'll be back in a few minutes. Is casual okay?"

"Yeah. Lunch is casual. If this goes well and we decide we want to do it again, I'll take you out for a fancy dinner. Then you can get all dolled up."

That worked for me.

I took off toward my bedroom and quickly stripped out of my clothes. Once I was in the shower, I thought about the fact that I was naked in my house taking a shower while a man I barely knew waited for me. Perhaps I should have been more cautious, but there was something about Holden that told me I had nothing to worry about. I didn't know if it was the fact that he worked for a well-known and highly-respected private investigation company in town or if it was the fact that he had contacted his brother to help me out until my studio was rebuilt. It could have been something else entirely. The one thing I knew for sure was that there was something innately good about him that seemed to always set me at ease.

After rinsing myself off in the shower, I hopped out and threw on a pair of jeans, a t-shirt, and sneakers. I made my hair look decent and put just a touch of makeup on. I was never one to wear a lot of makeup, but a little bit of under-eye concealer went a long way. That, some mascara, and a tinted lip balm did the trick.

"Okay, I'm ready," I declared as I walked back out to meet Holden. "Thanks for waiting for me."

I watched as he stood, walked over toward me, and allowed his eyes to roam over my face and hair. He gave me a genuine smile before he took my hand in his and moved toward the door.

Twenty minutes later, we were seated in a quiet, little café. We'd just placed our orders when Holden looked at me across the table curiously.

"What's the look for?" I asked.

He had sat back in his chair, crossed his arms over his chest, and shared, "I'm just sitting here trying to figure out how you got stitches in your foot only a few days ago and when I arrived at your place today you were in the middle of a workout."

I cocked an eyebrow and teased, "I'm a very determined girl."

Holden leaned forward, resting his elbows on the table.

His voice was low when he admitted, "I think I already figured that out."

Wow.

Okay.

Maybe I needed to rethink this.

Here I thought I was being fun and playful and could throw Holden off balance. Apparently, he was unaffected and could give back just as good as he got.

Backing off a bit, I explained, "As you know, the doctor told me I could start bearing weight after three days. I've been doing that slowly because I want to make sure I don't tear open the stitches. But I need to move and be active, so I've been spending a lot of time in my workouts on my hands."

His brows pulled together. "I'm sorry?"

"Well, as I'm sure you've already put together, yoga is a huge part of my life. Since I've been taking it easy on my foot, I've just shifted my practice for the last few days to inversions and arm balances. It's basically been a lot of variations on handstands. I've spent a ton of time upside down the last few days."

"I've got to see this sometime," he stressed, clearly intrigued.

I reached into my purse and pulled out the new phone I picked up the day after the fire since my old one had been destroyed.

"I have a couple videos on my phone of my practice the last two days if you want to see," I stated, pulling them up and holding it out to him.

Holden took the phone and watched with avid fascination. Occasionally, his eyes would widen in shock. I sat there and loved seeing every little nuance in his face when he saw me do something he found impressive.

When he returned my phone to me, he said, "That's amazing. I never would have imagined you had all that in you."

I let out a laugh and admitted, "I like to keep people guessing."

"Well, you've certainly got me wondering what else you're capable of."

There wasn't an ounce of humor in his tone. Evidently, Holden had no problem indicating he was thinking about naughty things.

I pressed my lips together. I'd been thinking about naughty things with Holden, too. Every night when I struggled to find sleep while curled up in his sweatshirt, I'd recall how it felt to be held in his arms. And then I'd think about how much I wanted to be curled up with him.

It had been a long time since I'd been with anyone. Up until the fire, I'd found that I'd finally gotten myself to a place where I was beginning to feel confident again. I had started accepting myself with my faults. Even now that the fire happened, I knew what I needed to do to keep myself grounded. But the peace I was feeling before the fire no longer remained.

Our food arrived, snapping me out of my thoughts. It also got me off the hook since I wasn't quite sure how to respond to Holden's words.

Once our waiter left, Holden switched topics.

"So, did you end up meeting with your landlord yesterday?"

"Yeah," I confirmed. "He's waiting to get the green light from the police, but once he does, he thinks it's going to be three to four months until I'm back in there again."

Holden nodded and guessed, "Well, my thought is he'll be getting the go-ahead soon considering we caught the guy with all the evidence on him."

"Really? Were you there?" I asked before I put a bite of food in my mouth.

He grinned and confirmed, "Yeah."

Holden then went on to tell me the story of how it all happened. Apparently, the suspect had been an upstanding member of the community until something happened with his business that led him to go off the deep end and seek revenge. When Holden caught him, he was about to set fire to a crowded tavern.

"I'm so happy you and your team were able to close this case. Do you get a lot of cases like this?"

"No," he started. "Most of the work we do is routine P.I. stuff like insurance fraud or infidelity cases. We occasionally have those missing persons' cases, but big stuff like this is rare. Usually, we only have this when the Windsor Police Department needs our help."

I nodded my understanding and pushed for more. "So, it's not usually dangerous then?"

Holden's head dropped to one side as he scrunched up his face. "I'm not sure how to answer that. I'm not going to lie and say it doesn't get dangerous at times. The majority of our cases are pretty standard, routine cases. But the ones that aren't can be very dangerous. It just really depends."

I didn't know why, but it bothered me to think that Holden worked on cases that were dangerous enough where he could get hurt.

As if sensing my concern, he stated, "I'm good at what I do, Leni. I've been doing this a long time and I enjoy it. It challenges my mind a lot, which is something I need."

That I could understand. I didn't even need any additional explanation. It seemed that Holden craved the mental challenge he got from his job at least as much as I craved the physical challenge I got from mine. And I knew what not having that would mean.

"So, now you need to tell me a little bit about this yoga," he requested.

"What do you want to know?"

"Anything. Have you always done it?"

I took in a deep breath and set my fork down. We were sharing things, getting to know one another. He'd shared a little about his work, so it was only fair I did the same.

"Movement has always been a huge part of my life. But it wasn't until I was in my first year of college that I realized just how much I enjoyed yoga. I started then and never stopped."

Holden's face grew curious. "What did you go to school for?" he asked.

After taking a sip of water, I replied, "I got a degree in business, but opening my own yoga studio wasn't the reason behind the degree. Had I realized going in that I wasn't ever planning to become a CEO of a major corporation like both of my parents, I'd have never enrolled."

His brows shot up. "Both of your parents are CEOs?"

I nodded slowly. "Yep. And they are both so disappointed in me for choosing such a lowly career. They hate what I do and want nothing to do with it or me."

Holden's jaw got hard. "Are you serious? You don't talk to them?"

Shaking my head, I answered, "I wish I were joking. And no, we don't talk."

"That's ridiculous," he muttered. "What about your siblings?"

I hesitated a moment, swallowing down the pain I felt at his question. "It's just me."

"Leni…" He trailed off.

I didn't want to get myself all worked up, especially in front of Holden, so I just shook my head and waved my hand in front of me. "It's fine. Really. They are who they are just as I am who I am. I've spent a lot of time worrying about what I can do, but if they don't want to support me, there's nothing I can do to change it. Life is what it is. I have to accept it and move on."

"How do you do that?" he wondered.

I shrugged. "I don't have much choice. If I let it consume my mind, it just brings me heartache. They're adults. I'm an adult. I have to look out for my well-being now and yoga gives me what I need. If my parents can't accept me as I am because they had some idea about who I was going to grow up to be, that's their loss. It's really a shame because in a way, I've still managed to become a CEO. My company just isn't nearly as large as theirs."

"What company do they work for?"

"Ford Communications," I stated.

Holden blinked at me. "Wait. Ford is your last name. Are you telling me that your parents own one of the biggest tech companies in the world?"

"That's what I'm saying," I sighed.

"Wow," he muttered, sitting back in his seat.

"Yeah, it's especially sad considering they refuse to listen to me tell them anything about my career."

Holden just stared at me in silence for a while. He eventually reached across the table, wrapped his fingers around my hand, and gave me a squeeze. "I'm sorry."

While I appreciated his show of support for me, there really wasn't anything either of us could do about my parents. So, we moved on.

The two of us sat and visited for a bit while we finished our lunch. Holden was great company. There was never a lack of conversation, and I truly felt like he was interested in getting to know me. He was a breath of fresh air and something I hadn't seen in a really long time.

After he paid the bill, he asked, "Are you ready to get out of here?"

"Yeah."

With that, Holden took me home.

When we arrived back at my house, I started to feel my mood shift. I was enjoying spending time with him and really didn't want him to leave.

I needed to be brave.

We were at my front door, and I had just slipped the key in the lock when I turned to him. "Would you like to come in for a little while?" I asked, my intentions clear.

Holden hesitated. "I probably shouldn't," he decided.

My shoulders fell, and I knew my disappointment was written all over my face. I gave myself a moment to accept his lack of interest in me. Just as I was about to open my door and let myself in so Holden could leave, he muttered, "Fuck."

My eyes shot to his. "What's wrong?"

Holden shook his head. "I guess I could come in for a little bit."

Smiling up at him, I didn't even look at the key in the lock as I opened the door for us. Holden pressed a hand to the small of my back and guided me in.

No sooner did we make it into the living room when I turned and pressed my palms to his chest. I slid them up and around his neck while I shifted the rest of my body close to his. Holden's arms instantly went around me.

The two of us stood there looking into each other's eyes for the longest time without saying anything. It felt like we were in slow motion until, suddenly, we weren't.

His earlier hesitation seemed to have worked itself out because the next thing I knew, Holden's mouth came crashing down on mine.

At first, it was just a firm kiss, his lips pressed against mine. Then, his tongue came, seeking more. I immediately opened for him, allowing him to deepen the kiss. As he did that, his arms tightened around me.

In that moment, I was all about feeling. I felt everything from the heat and possessiveness of his kiss to the warmth and security in his embrace.

Every inch of his body was solid.

Holden squeezed me just a tad tighter as he effortlessly lifted me off the ground and fell to his back on the couch. Once my body was on his, Holden's hands began to roam. They were in my hair, down my sides, and over my ass. I loved every second of it. Eventually, his hands came up and framed my face as he disconnected our kiss. His eyes searched my face, one of his thumbs stroking along my cheek.

"Holden," I whispered.

No sooner did I get the word out when he lifted his head and buried his face in my neck. His lips trailed kisses along the skin of my throat.

I was so turned on and needed more, so I rolled my hips over his erection. Holden groaned as his lips worked up to my jaw and toward my mouth. I sought more friction between my legs, my breathing becoming ragged.

"Please," I whimpered.

Holden sat up. "Leni, we have to stop."

"What?" I gasped. "Why?"

My bottom was resting in Holden's lap, my legs straddling his hips. We were both seriously turned on, so I was shocked by his hesitation.

"Sweetheart, I want nothing more than what you're offering right now, but I wasn't expecting this with you. I'm not exactly looking to get into something serious, so I'm not sure we should take this step."

No.

Was this his way of telling me he didn't want to be with me? The way he kissed me and touched me combined with the way he'd been treating me had me believing that he was seriously interested in me.

The thought that I'd read it all wrong was humiliating.

Feeling slightly embarrassed but very turned on, I groaned and dropped my forehead to Holden's shoulder. "I'm beginning to wonder if I'm experiencing some bad karma," I mumbled.

Holden's hands, which had been resting on my hip and thigh, tightened. "Why?" he asked.

"Clearly this is not turning out to be my week. First, my yoga studio is torched. Then, I'm hobbled up with stitches in my foot. Now, this."

I lifted my head and started to shift my body off his, but Holden stopped my movements.

When my eyes came to his, he hesitated briefly before he declared, "It's not bad karma, Leni. I'll give you the first one as being devastating, but the second two are not. Your foot needing stitches is far better than what could have happened that day. And this, right now, is far from being a bad thing."

I stared at him and harrumphed. "Maybe not for you. It's been a long time, Holden. So, getting all worked up and being turned down... well, I'm sorry, but that's all bad."

Holden didn't respond.

I stupidly continued, "I've got enough on my plate right now. This doesn't have to be a serious thing."

His eyes held mine a long time in silence. I was just about to speak again when he said, "I should probably get going now."

And just like that, the wind was out of my sails. We had just gotten back to my place, and now he was leaving. Only minutes after I spilled my guts and offered myself up to him with no strings attached.

When will you learn, Leni?

Holden must have noticed my despondency because he quickly added, "I'll be by tomorrow morning to take you over to the gym."

"Okay," I murmured, not looking at him.

"Leni?" he called.

I lifted my gaze to his.

"I'll see you tomorrow."

His voice was firm but strangely pained.

As much as I wished he'd explain the reason his voice sounded like that, I didn't press for it. Instead, I lifted myself from his lap and stood. Holden did the same, held my eyes a moment, and moved to the front door.

Then, I stood in the open doorway and watched as Holden walked away. The entire time I kept mentally kicking myself for, once again, never being able to hold back.

CHAPTER 4

Leni

IT WAS JUST AFTER SEVEN IN THE MORNING. SINCE I HAD A COUPLE hours until Holden was going to be coming to pick me up and take me to his brother's gym, I decided to get on my mat.

There was no denying I needed it. After we came back to my place yesterday following the celebratory lunch, I hadn't expected what happened. And considering Holden held back from taking things between us much beyond kissing, I'd been wound up ever since.

Being as forward as I was with him, I never imagined he would have turned me down. Now, I felt a bit foolish.

And that bothered me. Because feeling foolish wasn't me. Not since before I decided to take charge of my life and follow my heart have I really questioned the choices I made. I considered myself to be a smart woman, and I trusted myself to make good decisions.

But Holden's response to me yesterday had me wondering if I'd made a bad first impression. I really liked him; the kindness and concern he showed me meant everything. So, the thought that I'd scared him off had me feeling anxious most of the night. Between that and the trouble I was still having finding sleep since the day of the fire, the time on my mat this morning was more of a necessity than anything else.

I wasn't even ten minutes into my practice when there was a knock at my door. Much to my surprise, I opened the door and found him standing on the other side.

Shocked, I whispered, "Holden."

Without a word, he stepped inside, shut the door behind him, and pulled me close.

"I couldn't sleep at all last night," he started, lowering his mouth to mine. His lips were just barely brushing up against mine when he added, "The biggest mistake I made was walking out of here yesterday without giving in to what we both wanted."

I swallowed hard.

"Kiss me, Leni."

So I did. The second our tongues touched, my knees got weak. Holden held on to me with one arm around my waist and the other in my hair at the back of my head. We kissed a long time before I pulled my mouth from his and stepped out of his hold. Slipping my fingers through his, I led him to my bedroom.

No sooner did we step inside the room when Holden lifted me in his arms and tossed me onto the bed. I'd barely managed to process how easily he'd done that when I felt his fingers curl around my ankles so he could slide me close to the edge of the bed near him. Once I was where he wanted me, his fingers went to the waistband of my shorts. He yanked them and my thong down my legs.

Then, he disappeared.

Holden was no longer towering over me.

No.

He had dropped to his knees, thrown my legs over his shoulders, and put his mouth on me.

The second his tongue slid through me, he groaned.

I couldn't think. It had been so long since I'd had sex and even longer since I had someone's mouth between my legs, so I wasn't going to stop Holden, who clearly was a very talented man with his mouth.

One of my hands drove into his hair, the other stayed pressed against my nearly-naked chest. Holden's fingers were pressing into the flesh at my hips, the strength of his hold unwavering.

I loved it. That feeling of someone not wanting to let go of me. Even if only for this moment. And considering how I felt after Holden left yesterday, it was a relief to know that perhaps I hadn't scared him off by being open and honest with him.

His mouth had been expertly working me between my legs, quickly building me to an orgasm, when he was no longer there. Suddenly, he was standing again, tearing his shirt over his head.

I watched with avid fascination as the lean but muscular frame of his upper body flexed with his movements. He was stunning.

Holden snapped me out of my ogling when he ordered, "Top off, sweetheart."

Quickly, without taking my eyes off him, I removed my bra. Holden lost the rest of his clothes and rolled a condom over his impressive length before he joined me in the bed.

"These legs," he muttered as he trailed kisses from just above my knee up my thigh.

His hand was still gripping my thigh when he made it to my hip. Once he reached my breasts, he urged my legs around his back. I barely had the chance to let them settle there before he was filling me. Holden planted himself to the root and held himself there a moment, staring down at me.

I held his molten gaze briefly but couldn't stand it any longer. He'd managed to work me up so close to climax when he had his mouth on me that feeling him inside me not moving was pure torture. "Holden, please move," I pleaded.

Holden moved.

And everything about his movements were desperate, hungry, and carnal.

I loved it.

I loved the feel of his skin next to mine. I loved the look on his face. I especially loved the way it felt to have him moving between my legs.

"Holden," I breathed.

"Fuck, Leni," he groaned.

"I'm going to come," I warned.

Holden dropped his mouth to mine and kissed me as my orgasm tore through me. He didn't stop kissing or driving his hips in until, long after I found mine, he found his release and buried his face in my neck. I felt his weight for a fleeting moment before he lifted himself, touched his lips to mine, and declared, "Be right back."

Then, I watched as Holden walked from my bed to the bathroom. His backside was just as fine.

When Holden returned, he lowered his body to the bed, draped an arm across my abdomen, and propped his head up in his hand.

With his eyes on mine, I blurted, "That was nice."

He returned a grin and advised, "Yeah. So much so that I've decided we're not done yet."

A shiver ran through me. More of Holden Locke would not be a bad thing.

"Are you okay with that?" he asked.

I gave him a nod.

"Are you okay with that now?"

My eyes widened. *"Now?* Is that... can you... really?" I finally got out.

Holden let out a chuckle and clarified, "We'll need to work up to it, but yeah."

My gaze shot down his body. I licked my lips, shifted, and pressed a hand to his shoulder. Holden fell to his back, allowing me to start my exploration of his body. My kisses started at his lips, but gradually moved down. I took my time covering the solid planes of his chest and the dips and valleys outlining the muscles of his abdomen. By the time I reached his cock, it was semi-erect. I wrapped my hand around the base, heard him groan, and covered him with my mouth.

It took a little bit of time, but I eventually managed to work Holden up to round two.

And he expended effort to make sure the second round was just as phenomenal as the first.

A couple hours after Holden had arrived at my house that morning, the two of us were walking into his brother's gym. It was one of the few that I hadn't tried calling. As we walked through the front door and past the reception desk, Holden received nods of acknowledgment. Apparently, he was a familiar face.

He guided me to a room. The door was closed, but it was surrounded by windowed walls that offered a view into the office. With his hand at the small of my back, Holden reached around me with his opposite hand and opened the door. He ushered me in ahead of him.

We stepped inside, and I immediately noticed Holden's brother closely resembled him. The only difference was that Reece had a bit of an edge to his look. His hair was a bit longer, curling out from underneath the beanie he was wearing. He had tattoos up both arms instead of just one like Holden, and he had a pierced lip.

Reece stood and walked out from behind his desk with a huge grin on his face. Considering his resemblance to Holden, I already thought he was handsome. But once he smiled, I realized that he'd definitely make someone very happy one day. I didn't think it'd be possible for a woman to have that smile directed at her and not want to see that for the rest of her life.

"You must be Leni," he greeted me, extending his hand. "I'm Reece."

I shook his hand and returned, "Yes. It's so nice to meet you, Reece. Thank you for your willingness to help me out."

"Initially, I was doing it as a favor to my brother. But I've got to be honest... if you walked in here and asked me yourself, I'd have done it."

My eyes nearly popped out of my head at how forward he was. I didn't know what to say to that.

"Cool it, Reece," Holden warned. From the moment I met him, I found Holden's voice to be comforting and gentle. Except for the time he spoke in Zara's flower shop the day of the fire, he'd always been calm and collected. Now, it was the exact opposite.

Hearing it, I was concerned about where this was headed. I quickly turned to Holden, pressed my palm to his chest, and insisted, "It's okay. I wasn't offended."

Holden placed his hand over mine, squeezed, and maintained, "It's not okay with me. I don't need my brother hitting on my woman."

"Your woman?" Reece questioned him. "I didn't realize things had gotten serious between the two of you."

"They weren't before; they are now. So, like I said, cool it."

Reece turned his attention to me and said, "My apologies, Leni. Please, have a seat."

Holden and I moved to the chairs while Reece rounded his desk. Once we were seated, Reece dove right in.

"So, I don't know much other than the fact that Holden told me you need a place to work out of for a little while and why that is. What does your schedule look like?"

I didn't want to overstep or take advantage of Reece's kindness, so I explained, "I'd be happy to have a place to teach a few classes a week. I don't want to disrupt your schedule here or take up space that's being used for another class already. Aside from maybe being able to teach a couple classes every week, I really just need a place that's quiet where I can film."

Reece's brows drew together as Holden chimed in, "Film?"

Nodding, I look to him and clarified, "Yes. As much as I love teaching in-person classes, there just isn't enough money in it to cover my expenses. I can make some decent money doing yoga teacher trainings, which I've done once at my studio, but I don't schedule those consecutively or consistently. So, in order to have a steady income, I teach yoga online."

"Really?" he asked, seeming genuinely surprised.

"Yeah. I film my sessions and upload them to my channel. It's basically like having an online studio. Anyone who wants to take classes with me can do so by simply paying a low monthly subscription fee. And they can do it from anywhere in the world. I would have done it from my house, but I don't have a ton of room there. Besides, there's a certain look I've managed to maintain for my online students. I really don't want to ruin that."

Holden eyed me curiously. Whatever he was thinking he did not share. I didn't get to ask him either because Reece spoke.

"That's incredible. How much time do you need for filming and in-person classes? I've got the space, so I'm not worried about that."

"Like I said, I don't want to disrupt your schedule. I'll work with whatever you have available. If it's possible, I'd love to be able to teach classes here at least two nights a week and maybe two classes that are earlier in the day. I'll make whatever days and times you have work, though. I can do the filming whenever it's convenient for you. My online classes range from fifteen minutes in length all the way up to an hour and a half long. If you give me a specific set of days to work with, I'll adjust my filming schedule accordingly."

Reece glanced at Holden, smirked, and looked back at me. "I can give you as much time as you'd need for the filming. I've got a room that's not large enough to hold group classes in but should be perfect for your solo gig. With the in-person classes, I can accommodate more than you're asking for. My space for that is only being used half of the time that the gym is open."

I blinked in surprise. "Are you serious?"

Reece nodded. "If you can give me your email, I'll send over the current schedule for the classes that are being held. If there are any times when it's not being utilized and we're open, feel free to book it."

My hands squeezed the tops of my thighs. I was so excited and relieved. For the minor inconvenience of needing to drive a touch beyond what I did to get to my studio, it seemed as though I'd be able to continue working just as I did before the fire.

"Thank you," I exclaimed. "I really appreciate this so much." I turned my attention to Holden and whispered, "Thank you so much for setting this up for me."

His face softened as he reached over and gave my hand a squeeze. "You're welcome, sweetheart."

With that, I gave Reece my email address so he could send me the schedule. I also gave him my phone number in case he needed to contact me for any reason. Once I'd done that, Holden and I moved to the door to leave. I thanked Reece again before we left his office.

As we walked by the reception desk, one of the staff called out, "Catch ya later, Holden!"

"Later," he returned.

A few steps beyond the reception desk, I heard, "Lennox?"

Stunned, I stopped and turned around. That's when I let out a squeal of delight. "Connor?"

He blinked in surprise, opened his arms, and moved toward me. Connor pulled me into a hug, giving me a squeeze before he stepped back and put his hands on my shoulders. "Oh my God. I can't believe it's you. How are you?"

"I'm doing great," I replied. "And you?"

With a smile plastered on his face, he shrugged and stated, "Can't complain."

Just then, I heard Holden clear his throat beside me. Connor's hands fell from my shoulders as he looked over at the man standing beside me.

"Oh, gosh. I'm so rude. Connor, this is Holden. Holden, this is Connor."

Connor held his hand out to Holden. "It's nice to meet you, man. I've seen you around here before. You're Reece's brother, right?"

Holden shook Connor's hand and gave him a nod.

"So, are you still working over at—" I got out before he cut me off.

"Yeah, but it was touch and go there for a while."

I raised my brows in silent question. "Oh no. What happened?"

"Truthfully?" he challenged.

I nodded.

"You."

"Me?" I asked.

"They never expected you wouldn't be coming there after you graduated. They had to fill the spot they were planning for you, and they weren't happy about it."

"Okay, but the natural choice would have been you, considering we'd had numerous discussions about you joining the team I was putting together," I insisted. "You were going to be second in command for that department. They gave you what was supposed to be my job, didn't they?"

Connor shook his head. "No. They did a full round of extensive interviews for the position. I'm still your father's right-hand man, though."

"Really?" I asked, feeling slightly bewildered. "Wow. I never would have imagined they'd go through that when they knew you and I already had discussions about the plans for that project."

He brushed it off and asserted, "Things have settled. It's all good now. So, what about you? What are you doing here?"

I took in a deep breath and blew it out. "I'm sure you've heard about the serial arsonist," I sighed.

With a dip of his chin, Connor indicated he had.

"Well, it was my yoga studio that went up in flames less than a week ago," I began. "Since it's going to be a bit before all the damage is repaired, Holden talked to Reece about giving me a space to work."

"Wow, Leni, I'm so sorry to hear about your studio. That's awful. I'm happy to see you, but that's just horrible news."

"Thanks."

Connor simply stared at me in silence. It was then I decided to add, "Anyway, we should really get going, but I guess I'll be seeing you around if you come here often."

"Definitely."

With that, Holden linked his fingers with mine and led us out of the gym.

CHAPTER 5

Holden

FUCK.

It had already started.

And I had no idea how I was going to stop it.

She said she could do casual. She offered it with no strings. I was stupid enough to believe *I* could actually do it. The thing is that I was smarter than this. I knew better. And now I'd started something that I shouldn't have ever started.

On the surface, it might not have seemed any different from any other hookup I'd had over the years. But deep down, I knew it was different. I knew *she* was different.

Once. Only once before did I do something so stupid and not listen to instincts. And that one time ended in a world of hurt.

Now I was doing it again, and if I didn't find a way to keep it in check, this wouldn't end well.

When I finally dragged myself out of bed this morning following my sleepless night, I knew I'd be asking for trouble if I went to Leni.

But I couldn't stay away.

I couldn't walk away from her and what she was offering. Even though I managed to walk away before we took that step yesterday, something brought me back to her this morning. Now I was regretting it.

Not regretting her. No. She was incredible.

I simply regretted starting something with her that I knew I wasn't going to be able to keep casual. I knew it before I had her, and now I had not a single doubt.

For crying out loud, I was already calling her my woman. I felt it necessary to stake my claim to her in front of both Reece and Connor.

If I couldn't find a way to come up with a plan and do it soon, I had a feeling we were both going to wind up heartbroken. Even if for very different reasons.

Leni and I left Reece's gym and had just arrived back at her place. For most of the ride back, she reiterated just how thankful she was to me and Reece for helping her and giving her a place to work. If she wasn't talking, though, I wasn't either.

I tried to spend the remainder of the ride to her house getting my emotions in check. I wasn't sure I was successful in doing that when we finally pulled up outside because I found myself wanting to know more about the guy she seemed to be so friendly with just before we left the gym.

Leni looked over at me and asked, "I know it's getting late, but neither of us have had any breakfast. I'd love to express my gratitude for what you've done for me by making you something to eat this morning. Do you have time to come in or do you need to get to work?"

Considering how things changed between us this morning, and the fact that I was still curious about Connor, I said, "Since I knew I was taking you to the gym this morning, I planned to only work half a day today. I've got time to come in if that's what you want."

I didn't know who I was trying to kid. It was what I wanted. I liked being around Leni. She had this natural ability to let it all hang out and didn't seem to have any reservations about it, either. In that sense, she was the opposite of me.

After shooting a gorgeous smile my way, she confirmed, "That's what I want."

Five minutes later, I was watching Leni as she moved around her kitchen. She had pulled out a pan, toast, fruit, and eggs. Seeing that, a thought popped into my mind.

"Is it safe to assume from the eggs that you're not vegan?" I asked.

Leni stopped moving, looked up, and worried, "Are you?"

I shook my head. "No. My meal from yesterday's lunch should have given that away, but I thought that was a big thing with people who practice yoga. Since you had a salad yesterday, I just assumed."

She got back to what she was doing and stated, "It is. Some people are very strict about it and go so far as to say that anyone who isn't vegan isn't a real yogi." Leni shrugged her shoulders and continued, "Over the years, my diet has definitely changed. I'm mindful of the food that I do consume, but I have to do what's best for my body. So, while I don't eat a lot of meat, including zero red meat, I do still have eggs and fish. Either way and despite what some might say, my choice of food doesn't make me any less qualified to do what I do."

"Do you get a lot of grief about it?"

She sighed. "Occasionally people will offer unsolicited advice. I'm in the public eye because of the way I've built my business and what I do, so I guess it's par for the course. I do my best to shrug off the nasty comments. I do that mostly because for every bad comment I receive, there are hundreds of positive ones. And ultimately, I've dealt with worse than faceless people on the internet."

There was my perfect opportunity to learn more about her. I took my shot.

"Does that worse have anything to do with your family?" I asked, hoping I wasn't opening old wounds for her.

"Mostly," she answered. "But there really isn't much more beyond what I already told you about them. I probably shouldn't have brought it up, but it's the best comparison I can make."

"What do you mean?"

She held up an egg and asked, "Scrambled okay?"

I nodded.

Leni started cracking eggs into a bowl. As she did that, she returned to our conversation. "All I meant by what I was saying was that at a certain point, I started making my own decisions about how I'd live my life. I stopped allowing my parents to choose what they believed was best for me. If I'm not going to listen to them, I'm certainly not about to let the opinions of a few people who've never met me influence how I live my life."

While she poured the whisked eggs into the frying pan, I pressed for more, but did it discreetly. "Based on your conversation with that guy today, it certainly seems like your parents were torn up about your choice."

Leni pursed her lips and narrowed her eyes, clearly thinking about it. Eventually, she shared, "Yeah, they were only torn up about the fact that they could no longer control me. They didn't once take into consideration how torn up I was when I walked up to get my diploma and looked out into a crowd of people to see nobody there for me."

Suddenly, I felt angry on Leni's behalf. Part of me

wondered how someone could do that to their child, while the other part of me understood what Leni felt all too well.

"I'm sorry to hear that," I lamented. "You mentioned your grandmother before. She didn't go?"

Leni shook her head. "No. But it's not because she didn't want to. Getting around is not easy for her. She's in an assisted living facility and doesn't drive. Even though she moves slow, she would have loved to have been there if she had someone that was willing to take her. Given that my father is her only child, and he had no plans of making an appearance, there was no way she was going to be able to get there. I hate that she had to miss it because I know she's proud of me."

I couldn't say I fully understood why her parents were acting that way. It wasn't like Leni hadn't made something of herself. She'd simply chosen a career path that was unconventional in their minds. It hardly seemed like a good reason to abandon your child. Then again, I wasn't sure there ever really was a good reason.

Not wanting to continue talking about something that didn't really have good memories for her, I decided to shift topics a bit.

"So, what is it that made you start doing yoga?"

"I started right after I graduated high school. It helped me to deal with a lot of the anxiety I felt over the pressure I was feeling from my parents," she started. "Don't get me wrong. My parents gave me every opportunity. I'm thankful for what they did, but it all came with strings attached. They were happy to give what they did when it meant they could control me. After I'd done yoga for a few months, I started feeling like I was in control of myself again. My practice became a huge part of my life. It called to me in a way I'd never felt anything before then."

That made sense. I understood a lot of what she said and

surmised, "And that's when you decided it was what you were meant to do with your life."

As she nodded, she started serving the eggs on each plate. At the same time, the toast had finished in the toaster. She grabbed it, put it on the plates, and confirmed, "Yeah." I was surprised there was no bitterness in her tone or her expression. I didn't expect she'd feel that over her choice, but I believed it would have been understandable that she might have some lingering over the situation with her parents.

"How long ago did you graduate?" I asked.

Leni laughed as she held a plate out to me and retorted, "Is this your way of trying to figure out how old I am?"

"No," I instantly replied, taking the plate from her. "But I guess it's information I should know about you, don't you think?"

Her eyes studied me. I presumed she was trying to decide whether I was telling the truth. Ultimately, she answered, "I graduated six years ago. I'm twenty-seven. You?"

"I'm thirty-two."

She smiled and moved out from behind the counter toward the table. I followed her and sat down across from her.

"What about you?" Leni asked.

"What about me?"

"Your family," she clarified. "Do you have any other siblings?"

I wasn't sure I was prepared to go down this road. Even still, I replied, "Nope. Just Reece. But he was more than enough. Trust me."

Leni let out a laugh. "It's great that you two are so close."

Nodding, I agreed, "Yeah. As much of a pain in the ass as he can be sometimes, I don't know where I'd be without him."

"I'm happy you have that," she said. "How about your parents? Are you just as close with them?"

At her question, I stopped eating and took in a deep breath. As I slowly let it out, Leni interrupted, "I'm sorry. Don't answer that."

"What?"

She offered a sweet smile and explained, "When I'm feeling anxious about something, I do the same thing you just did. I breathe. Big, deep inhales. Slow exhales. I guess I'm assuming that whatever the story behind that breathing you just did means that there's something painful for you. You don't have to share if you're uncomfortable."

Leni surprised me. Her parents were fools because she was clearly a wise woman. "I appreciate that, Leni. But you shared with me, so I think it's only fair I do the same with you."

Her face lit up at that. Seeing it, I secretly wished I'd listened to her and not shared. Because that look on her face could ruin me. After we had whatever this was between us this morning, I had to find a way to take a step back. I'd give what I could this morning and then I'd shut it down. It was best for both of us. I ultimately continued, "My mother left when Reece and I were kids. We haven't seen her since. My father is now remarried, and my brother and I are very close with our dad, Troy, and our stepmom, Eva."

Leni nodded in understanding but didn't press me for more information. I had a feeling she knew this really wasn't something I was interested in discussing. Sadly, I knew that if she'd asked, I might have shared. But because she didn't, I took the easy way out and never offered more.

Leni

With my eyes closed, my arm reached out to my nightstand. My hand felt around in the dark for my phone because it was ringing. When I found it, I opened only one eye to see the name on the display.

Holden.

Suddenly feeling very awake given this was the first he'd reached out to me in the last three days, I answered.

"Hello," I rasped.

There was silence a moment before I heard him say, "You're asleep."

"Yeah," I confirmed. "Is everything okay?"

Hesitation again before Holden shared, "I just pulled into your driveway."

He was here.

I sat up in the bed, swung my legs over to the side, and asked, "You're here?"

As I walked toward my front door, I blinked my eyes several times.

"I didn't think you'd be sleeping already," he replied. "I wondered if you'd want some company for a little while."

I couldn't help but wonder what else he thought I would be doing at this hour besides sleeping. Even still, I definitely wanted his company.

Before I could respond to him, I made it to the door. I unlocked it and opened it. Holden was standing in the driveway, leaning against the front passenger side fender of his car.

With the phone up to his ear, Holden's eyes ran over my body. It was then I realized I was standing there in the cool night air wearing nothing but a pair of panties and a camisole.

Holden's gaze locked on mine as he pulled his phone away from the side of his head, tapped on the screen, and slid it into his pocket. Then, he walked toward me. And he walked like a man who had a purpose. I had a feeling it would be mere moments before he showed me what that purpose was.

I never took my eyes off him.

When he made it to within a few feet of where I was standing in the doorway, I expected him to stop. But he didn't.

Holden continued to close the distance between us until I was close enough to touch. While the pace of his strides had slowed, the movement of his upper body did not.

He reached out, slid one arm around my waist, and lifted. His other hand settled on my bottom as my legs instinctively wrapped around his body, my ankles crossing behind his back. My arms went over his shoulders and my hands drove into his hair.

Holden had just barely stepped inside the door when I vaguely heard him kick it shut behind him. I couldn't focus on that, though. Because the next thing I knew, Holden's mouth was on mine, and he was walking us through my home.

In any other case, I probably would have marveled at the fact that he seemed to have no problem navigating my house in the dark while he carried and kissed me. But right now, I couldn't.

All I could think about was the fact that he was here. I hadn't seen or spoken to him in days, and I had missed him terribly. So, all of my focus was on him.

Holden's mouth disconnected from mine when he lowered me to my back in my bed. His body was bent over mine, and he began peppering kisses along my collarbone and down my chest.

He yanked my top down, exposing one of my breasts, and instantly captured my nipple in his mouth. My legs, which were still wrapped around him, tightened. I lifted my hips from the bed, seeking pressure between my legs. Holden knew what I wanted—what I needed—and gave it to me. He pressed his weight right where I needed it, causing me to roll my hips.

"Holden," I breathed.

"Can't stay away," he groaned as he moved his mouth to my opposite breast, his hand toying with the other. Coming from him, I didn't know what that meant, and it made me wonder if he was trying to stay away.

I wasn't able to concentrate on that, though. Because when it seemed he could no longer take the torture he was delivering to both of us, Holden lifted his body from mine, whipped his shirt over his head, and moved his hands to the waistband of his jeans.

"Panties, sweetheart," he said, his voice husky.

Understanding what he wanted, my hands flew to my hips and slid under the fabric of my panties. I lifted, pushed them down my legs, and tossed them aside. Then, I removed my camisole, belatedly noticing Holden rolling a condom on.

Holden lightly touched his fingers to my thigh and jerked his head up. "Scoot back," he instructed.

I shifted my body back in the bed as he put a knee to the mattress and joined me.

Seconds later, Holden slid inside. I had him back.

And I loved it.

He cradled my hips in his hands, his grip firm and strong. Then, our bodies and my bedroom illuminated by the full moon outside my window, Holden watched.

He watched as he tortured me.

There was no other way to describe it. Holden was torturing me.

Slowly.

He pulled back as torturously slow as his languid thrust in had been.

And while I might have wanted to complain, I couldn't. Because I was too focused on the intensity of gaze. It was directed right at the spot where our bodies were connected. From the little I could see in the moonlight, I knew I liked what I saw on his face too much to say something that would stop him from looking at me that way.

So, I didn't.

I simply allowed myself to enjoy it. To enjoy him and what he was giving me.

And there was a lot to enjoy.

It seemed to take Holden no time at all to build me up and have me on the verge of an orgasm. While I knew part of that had to do with the fact that it had been a few days since we'd last done this, I had no doubt that it had more to do with the fact that it was him.

Clutching the blanket beneath me in my hands, I moaned.

I moaned and gasped and panted.

Finally, pleasure tore through my body. Holden continued to move slow, helping me ride the wave until it left me.

Then, his hands left my hips, as he lowered himself down to one elbow, and brought a hand back to grip my thigh. He clutched it tight against his waist as he relentlessly powered into me, quick and unyielding.

I held on. Craving it. Needing it. Loving it.

And then it happened. The quickening of the sound of his grunts and groans filled the air around us. Moments later,

I watched, completely captivated, as Holden found his release and came apart above me.

When he finished, though, everything changed.

Holden didn't collapse on top of my body.

He simply shifted, pressed a kiss to the side of my face, and pulled out. Getting to his feet beside the bed, he walked to the bathroom without a word. And when he came back in the bedroom afterward, he still didn't say anything.

I was in the bed, still on top of the blankets, right where he left me. Holden joined me in the bed and immediately began kissing down my body until his mouth was between my legs.

The worry I had felt when he walked away without a word had vanished. I figured more of this with him was a good thing. So, I enjoyed it. Holden took care of me with his mouth before he initiated round two, this one with me on top.

But it was after that when I'd realized that I hadn't been wrong.

Because when we finished, Holden moved to the bathroom again to dispose of the condom. And when he returned this time, he bent down and grabbed his clothes off the floor.

I stayed there in bed, too shocked to speak or move, and watched him.

Once he had all his clothes back on, he put a hand on the bed beside my shoulder and leaned down. His face was inches from mine when he shared, "I had a good time, sweetheart. I'll call you."

It took everything in me not to react the way I felt.

Instead, I managed to swallow it down and give him a quick nod.

Then, Holden touched his lips to mine and said, "I'll take care of locking up."

"Okay," I rasped, feeling uncertainty like never before. "Night, Leni."

With that, Holden stood and walked out.

I felt the sheet slide down my back and immediately knew what was happening.

It was Sunday evening, or perhaps very early Monday morning.

I hadn't seen or spoken to Holden since he left my house on Thursday night. But he called me earlier in the day today. He asked if I was going to be around tonight.

I was and told him so.

Of course, I had assumed he meant earlier in the evening.

Apparently, I had misunderstood.

Because while I had gone through the trouble of making sure I had food prepared for dinner, Holden never showed. Instead, I waited around for a man who let me down by never showing.

Or, at least, not until now.

Whatever time it was.

I was on my side, facing away from Holden. The sheet had stopped moving once it reached the top of my ass. Then, I felt the feather-light touch of Holden's fingers on the exposed skin of my back since I was only in a pair of panties and a bralette. I hated that my body reacted to his gentle touch the way that it did.

Especially when he'd let me down the way he did.

His fingertips traced down my back and over my hip before I felt his lips on the curve of my waist. He was, slowly but surely, undoing me. Holden's mouth and hands on my body were too much to resist, and I had to admit that I wouldn't be able to deny myself.

I shifted to my back. My eyes fluttered open, and once again, I could see the outline of Holden's body in the moonlight. It seemed he had stripped out of his clothes before he started touching me.

His palm was pressed flat to my abdomen as he moved his face up toward mine. He kissed my chest, my neck, my jaw, and my lips. Then, he pulled back just a touch and whispered a pained, "Missed you, sweetheart."

Hearing that, hearing those words, my sadness was gone. I slid my fingers up into his hair and surrendered to him. I kissed him back, hoping I was communicating that I felt the same.

I didn't know for sure how long it was, but it felt like hours had passed as Holden and I connected with one another again. Though, our connection was only ever physical.

Because once again, when he was finished with me, Holden kissed me, told me he'd lock up, and left.

And I was stuck wondering if I hadn't made a mistake that was going to leave me heartbroken.

CHAPTER 6

Holden

I HAD NO IDEA WHAT I WAS DOING, BUT I KNEW I NEEDED TO figure it out quick.

Because I wasn't sure how much longer I could continue to do what I was doing. Not only was I struggling with it, I also knew it wasn't fair to do to Leni.

The problem was that I had no clue how to stop.

It was late Monday morning, and I was struggling focus on work. Unfortunately, I felt like an ass. Mere hours ago, for the second time, I'd done something I had told myself I wasn't going to do again.

I made that promise to myself days ago when I walked out of Leni's place the first time I'd gone to her in the middle of the night. Just getting myself to go there had been difficult.

The truth was, when I left Leni's place following the trip to Reece's gym, I decided I was going to do what I needed to do to make sure I didn't fall into a place I feared. I had no problem admitting to myself that I was afraid. Afraid of what a woman, especially a woman like Leni, could do to me.

But as the days passed, I couldn't stay away. Leni's pull was far too strong, and after three days, I finally gave in. I did it only after I promised myself that I was going to stick to her original offer. This didn't have to be a serious thing.

I could do that.

I'd done not serious with other women before her. I could do it again.

I was such a fool.

A fool to believe I could keep it as just that. Even if I thought I could, I knew I should have stopped myself after the first night. Seeing that look on her face when she realized I wasn't staying. When she realized I was giving her precisely what she told me we could have between us.

It was like taking a knife to the gut.

Somehow, I powered through the feeling it gave me to see that look and left her alone in her bed.

Apparently, I was a glutton for punishment because I ended up going back for more only hours ago. I shouldn't have done it. Twice now I walked out of her place, leaving her sad and alone. Leni did her best to hide it, but I could see it.

This was killing her at least as much as it was killing me.

Now, I was sitting here at work and couldn't think about anything but her. The way she looked, the way she moved, the way she laughed. Most of all, the way she made me feel.

Before I could become even more consumed with her, my attention was directed to the sound of my co-worker's voice.

"I know that look," Tyson said, as he sat down in the chair on the opposite side of my desk.

I shot him a look that I hope communicated I was not in any mood to be hassled.

Tyson ignored my look and continued, "You've got trouble with a woman."

I let out a grunt. He had no idea.

"Now's not a good time, Tyson," I returned, refusing to acknowledge his words.

"Sure it is," he insisted. "You've got problems; I'm here to help. Is this about the yoga girl from the fire?"

Tyson was relentless, and I knew he'd persist. It would just be better to treat it like a bandage. Rip it off and get it over with.

"Her name is Leni," I corrected him.

My friend and co-worker sat back in his seat and said, "Now we're getting somewhere. Tell me about Leni."

Shaking my head, I replied, "There's nothing to tell."

Tyson's brows shot up. "Nothing?" he repeated.

"Nope."

"You do realize that I'm in the same profession as you, right?"

I let out a sigh. "What are you looking for me to say?" I asked.

He threw his arms out to the side and answered, "I don't know. But it's clear there's something on your mind with her. Enough that I can see it and know that it's not nothing. What's going on with the two of you?"

I didn't respond. Mostly because I still didn't know what to say, but also partly because I believed that if I talked about her, I'd share the things that drew me to her.

Tyson pressed, "Locke, brother, it doesn't take a genius to see that there's something different happening here. You come here and do what you've got to do, but there's some distraction. The last time you were distracted, it was for all the wrong reasons. I'd like to think the thing that's taking your attention now is for the right reasons."

It was no surprise Tyson recalled my reaction to the end

of my engagement. It took me some time to get past what happened with my ex, and all my co-workers knew how hard it had been. It was like I was my dad when he had been trying to cope with the fact that my mom left us.

I shrugged and explained, "Maybe Leni could be, but I'm not going to find out. I've decided I need to put a stop to what was developing between us. I thought we could do the no-strings thing, but we can't."

He cocked an eyebrow. "You can't?"

"No. Not only because I can tell it's not sitting well with her, but also because I'm struggling to keep it just that."

"I'm failing to see the problem," Tyson started. "If neither of you is okay with it, why not just make it the real deal? You know you can have a relationship?"

No.

There was no way.

I didn't think I'd be able to survive a relationship with Leni. I had no doubts that when it was good, it would be really good. But if it went south, there wasn't a question in my mind that I'd be miserable.

"I'm not cut out for that," I responded.

"That's a lie," Tyson shot back.

I stared at him in shock. He clearly had no issue calling me out. "Excuse me?"

Shaking his head, Tyson assured me, "You are. It's like you forget that we all got to see you in a serious relationship before, Holden. That girl was your top priority. Maybe she wasn't the right one for you... that doesn't mean nobody will be. You'd be foolish not to try."

I didn't tell him that I thought I'd be foolish to pursue this further with Leni. As much as I wanted her, I simply couldn't pretend. I didn't think it was fair to her that I pretended I could get somewhere with her that I had serious doubts about my ability to do. And even though my recent behavior might not have shown otherwise, I truly did not want to hurt her.

"I just can't do it," I told him. "I'm not sure I can take the risk."

The silence stretched between the two of us. Tyson shifted in the chair and stood in front of my desk.

"I think you're making a mistake," Tyson started. "Obviously, you didn't ask my opinion, and I can't force you to do anything that you don't want to do. But I think you've made it clear that this is something you want. If you don't go after what you want with her, you're going to regret it."

With that, Tyson turned and walked out.

Five minutes later, I was still sitting there wondering if my friend was right. Would I regret not taking a chance on Leni?

Ten minutes after that, all I'd come up with is that I knew I wanted that sweet reward. Sadly, nobody could give me the guarantees I needed.

Leni

Distraction.

That's precisely what I needed.

I didn't want to focus on the anxiety I was feeling about the unknown. Over the years, I'd learned to let a lot of things go and how to effectively do it, but I only managed to accomplish that by shifting my mindset through my yoga practice.

And since I had a lot of uncertainty swirling in my mind

surrounding my relationship with Holden, I needed today's yoga class more than ever.

It had been a week and a half since Holden brought me in to meet his brother. Reece and I worked out a schedule that was accommodating to the both of us. In fact, I was able to add a few extra classes that I hadn't originally planned on because Reece had the time and space for it.

Unfortunately, it had also been a week and a half since Holden and I had a real conversation. I had seen him twice since the morning I made him breakfast as a show of thanks, but we didn't really do much talking in those instances.

I didn't mind the physical closeness with Holden. How could I? He was a marvelous lover, but I was disappointed that the conversation between us seemed to have stopped. The first night I was too stunned by the change in him to say anything about it. When I thought about it after the fact, I wasn't sure it would have mattered anyway.

In the moment that night, it didn't even really cross my mind. I hadn't seen it for what it was until after he left. Truthfully, I had just really enjoyed being with him again for the first time in a few days.

But when it happened again on Sunday and he left shortly after two rounds of lovemaking, giving me more of the same emotional distance, I started to wonder if this was what things would always be like between us.

Now, it was Wednesday. I hadn't heard from him since he left on Sunday, and I needed something to distract me from the constant state of panic I'd been in when I realized the mess I'd gotten myself into.

So, today's yoga class was going to be all about busting anxiety. I planned to put in a lot of balance postures into the class today because I found that the concentration necessary to keep my body balanced always took my mind off anything that was worrying me.

There was still a good ten minutes left before class was set to start. Some familiar faces had already started arriving. It wasn't uncommon for me to see that happen. Oftentimes, some of my students would come in and practice a little meditation before class began. Typically, I'd just give them a smile and a nod when they came in and let them do their thing until I was ready to start class.

When the door opened again, I shifted my gaze to it and saw Zara walking in. There was another woman walking in with her that I hadn't seen in quite some time. I didn't know they knew each other but was happy to see them both.

Zara was with one of my friends from school, Lexi Townsend. In fact, Lexi and I had gone to high school together, and halfway through my freshman year in college, she had transferred to my school.

"Hey, ladies. I didn't know you two knew each other," I greeted them.

Zara nodded as Lexi smiled. Zara shared, "Yeah, I actually met Lexi recently. I'm going to be doing the flowers for her upcoming wedding. Her fiancé works at Cunningham Security, too. She heard about your studio, and we both wanted to show our support by coming to your first class since the fire."

"I'm warning you now that I know nothing about yoga, so you can't laugh at me," Lexi stated. "I figured I'd do something to tone up a bit before the wedding."

I stood from where I was seated on my mat at the front of the class and promised, "I would never laugh at you. This specific class is meant for all levels, so I'll be sure to offer plenty of modifications for everything. Congratulations on the engagement. I'm so excited you both came."

"To be honest," Zara started. "I've been craving taking a class, so I'm so excited Holden managed to get something figured out to help you out until the studio is rebuilt. I almost wonder how I survived before I found yoga."

I let out a laugh. "You and me both, girl," I agreed with her.

"Speaking of Holden…" Lexi trailed off.

I rolled my eyes and reasoned, "So this isn't really about toning up before the wedding, is it?"

She shrugged, feigning innocence. "Of course, it is. I can't help that there's other juicy gossip happening at the same time."

"I'll believe that when you show up to a few more classes," I teased her.

"I will. Just wait and see."

"So, how are things going with you and Holden?" Zara asked, redirecting us.

I sighed, unsure of what to say. As I told Holden weeks ago, I didn't have friends that lived close by. The people that I did have meaningful friendships with I'd met through yoga. When I went to a couple different yoga teacher trainings over the last few years, I'd fostered connections with some incredible people. But none of them lived in Wyoming. Sure, Zara was one of my students, but she was also a friend and fellow business owner. While I'd originally reached out to Lexi years ago when I first opened my studio, we hadn't kept in touch.

Standing in front of them now, I realized it wouldn't hurt to forge a deeper bond with these two women.

"I honestly don't know," I admitted. "I think I made a huge mistake."

"What did you do?" Zara asked.

"I lied to him."

After noting the shock on their faces, I felt my mood plummet.

"What do you mean you lied?" Lexi asked. "About what?"

Keeping my voice low, I explained, "I told him I could do a no-strings-attached affair. It had been a while since I'd been with anyone. He's so good-looking, a magnificent kisser, and there was clearly a mutual attraction between us. At first, Holden didn't take me up on it. But less than twelve hours later he showed up on my doorstep telling me that he shouldn't have denied us both from having what we wanted."

Zara and Lexi were staring at me intently when Zara concluded, "And now that you've both given in to the physical attraction, you want something more. Am I right?"

I nodded.

"Okay, but why is that a problem?" Lexi wondered. "Did he say that he didn't want anything more than just a physical relationship?"

"The whole reason I offered a no-strings-attached affair was because he had said he wasn't looking for anything serious. When he showed up and gave in to the attraction between us, he didn't exactly hold back in any other realm. I mean, he told his brother I was his woman for crying out loud."

Understandable confusion washed over their faces.

"So, did something happen that's making you think there's a problem between the two of you?"

I glanced at the clock, realized I still had another four minutes before class was going to start, so I went on and shared, "Everything was mostly great up through last Monday. Then, he called and showed up on Thursday night. It was all about phenomenal sex. I was fine with that. But after he left, I didn't hear from him until Sunday when it happened again. I haven't heard from him since. I guess I didn't really think it through enough, and I'm mostly to blame for my current predicament. I mean, I told the guy we could do this without strings."

Zara contemplated my words a moment before she asked, "Did you ever actually believe you could do this without strings?"

I let out a laugh and admitted, "I think I tried to convince myself of it in the heat of the moment."

"Yikes," Lexi murmured.

"Have you tried talking to him?" Zara asked.

"That's the thing," I started. "When we first started this thing between us, he talked with me. I'll admit he wasn't very forthcoming with a lot of stuff, but there was at least something. Now, there's almost nothing. I've tried talking to him. Not about this, but just in general. He seems happy enough to listen to me talk, but the minute I ask anything about him, he basically shuts down."

"Keep trying to talk to him," Lexi ordered. "Whatever you've got to do to make it happen, just do it. Withhold sex if necessary. But no matter what, if this isn't working for you, you have to let him know."

I knew that. I really did. I just found myself so consumed by him when he was around that I seemed to lose my ability to function properly.

"I have to," I said. "I just need to figure out how to do it."

"If you need to talk about it, Leni, just call. You have my number," Zara offered.

"Mine too," Lexi added.

"Thanks, girls. I really appreciate it," I returned. "We should probably get ready for class."

With that, I returned to my space on my mat while Lexi and Zara joined the rest of the students on their individual mats.

Sitting there, I looked out at my class and realized it was larger than normal. While most of the faces were familiar ones of students who'd been coming to my studio previously, there were quite a lot of unfamiliar faces. It was then I gathered that Reece must have done some work to get me a few new students.

At that knowledge, I took in a deep breath, smiled, and said softly, "Hi, yogis. Thank you so much for coming to class today. I'm seeing a lot of familiar faces here. I appreciate all of my regulars for making the journey here to practice with me. And to all the new students here today, I hope you enjoy this class, so I can see you more often. Today, we're going to be focusing on reducing our stress and anxiety through a bunch of balance postures and breathing techniques. Before we begin, I want you to take a moment to think about what it is that you need to let go of, whether in the physical or emotional sense and let that sit in your mind for just a moment. I'm going to ask you to acknowledge whatever it is that's taking up space in your mind or your heart, and by the end of class, our goal will be to let it go."

With that, I instructed my class to sit in half-lotus pose, close their eyes, and just focus on their breath. Then, right along with my students, I spent the next hour working through what was causing me stress, finding a way to shift my mindset, and focusing on something else.

While I always found the time on my mat to be productive, today's class was, by far, the most therapeutic session I'd had in a long time.

Following class, I took some time to talk with my students. Many of my regulars from my studio extended their heartfelt sympathy at the loss I'd suffered, offering a helping hand if needed when the time to rebuild arrived. I also introduced myself to some of the new faces, hoping I was cultivating what would end up being a long-standing relationship.

When the room had emptied out, I started rolling up my mat and the few extras I'd brought along for those who might not have had one. That's when I heard the door open.

I turned around and saw Reece walking toward me.

"I was just thinking about you," I stated.

He cocked an eyebrow and smirked at me. "Is that so? I'll take that as a compliment."

I laughed and corrected him, "Not like that. What I meant to say was that I was thinking that I wanted to come out and talk to you before I left here tonight."

"The fact that I'm on your mind at all is enough for me," he teased. "So, how did it go here? Was everything alright?"

"It was," I started. "I was actually really surprised to see so many new faces here tonight. Am I to assume that you went above and beyond to promote this class for me?"

Reece grinned. "Well, it was for me, too," he assured me. "The truth is, we've had quite a few requests over the years for yoga classes, but I've had a heck of a time trying to find someone to teach them regularly. I figured if I could bring in some additional business, we could work out an arrangement that'll have you staying on, even if only on a part-time basis, after you're back up and running in your studio."

I had to admit that it was a reasonable request and a great idea. It would have been foolish of me to turn down the opportunity to reach more students. If they came to Reece's gym out of convenience but enjoyed the classes enough, they might be willing to travel to my studio on the days I didn't come to the gym. Plus, I felt compelled to show my appreciation for him helping me out.

"I think that's an excellent idea," I said. "I'm more than willing to talk about that when the time comes. I'd love to try to find something that works for both of us."

Reece's eyes widened in surprise. "Really? I was mostly joking, but I'm definitely excited that you're willing to consider it. And so many of my regulars here will love it."

"Yeah, I was being serious," I insisted.

"That's great news, Leni. This is certainly one of those times where I'm grateful my brother decided to not stand in his own way," Reece declared.

I didn't know what Reece meant by that, but at the mention of Holden, I felt myself starting to unravel a bit. Suddenly, I was worried that I was going to undermine all of the hard work I'd just put in to release the tension that had built up in my body over the situation with Holden.

"Or maybe he hasn't gotten out of his own way," Reece stated, snapping me out of it.

I shook the negative thoughts from my mind. And even though I heard what he said, I still asked, "What?"

"The look on your face tells me that Holden's struggling with you."

My eyebrows shot up. "Struggling with me?" I asked, even though I thought that was the understatement of the century.

Reece just nodded.

Perhaps I should have let it go at that, but I couldn't help myself. I really liked Holden. I enjoyed being around him, I loved the compassion and care he'd shown me from the moment we met, and I thought we had been doing a great job of building something until he suddenly stopped.

So, while I didn't want to do something that could upset Holden if he found out I was discussing what we had between us with his brother, I decided to tread carefully. Ever since I made a choice to follow my heart years ago, I'd found it very difficult to hold myself back from anything. Finding out what might have caused the change in Holden was one of those things I couldn't just overlook.

"Is there something I should know?" I asked cautiously.

Reece shook his head and sighed, "Nothing that I can share."

A wave of disappointment flooded me as my gaze dropped to the ground. Reece must have noticed because he urged, "Be patient with him."

I brought my eyes to his, and he continued, "I know he feels something strong for you, Leni. But he's got stuff that holds him back from going after what he might really want. Give him time. I promise that once he finds a way to surrender to how he feels, you won't regret giving him that chance."

I swallowed hard at the news Reece just delivered. The thought of Holden battling something and not knowing how to get past it hurt my heart. With the newly imparted wisdom Reece shared, I decided I could be patient. I'd give Holden more time. My hope was that he wouldn't need much, though.

"Thanks, Reece," I finally said softly.

He gave me a quick nod and replied, "It's getting late, so I'll let you get going. I just wanted to come in and check to see that everything ran smoothly with your first class here."

"It did. Thank you again."

"No problem."

With that, Reece walked out. I stared at myself in the mirror, took a few deep breaths, and walked out a couple minutes after he did.

Just as I was approaching the front reception desk, I saw Connor walking away from it.

"Hey, Connor," I greeted him.

He smiled at me and recalled, "Hi, Leni. Oh, that's right. I remember seeing the advertisement about the yoga class. Tonight was your first one, wasn't it?"

I nodded. "What are you doing here? I thought you came here in the morning."

Connor shook his head. "I only do that on days when I know your father is coming into the office later or if he's out of town. I still work the same number of hours but prefer to get a workout in early and stay later at the office when it's possible. Sometimes after a long day at Ford Communications, it can be difficult to find the motivation to come and get a workout in."

"I bet," I returned. "I commend you on making it here tonight, then."

Connor laughed. "No doubt it was a struggle."

"Well, I won't delay you in making it happen any longer."

He shook his head. "It's okay. I miss being able to talk to you. I'm so glad I bumped into you here last week. It was nice to reconnect after all these years."

"Absolutely. It's great seeing you again, too. But I've got to get out of here now. I still have some work I have to get done tonight before I get to bed. I'm sure I'll see you again soon now that my classes have started."

"Sounds great. Take care, Leni."

"You too, Connor."

At that, I continued my journey to the front door. On the way there, I looked over toward Reece's office. His eyes met mine, and it seemed like he was in deep thought. I offered a friendly wave.

Reece smiled and jerked his chin up.

Then, I stepped outside and took in a deep breath of the fresh air. When I let it out, I did so with a renewed sense of faith in my non-relationship with Holden.

We were new.

Maybe he just needed some time.

CHAPTER 7

Leni

I HAD BEEN INCREDIBLY CLOSE TO GIVING UP HOPE.

Currently, it was early Friday evening, and it wasn't until a few hours ago that I received a call from Holden. Seeing his number come up on my phone's display left me feeling a bit shocked.

Wednesday evening, following my first class at his brother's gym, I sent Holden a text.

I just taught my first yoga class tonight, and it was a huge success.

It was nearly thirty minutes later when he responded.

Congratulations! Happy to hear everything is working out there for you.

Me: None of it would have happened if it hadn't been for you. I feel like I can't thank you enough.

Holden never responded to my last text.

Even though I tried to keep Reece's words in the back of my mind, the emotional distance between Holden and I really started to feel unsettling.

But today, he called.

I got to hear his voice for the first time in nearly a week. A voice that brought me so much comfort on one of the worst days of my life. I loved getting that voice back.

After I answered his call, he asked, "Hey, sweetheart. How was your week?"

It took me a minute to pull myself together, but I eventually found my words. "Good. Great, actually. I've been keeping myself busy with classes, filming, and editing. How about you? Did you have a good week?"

"Mostly," he replied. "It's been pretty quiet at work. I've been working on a few smaller cases, so nothing too crazy."

"That's good."

I wasn't sure what else to say. I hadn't been expecting his call, and I was still feeling a bit caught off guard. Thankfully, I didn't have to try too hard to think of something to talk about because Holden said, "I was hoping you were free tonight. Do you have any plans?"

I was torn. I really, really wanted to see him. But part of me wondered if I could handle having him come over simply to connect physically.

"I don't have any plans," I answered.

A moment of hesitation before he responded, "Well, if you're up to it, I'd like to take you out tonight."

Butterflies fluttered in my belly. Holden wanted to go on a date.

"Really?" I asked.

I realized after I said it that it probably wasn't the best thing to say. If he was, as Reece put it, struggling with this thing between us, me making my shock over him wanting to spend time with me outside of the bedroom wasn't going to make it any easier on him.

I couldn't read the tone of his voice when he said, "Yes, Leni. Really."

Instantly, I agreed, "Yes, I'd love to go out with you tonight."

"Dress casual," he instructed. "I have something planned that I think you'll find fun."

"I can do casual," I assured him and instantly regretted my choice of words. Casual was the exact opposite of what I was finding I could do.

"I'll pick you up around five-thirty. Does that work?"

"That's perfect."

Now, it was just a few minutes before five-thirty, and I was bursting with excitement. Not only could I not wait to see Holden, but I also couldn't wait to see what he had planned for us tonight.

Of course, I was also excited that we were going on an actual date. Truthfully, as eager as I was to find out where he planned to take us tonight, I really didn't care where we were going. This was the first real date we were going on. I didn't consider our lunch date after he and his team caught the arsonist to really be a date. At least, not the romantic kind, even if we ended it by kissing each other on my couch.

When there was a knock on my door a few minutes later, I struggled and forced myself not to run over to open it. But in all honesty, I definitely found myself scurrying toward it. The minute my eyes locked on Holden's I wanted to cry. I had truly missed him this week.

At the same time, as much as I wanted to throw myself into his arms, I held myself back. Luckily, Holden took a step toward me, slid one arm around my waist, the other around my upper back and pulled me close. He buried his face in my neck and took a deep inhale. I couldn't do anything but hold on tight and enjoy the feeling of being in his arms again.

After several long moments of silence while we held each other, Holden kissed the skin where my neck met my shoulder. He did it slowly and repeatedly. And it took everything in me not to moan at the feel of his lips on my skin.

Eventually, Holden loosened his grip on me and pulled back to look in my eyes. "Missed you, Leni."

He was going to make me cry. It was then that I realized perhaps I had made more out of things than was necessary.

It was hard for me because I'd become so accustomed to diving in without any reservations for so long. And every time I'd done that up until now, I'd never once regretted it. When I believed that Holden wasn't really interested in me beyond a physical relationship, it made me question myself for the first time in a really long time.

"I missed you, too, Holden. So much," I told him.

He let that settle a minute before he asked, "Are you ready to go?"

I nodded, moved to grab my purse and keys, and locked the door.

Twenty minutes later, I found myself falling harder for the man beside me. He had taken the time to really think about a great idea for a date with me. I appreciated his effort to make sure it was something he truly believed I was going to enjoy.

And his efforts were not in vain.

Because I was beyond thrilled to be taking trapeze classes with him.

"I can't believe you planned this," I exclaimed. "This has got to be the best idea anyone has ever had."

Holden shot me a huge grin and asked, "Have you ever done this before?"

I shook my head. "No. But I've always wanted to try it."

"I was thinking about where I wanted to take you on a date and realized that because you love yoga so much, it needed to be something that would keep us active."

"Obviously, I can't say for sure just yet, but I'm willing to bet this is going to go down in my book as the best date ever," I insisted.

Holden looked proud of himself for his efforts. I leaned into him, and after a moment of hesitation, he put his arm around my shoulders and gave me a squeeze. That small gesture did so much. It made me feel the best I'd felt in days.

Before we could get started, Holden and I first needed to go through the fifteen-minute introduction for the class, which was where we learned about the harness system, the calls, and the body positions. By the time that ended, I was bursting at the seams with excitement to strap in and start flying.

"Are you okay?" Holden asked as I practically bounced out of my shoes beside him.

My head bobbed up and down furiously as I continued to grin from ear to ear. "I'm fantastic," I chirped. "I'm just anxious to get started."

"I guess that's my confirmation that this was worth all the time I took to plan it," he declared.

"No doubt about it," I assured him.

For the next two hours, Holden and I had an absolute blast.

Apparently, I'd done really well because I was given the chance to try a catch. According to the employees, it was rare for someone to come in and do a catch at their first class. I was so excited about it, determined to do it, and asked if I could. They liked the control I had over my body and the ease with which I learned to do everything else, so they agreed to it.

Holden didn't mind and even snapped a few pictures and took a video for me.

I knew this was a date I'd never forget.

When our session was over, Holden called a local

restaurant and ordered food to go. "I'd prefer to have you to myself for the rest of the night," he explained his reason for not taking me out.

Since I'd had such an amazing time with him at the trapeze classes, and he was taking the time to feed me, I said, "It makes no difference to me where we eat as long as you're with me."

That statement caused Holden to stop and stare at me. As quickly as it took hold of him, it let him go.

Then, we got in his truck and went to pick up dinner.

It wasn't much later when Holden surprised me again. After we got our dinner, he didn't drive back to my place. Instead, he drove us to his. It was the first time he was bringing me to his place; that had to mean he was making small steps in the right direction.

Holden lived in a townhouse in a quiet neighborhood not too far from where I lived, and I had to admit to myself that I liked knowing he was that close to me.

Holden parked, came around to open my door, and took the food from my hands.

I was too stunned to bring myself to say anything, so I simply walked beside Holden into his house.

And the shock didn't end there.

Holden and I had sat down to eat and had gotten a few bites of our food in when he surprised me by asking about something I thought he had no interest in.

"So, everything is going okay with your classes at Reece's gym now?" he asked.

It caught me off guard because the last time I tried to talk to him about it, though it was only through text message, he never engaged in the conversation. I took a minute to think about it and realized that it only seemed to be when I mentioned Holden himself that he shut down. Perhaps it was best to avoid discussion of him for the time being while he got used to the idea of me.

Nodding, I finished chewing, swallowed, and replied, "Yes. I've only held one so far, but it was great for a multitude of reasons."

"Really? Like what?" he pressed.

Okay. That was a good sign. He wanted to know more.

"Well, I think the biggest thing for me was finally just knowing that I had a place to work and hold classes. I love what I do, so the idea that I wasn't going to be able to do it for a few months was really messing with my head. Even if I only had two or three students, I would have been happy."

Holden's brows pulled together as he brought his food to his mouth. "Was it a large class?" he asked before taking a bite.

Smiling brightly at him, I shared, "One of the biggest I've ever had even when I was in my own studio."

Confusion marred his features briefly, but it lasted on a few moments. Realization suddenly dawned, and Holden murmured, "Reece."

"Yes," I confirmed with a nod. "I had actually planned to go out and talk to him right after class, but he walked in as I was rolling up the mats. Much like you just did, I had guessed that he was the reason behind it. He confirmed that he'd done a little promoting for the class but also insisted that he had something to gain by it."

Holden chuckled as he sat back in his chair. "Let me guess," he started. "He wants you to stay on even after your studio is rebuilt."

"How did you know that?" I asked.

Shaking his head with a grin on his face, he pushed his

empty plate back and explained, "I'm not an idiot. I know how my brother works, so this doesn't surprise me."

"I'm not upset about it," I assured Holden in case he worried that his brother had offended me.

"Are you going to do it?" he asked, his tone unreadable.

I hesitated to answer immediately because I wasn't sure how he'd react to my decision. Ultimately, I decided there would be little I could do to control his reaction, so I simply answered, "I didn't make any official commitments, but I did tell Reece that I'd be open to working something out. I'd love to be able to express my gratitude to him for doing this for me, so if I can teach a couple classes a month doing something I enjoy while bringing in extra business for him, I'm willing to do it."

Holden kept his eyes on me in silence while he assessed me. Then, he noted, "Reece will be happy about that."

I didn't know if Holden would be put off by my question, but he gave me no indication otherwise. So, I pushed my plate away, took in a deep breath, and asked, "What about you?"

"Me?"

Nodding, I clarified, "Yeah. How do you feel about it?"

Holden tipped his head to the side and remarked, "I'm happy for you if that's what you want to do. Why do you ask?"

I shrugged. "I don't know. I was just curious if you had an opinion about it."

"I'm not sure I'm in a position to have an opinion about it," he started. "If this arrangement is something that works well for you and for Reece, then I think you should do it. But it's really not my place to tell you what to do."

Hmm. Holden didn't think he was in a position to have an opinion about me working at his brother's gym. While I understood that he had no control over the decisions I made,

I still valued his input. It still mattered to me what he thought about it.

Perhaps from his perspective, especially if he was struggling to open himself up to me, we weren't at a stage in our relationship where this was something he was comfortable doing. I felt disappointed, but also thought it was wise to be understanding. Just because I moved at warp speed didn't mean everyone else would.

This date was a huge step in a positive direction. So, even though it wasn't all perfect and exactly how I had hoped, it was still something. Holden was trying to give me something. I wasn't certain if he knew that or set out to do it, but it meant a lot.

And because I appreciated his efforts, I thought he should be rewarded. I pushed forward out of my chair and moved toward him. Holden slid his chair back and reached a hand out to the side of my upper thigh as I got close.

I straddled his lap and brought myself chest to chest with him.

"I had an amazing time today," I shared. "This was the best date I've ever been on."

Holden's grip on my thighs grew tighter as he returned, "I had a great time with you, too."

Leaning forward so that my mouth was just inches from his, I praised him. "You're a smart man," I started. "This wasn't just a simple dinner and a movie date. You took the time to pick something that I'd truly enjoy."

"I'm happy to hear that," he whispered.

"Do you know what that means?" I asked.

He gave a slight shake of his head indicating he did not know.

Smiling against his lips, I declared, "It means I have my

work cut out for me to give you the best night you've ever had."

Holden cocked an eyebrow and wondered, "Do you think you can do it?"

I touched my mouth to his, kissed him once, pulled back, and promised, "I plan to give it all I've got."

Then, I kissed him again. This time, it was much longer and included tongues, touching, and moaning. We ended up removing our tops right there. Holden's mouth was all over me until he lifted me from his lap and shifted my bottom to the table where he started removing my bottoms. The minute they were gone, he ran his lips and his tongue along my legs.

His grip on them tightened, and with his mouth on the inner part of my knee, he rasped, "Your legs are gorgeous, Leni."

My thighs clenched, but he held them apart. "Holden," I breathed.

"I've never seen another pair of legs this beautiful in my whole life," he went on.

So it seemed Holden could share his feelings. Of course, this was related to our current, or pending, physical connection. Considering I'd had a rough week of thinking he wasn't going to give me anything, I'd take this for now.

But I was going to be in charge of delivering the fun.

"I'm supposed to be making this night the best you've ever had," I reminded him.

Holden stopped moving his mouth over my body, stood from his chair, and looked down at me. His eyes were burning with desire. I held his gaze waiting for him to say something.

He didn't.

At least, not immediately.

Instead, he lifted me from the table and carried me

through his house. He climbed the stairs with me in his arms and took us to his bedroom. Once he brought me to my back in his bed, he positioned himself next to me on his back.

Then, he ordered, "You better get to work then."

Not wanting to waste a moment, I sat up immediately and got to work. I couldn't remember a time where I put as much effort into something as I did with pleasing Holden. When we finished, I had no doubts I'd accomplished what I set out to do.

It wasn't because he told me that I had. Instead, he communicated it another way. Holden shocked me once again when he slid under the covers after returning from disposing of the condom. I thought he was going to initiate another round of sex, which I wasn't sure I had the strength to endure at that moment.

But he didn't.

Instead, he rolled his body toward mine, urged me to my side, and hooked an arm around my waist.

Yes, that's right.

Holden spooned me.

And while it might have seemed like such a small thing to anyone else, I knew it was huge for us.

So, I allowed myself to feel happy about it. I loved seeing the effort Holden was making. If what Reece said was true and Holden was going to need me to be patient, it gave me comfort that Reece wasn't wrong. Because what Holden was giving me now told me that I wouldn't regret it if I could find it in myself to be patient with him. Maybe things hadn't gotten deep between us, and maybe Holden was still struggling to give me parts of himself. But from the minute he called me this afternoon until now, curled up tight in his arms, I didn't have it in me to be the least bit disappointed.

Holden

I couldn't do it.

I tried to stay away, but I couldn't.

And I didn't like that because it didn't make sense. Life for me was always about doing what was logical. Common sense told me that putting myself in a situation to be hurt again was foolish.

But for nearly a whole week, Leni never left my thoughts. I felt like I was going crazy not being around her.

So, I gave in to my reckless heart for the first time in a really long time.

I decided to take a risk. But I was going to be cautious.

Maybe it was a bad idea. Maybe I was setting myself up—setting us both up—for disaster. I didn't know what else to do, though.

Never before had I ever been consumed with such a strong pull to a woman. Yes, I'd been engaged before, but I hadn't ever been fighting myself not to go all in when I took that risk.

Now, I was fighting myself and struggling to stay away from this woman. This beautiful woman who had made me forget tonight, even if only for a few hours, that I was supposed to be guarding my heart.

Holding her in my arms now with her gorgeous, sleeping body pressed against mine, I remembered.

And as my arm rose and fell on her side with each breath she took, I silently hoped for strength. Because even though I called her earlier today believing I was just going to find a way to connect with her again, all it took was hearing her voice. One word was all she had to say, and I caved. Suddenly, the plan to call and keep things as she had offered from the start went out the window.

So, I needed to find a way to always remember and stay strong.

Willpower, which I currently seemed to be lacking, was the only thing that would keep me from making emotional decisions.

Just as I closed my eyes and inhaled the scent of Leni, I prayed that my logical brain wouldn't continue to falter. When I woke in the morning, I needed to be prepared.

Because I knew if I wasn't, the moment Leni looked at me, I'd easily surrender to her all over again.

CHAPTER 8

Leni

As much as I didn't want to leave Holden's warm embrace, I needed to know what time it was. Begrudgingly, I ended the best night of sleep I'd had in the last week, opened my eyes, and rolled away from him. I slid out of the bed and stood at the edge of it looking at Holden as he slept.

He was exquisite… in more than one way. I simply couldn't get over it.

After giving myself a few moments to take him in, I slid one of Holden's t-shirts over my head and went in search of my phone. I found it, noted the time, and realized I had two-and-a-half hours left before my yoga class was set to start this morning.

When I walked back into the bedroom, I saw that Holden had rolled to his back and was looking up at me. His eyes roamed over me, from top to toe, before he asked, "Where did you go?"

I held my phone up in front of me and answered, "I needed to check the time. I have a class this morning."

"What time?"

Moving toward him, I stopped right next to his side of the bed. Then, I replied, "Two and a half hours."

Holden grinned at me but said nothing.

"What's that look for?" I asked.

His hand reached out and landed on my hip. It was there only briefly before he began trailing his fingers down over the fabric of his shirt until he reached the hem. His fingers lightly caressed the skin on my upper thigh.

"Plenty of time," he whispered.

I pressed my thighs together in anticipation of having him between my legs again. Holden noticed me squirming, brought his eyes to mine, and smiled. Then, without warning, he quickly sat up in the bed, slid one arm around my bottom, another around my back, and pulled me into the bed with him.

Once there, he slid his shirt up and off my body before he used his time wisely.

An hour later, Holden and I were in his truck on the way back to my place. After having his way with me this morning, we dragged ourselves out of bed and got dressed. Holden decided to treat me with breakfast and made a quick stop at a bagel shop on the way to my house.

When we pulled up outside my house, I looked over and said, "Thank you so much for such a wonderful night last night. I really had the best time."

Holden's hand reached out to cup the side of my face. His thumb stroked over the skin of my cheek before he replied in a gentle voice, "You're welcome, sweetheart. I had a really nice time, too."

I didn't want to leave him just yet, so I leaned across the center console, touched my fingers to his face, and pressed my lips against his. Holden's hand gripped my hair at the back of my head as he moaned against my mouth.

Following a brief make-out session, I pulled back and searched his face. "I should get going," I rasped.

"Yeah. Let's try to focus for the next hour on getting you ready and fed, so we can get you over to the gym on time," he agreed.

My brows pulled together. "Let's?" I asked.

Holden dipped his chin in response.

"What does that mean?" I wondered.

He let out a laugh. "Why do you look so confused?"

"What you said indicates that you're not leaving," I explained.

Holden gave me a peck on the lips and confirmed, "I'm not." Then, he pulled away, opened his door, and exited the truck. I sat there, dumbfounded, as I watched him round the front of the vehicle.

When he opened my door, I turned and asked, "Are you staying with me?"

Holden didn't immediately respond. His eyes roamed over my face for a bit before he said, "Yeah."

"Really?" I pressed, making my shock even more evident.

"Yes, Leni."

With that, he plucked the bag with our breakfast from my lap and held his other hand out to me. I placed my hand in his because I couldn't do anything else. Holden's one-hundred-and-eighty-degree turn had me feeling a bit off balance.

"I've got to get a workout in this morning as well, so we can ride over together. While you teach, I'll get in my own workout."

"And then what?" I questioned him.

He shrugged. "I'm not exactly sure. I just know I'm not done with you yet."

Yet.

I didn't like what that three-letter word implied. But without any real time left to process that word, that statement, or Holden's complete turnaround, I did all I could do and simply went with the flow.

Once inside, Holden and I ate breakfast. After, I went to my bedroom and got myself ready for my class. When I walked out in a pair of my yoga shorts, a sports bra, and a crop top, Holden stood from the couch and moved toward me with a devilish grin on his face.

With my body being held tight to his, he brought his mouth to my ear and asked in a low tone, "Do you know what these outfits do to me?"

I barely managed to shake my head, but I whispered my reply, "No."

Holden shared, "The first time I saw you on the day of the fire standing outside your studio, you were wearing an outfit like this one. Did you know I couldn't get that image of you out of my head for days?"

I swallowed hard at his admission because it seemed Holden was making baby steps in opening up to me. My body remained still, my breath frozen in my lungs, as I waited for him to tell me more.

"Sometimes I still can't," he added.

He was killing me.

One of his hands dipped down over the curve of my ass. He squeezed and continued, "I hated seeing you so devastated, but still thought you were the most beautiful woman I'd ever laid my eyes on."

"Holden," I breathed.

"You're incredible, Leni."

I tipped my head back and looked up at his face. It was filled with adoration. Seeing that made my heart swell. And it was this very moment, being held in his arms with his sweet words filling my head, that I found myself unable to regret diving in head first and leading with my heart.

As much as I didn't want to ruin the moment, I knew

we needed to get going if I was ever going to be able to leave. I brought my cheek to his chest, took in a deep breath, and let the warmth of him surround me for just another minute.

"We should leave," I finally said.

Holden gave me one last squeeze and a kiss on the top of my head before he agreed, "Good idea."

"So, what's the problem you're having?"

Holden and I were standing in Reece's office. I'd just finished teaching while Holden got in his workout. When we walked into the gym this morning, Reece saw us, greeted us, and told Holden he had a situation he needed his help with when he was done with his workout.

Holden was ready to help his brother immediately, but Reece insisted he had a few phone calls to make anyway.

Now that we'd both finished what we originally came here to do, Holden wanted to see what this situation Reece was having was all about.

"I'm stuck right now on this construction," Reece began. "You know how we're renovating and putting in an aquatics addition to the gym, right?"

Holden nodded. "Yeah."

"Well, I've been fighting to get approval for the last step in this process, but I can't seem to get them to give it to me so that the construction crew can do what they need. Once I have that approval, they can finish up and I can finally have the cement poured for the pool."

Wow. Reece was adding a pool to the gym. This was

particularly exciting to me because I loved swimming. It was just another means of movement for me.

"Has the town cited any specific reasons why they aren't giving you the approval?" Holden asked.

Reece shook his head. "It's not a matter of there being an issue with any of the work that's been done up to this point. It's simply because they seem to want to drag their feet. The zoning officer doesn't work every day. This is just something he does on the side, so for the few hours he works each week, he's not getting much done. From what I've heard, I'm not the only one in this position."

"What days does he have hours?"

Reece gave Holden a look of disbelief and declared, "Mondays and Wednesdays from one o'clock to four o'clock. That's it."

Holden shook his head. "You've got to be kidding me."

"I wish I was."

After a brief stretch of silence, Holden instructed, "Alright. Get his information over to me along with any paperwork I'd need. How long has this guy been dragging his feet?"

"We should have had the approval three months ago," Reece stated.

"That's ridiculous," Holden grunted. "I'll stop in to the town office on Monday at one and get this taken care of for you."

Relief washed over Reece. "Thanks. I hate to burden you with it, but I'm out of time and patience. If you can make this happen, I'll owe you one."

Holden shook his head, put his arm around my shoulder, and curled me into his body. I had no choice but to press my palm to his toned and defined midsection. "No thanks needed. And you don't owe me. You took care of my girl. We're even," Holden insisted.

Reece's eyes went from his brother to me. He shot me that same look I saw the night I was leaving the gym. I couldn't quite read it, and that unsettled me a bit. Even still, I offered a smile. Eventually, Reece returned one and directed his attention back to his brother. "Keep me posted, yeah?"

Holden gave him a nod. "We'll see you later, Reece."

"Later, guys," Reece responded.

"Bye, Reece," I said as Holden moved us toward the door.

No sooner did we step out of Reece's office and close the door when our attention was drawn to a woman who'd stopped right in front of us. She was eyeing me in a way that I did not like. I was just about to say something when the sound of Holden's voice stopped me.

"What do you need, Tanya?" he asked.

Her eyes shot to him, moved over his body in a way I really didn't like, and she smiled. "I was just coming over to introduce myself to the new yoga instructor. Reece was promoting that class last week and I hadn't realized you both knew each other."

I wasn't sure I understood why Holden and I knowing each other was this woman's business. Unfortunately, I didn't get an answer to that because Holden never responded to her.

Tanya extended her hand to me, "Hi, I'm Tanya."

Despite the bad vibe I got from her, I decided to be a big girl about this. I took her hand, shook it, and returned, "I'm Leni. It's nice to meet you, Tanya."

"Leni," she repeated my name. "So, are you teaching yoga classes here regularly then? I've always wanted to take a class, but Reece seemed to have trouble securing someone to fulfill that role."

"I'll be teaching here regularly for the next few months while my studio is being rebuilt," I started. "After that's up and running again, I'll probably come here and offer a couple classes a month."

I could tell she wasn't the least bit excited at that prospect as her eyes darted back and forth between Holden and me. Ultimately, she declared, "Well, maybe I'll stop in to take one of your upcoming classes then. It was nice to meet you, Leni."

"You too, Tanya."

Tanya directed her gaze to Holden. She tried to come across as seductive, but it was overt and anything but. "As always, it's been a pleasure to see you, Holden."

The way she said that made me think that there'd been more than just glances between them at some point. Sadly, that thought churned my stomach.

Holden replied, "Tanya."

At that, he ushered me past her and around the check-in desk.

We didn't speak to each other as we walked to his truck, but once we were inside it, I blurted, "I'm sorry if there was ever anything between you and Tanya, but I've got to say this. I do not like that girl."

Holden let out a laugh and assured me, "There was never anything between me and Tanya. She wanted there to be, but I was not interested."

I felt myself relax at that news. Even though I never suspected Holden to be the kind of guy who'd cheat, it didn't make me feel all warm and fuzzy to think that a woman he'd been with would be sniffing around. The way she looked at him was enough to make me want to claw her eyes out, though.

"Does she know that you're not interested?" I asked as Holden pulled out of the parking spot.

"I told her several times already," he insisted.

I looked at Holden and said, "I don't think she understands that."

"Leni?" Holden called.

"Yeah?"

He came to a stop at a red light and looked over at me. "I don't care if she understands that or not. I'm not interested in her. I never was. But even if I had been, the second she decided the way to get my attention was to sleep with my brother would have been the second I no longer cared to get involved."

My eyes widened in surprise. *Tanya slept with Reece just to get Holden's attention?*

"She slept with your brother?"

"Yep."

I sat back in my seat and gazed out the windshield. "Wow."

"Trust me, Leni. You do not need to be worried about Tanya."

Holden knew I was feeling uncomfortable about the situation and was doing his best to ease my mind. Even still, I had to save face. "I was *not* worried about her," I stressed.

"If you say so," he teased.

"I wasn't!"

Holden reached across the center console and curled his fingers around my wrist. He lifted it up and placed it on the armrest between us. Then, his forefinger traced patterns on my palm. "Okay, sweetheart. I believe you."

I wasn't sure if he truly meant that or if he was just trying to calm me down. Either way, it worked. I allowed Holden to continue caressing my palm as I thought about how grateful I was for what he'd given me earlier that morning.

And as the thoughts ran through my mind, I realized I needed to make a trip to see the one person who'd be happy to hear all about the man in my life and all the wonderful things he'd done for me.

CHAPTER 9

Leni

"GOOD AFTERNOON, LENI. IT'S BEEN A FEW WEEKS SINCE WE last saw you."

I stared back at Pauline feeling a twinge of guilt. Pauline was the receptionist at the assisted living facility where my grandmother stayed.

"I know," I started. "There's been a lot going on, and I just couldn't get over here. I've gotten just about everything sorted now, though, so I should be back to my regularly scheduled programming now."

Pauline gave me a friendly smile. "Well, it's good to see you again. Audrey is going to be so excited to see you today."

I felt my insides warm at the mere mention of my grandmother's name. Pauline wasn't wrong. My grandmother was going to be beyond excited to see me today, the same as she always was every time I came to visit her.

"I feel the same about seeing her today, too," I assured Pauline.

"You can head on back. She should be in her room now, watching her favorite morning program."

I shook my head in mock disappointment. "That's never going to stop, is it?" I asked.

"She's pretty set in her ways," Pauline replied. "I wouldn't bet on it."

"Figured as much. Thanks, Pauline. I'll see you later."

With that, I walked to the double doors where Pauline buzzed me through so I could make my way down the hall and around the corner to my grandmother's room.

When I made it to her door, I tapped lightly before I went inside. Her eyes left the television and came to me.

"Am I interrupting?" I asked, shooting her a knowing smile.

"My darling girl," she beamed. "You've got perfect timing. This mother-daughter duo is about to reveal to the ex-husband and father that for the last three years they've been working together as a sugar baby team."

I shot her a look of utter disbelief. "I don't think I'll ever come to terms with the fact that you watch this salacious stuff."

"There's nothing wrong with it," she insisted. "Besides, watching this makes for great conversation at bingo night."

I guess she had a point there.

"Come watch with me," she ordered.

I had no choice but to walk over and sit down next to my grandma while we watched the rest of her show.

When it ended thirty minutes later, she turned off the television and continued to stare at it. She did it for so long, I began to wonder if something was wrong.

"Grandma?" I finally called.

She didn't look at me when she deadpanned, "You've got to admit it's not a bad way to make a living."

Not understanding what she was talking about, I asked, "What?"

"The mother and daughter," she clarified. "They've got a good thing going. Look at the life they're living."

"Don't tell me you're having regrets you didn't think to do this," I teased.

She shrugged. "You can't deny they're having the time of their lives, Leni. And really, who are they hurting? The men know what they're getting into, and mama and her girl are traveling the world."

"What about the father?" I questioned. "Don't you feel the least bit bad for him? Maybe not over the ex-wife, but what about his daughter?"

For the first time since the show ended, my grandma turned to look at me. "He left them," she started. "They did what they had to do to survive while making themselves happy. If he wasn't there to support his daughter then, he doesn't really get a say in what she does now. Especially considering she's an adult. You, my darling girl, should understand that more than anyone."

I loved my grandma. It didn't matter to her that my father was her son. She believed whole-heartedly that he was wrong for all but disowning me, and she refused to hide her dismay over it.

"I guess you're right," I agreed.

She laughed. "Of course I am. When am I not?"

Grandma was also a little spitfire. She knew who she was, remained confident in that, and never let anyone tell her any differently.

"So, tell me. Why has it been a few weeks since I last saw you?" she asked.

"Where should I start?" I wondered.

"The beginning is usually the best place."

Nodding, I sat up a little straighter. I took in a deep breath and let it out. No sooner did I do that when she pointed out, "Deep breaths... this is going to be big."

I couldn't help but laugh. She knew me so well.

When my laughter died down, I launched in and told her everything. I started at the beginning and told her all about the fire and the complete destruction of my studio. There was no way to tell her about that without telling her about Holden, not that I had any intentions of keeping him a secret from her anyway.

I gave her all of it.

I told her about all of the kindness and compassion he'd shown me from the minute I met him. She learned about the things he did to secure a place for me to work from until my studio was rebuilt. And I even shared how he took the time to plan the perfect date for me a few days ago.

When I finished, I sat there and waited for her reaction.

"You were inside the building when it was on fire?" she struggled to ask.

"Yes," I confirmed. "But other than needing a couple stitches in my foot, I was completely fine. I didn't have any other injuries that needed to be treated."

"What about the studio?" she asked.

"It's being rebuilt," I replied. "The landlord is getting it taken care of, so there's nothing for me to do there until it's ready for me to move back in."

She looked me over and nodded slowly as though she was trying to assess whether I really was okay. I loved her for it and gave her the time to do it.

"Alright," she eventually said. "Now tell me the truth about this boy."

I cocked an eyebrow and advised, "He's so not a boy, Grandma."

She got a devilish look in her eyes. "Of course not. But until I know the truth and that he's worthy of you, he's not a man."

"What makes you think I lied to you about him?" I wondered.

Shaking her head, she insisted, "I don't think you lied at all. I just know that there's something you haven't yet told me."

I didn't plan on hiding anything about my relationship with Holden from her, but what I really needed to discuss with her about it wasn't the kind of thing I had planned to lead with. I didn't think it would be the best to present him in a negative light right off the bat.

"I'm falling for him," I said softly. "And I'm worried he's going to walk away and break my heart."

My grandmother reached out and took my hand in hers. "He'd be a fool," she asserted.

"You're supposed to say that. I'm sure you'd be going against some grandmother code if you didn't."

"You're right. But I'm also not lying. Now, explain why it is that you think he'll walk away from you."

I honestly didn't know. Even though there'd been tremendous strides on Friday and Saturday in the progression of things between us on an emotional level, it still concerned me that I'd had so many doubts before that phone call on Friday afternoon.

"When things had started between us, they were good. Everything was just as you'd expect with something new. He asked a lot of questions and showed an interest in getting to know me. I was the same, but every time I asked anything that wasn't just superficial, he closed down on me. Just when I thought things were headed in the right direction, he went an entire week without once reaching out to me. I did send him a text that he replied to, but beyond that there was nothing."

I paused a moment, recalling the feelings I felt that week.

The person Holden had shown me that week conflicted with the person he'd given me prior to that point.

Sighing, I continued, "When he called me on Friday asking to take me out on a date, I was so excited. And from the moment he picked me up, it was perfect. Even yesterday was great, perhaps even a little better. He started sharing a bit more about how he felt about me. It's a good sign, but I'm still worried because I don't understand where the silence last week came from."

Giving my hand a squeeze, my grandma said, "This thing is still new between the two of you. But you're a catch, my darling girl. If he's a smart man, I'm sure he realizes just how precious you are. And it might be a bit much for him to cope with how strongly he feels for you so quickly."

"I'm not convinced that's what it is," I said.

"Then what else am I missing?" she asked.

I bit my lip, not completely wanting to recall the conversation. I pushed past the anxiety and murmured, "I talked to his brother one night following my yoga class. He indicated that I needed to be patient with Holden."

"Did he tell you why?"

I shook my head.

"So what do you want to do?"

"Aren't you going to tell me what I should do?" I practically pleaded.

"No," she stated firmly. "Why would I? And honestly, how could I? You're the girl who has this unbelievable ability to leap into something based on what you feel and you're really good at it. You've always followed your heart. And not once has it ever led you astray."

I rolled my eyes. "Tell that to the girl without any parents," I muttered.

"Leni, look at me," she demanded.

When I brought my eyes to hers, she asserted, "The fact that your parents aren't in your life does not mean that your heart steered you in the wrong direction. That is all about them and the choice they made. Your mom and dad aren't leading with their hearts. And when that's the case, there's bound to be disappointment. They're not motivated by what feels right. You are."

I held her gaze as she continued, "But aside from the fact that they aren't around right now, I know that you are the happiest I've ever seen you. When you were working there, you were feeling weighed down. You'd walk through my door, and it was like I could see you physically carrying the stress on your shoulders. And the minute you surrendered to your heart and took charge of your own life, you started soaring."

She brought her hand to my cheek, stroked her thumb along it, and pleaded, "Don't stop listening to your heart now. You'll regret it for the rest of your life if you do."

I pressed my lips together in a smile and struggled not to let any tears fall. When I managed to win that battle, I proclaimed, "I love you, Grandma."

"My darling girl," she started. "I love you, too."

For the next few hours, I stayed at the assisted living facility and visited with the only blood relative I had left in my life. We moved beyond the conversation about my relationship with Holden to much lighter topics. Grandma filled me in on all the latest juicy gossip amongst her cohorts. She never failed to make me laugh.

When it was time for me to leave, I felt myself getting emotional. For some reason, I started thinking about the fact that one day I'd no longer have this. My grandmother still had a young, fiery spirit, but she was still rapidly approaching her nineties. I couldn't imagine how I'd ever survive without having her in my life. I did my best to rid my mind of the negative thoughts and promised myself that I'd make it a priority to come and see her every week.

Not only did I know I needed that, but I was pretty sure she did, too.

Later that night, when I was curled up under my blankets and ready for bed, my phone rang. My belly began to tingle at the sight of Holden's name on the display.

"Hello?" I answered.

"How was your visit with your grandmother today?" he asked.

I loved that he was calling to check in and see how my day with her had gone. "It was great. With the fire and everything else I've had going on, I hadn't been over to see her in a few weeks. It was really nice to have the chance to catch up with her."

"I'm happy for you," he said. "Did she take the news of the fire okay?"

That he cared about her mental state after learning her granddaughter had been trapped inside a burning building melted my heart.

"Initially, she was concerned about my well-being. As soon as she confirmed that I didn't suffer any serious injuries beyond needing the stitches in my foot, she seemed to relax a bit," I shared.

"That's good."

"Yeah. How was your day today?" I asked.

"Missed you," he replied softly.

Yep, there was no doubt about it. I was definitely going to continue doing what my grandma told me to do. Hearing those words from Holden, I knew I was going to follow to my heart.

"I missed you, too."

"So, I have something to ask you," he stated.

"Sure. What's going on?"

There was a brief pause before he mentioned, "My family is having a small celebration next weekend for my grandparents' seventieth wedding anniversary. I'd really like to have you there as my date."

It seemed Holden was no longer taking baby steps.

"I'd love to join you," I bubbled. "Can I get fancy for this or is it casual again?"

"You can do fancy," Holden confirmed. "In fact, I'm really looking forward to seeing fancy on you."

I felt myself smiling on the inside as I recalled his words to me Saturday morning. It felt good to know that he liked the way I looked.

"I'll do my best to make you proud then," I promised.

"I can't wait to see it."

Neither of us said anything for a few long seconds. Finally, Holden broke the silence. "Are you heading to bed?" he asked.

"No. I'm already there."

I could hear the amusement in his tone when he responded, "Alright, then I'll let you go, sweetheart."

"Okay."

"Goodnight, Leni."

"Goodnight."

At that, we disconnected. I stretched my arm out to put my phone back on my nightstand. Then, I curled up tighter under my blanket with a smile on my face. Having Holden lying beside me in bed would have been my first choice but talking to him before I went to sleep and getting invited to one of his family's celebrations was easily a close second.

On that thought, I closed my eyes and felt myself easily drift.

CHAPTER 10

Leni

"ARE YOU HERE?" ZARA ASKED.

"I'm leaving my house now," I answered into the phone. "I should be there shortly. Are you still good on time?"

"That'll be perfect timing," she replied. "I'll see you soon."

I disconnected the call with Zara, turned on my car, and backed out of the driveway.

I was running a bit behind schedule today. It was late Tuesday afternoon, and I'd spent the earlier part of my day at Reece's gym continuing the filming of a couple training videos. As was often the case with my yoga practice, I was feeling inspired by the circumstances in my life and used that inspiration to create a program for students who might be feeling similarly.

I'd done this regularly over the years. No matter what situation was, I coped with it through my practice. So, if I was feeling stressed, I'd create a program that my students could turn to when they were feeling the same. When things in my life felt good and I was feeling powerful, I'd create different strength and conditioning classes for them. Or if my body or my mind was feeling fatigued, I'd work on a restorative program to help with recovery.

This had become such a huge part of my life and my business, and it was something that so many of my students appreciated. As long as it was providing a benefit for myself and others, I'd continue to create classes and programs by being vulnerable with whatever was going on in my life.

For the better part of the day Monday, all I did was film. I had a couple extra classes I wanted to film to complete the program, so I went in early this morning to get them done. Afterward, I came home and immediately got to work on editing my content. Unfortunately, I got so caught up in it that I lost track of time and realized I was going to be late.

I reached out to Zara around lunchtime yesterday and told her about the invitation Holden extended to me. When I told her that he mentioned I could get fancy for the occasion, she insisted we take one afternoon this week to find my fancy. Since I was holding classes all week this week, with tonight being the night that I was holding the latest class, we decided this was the best day to do it.

So, even though I'd realized I was behind schedule, I worked as fast as I could to get myself ready and out the door. Now, I was finally on my way, but still fifteen minutes late. Thankfully, it sounded like that was going to work out perfectly for Zara.

When I finally pulled up outside her place, she walked out, locked up her shop, and hopped in my car.

"Sorry I'm late," I lamented as I pulled away from the curb.

"Oh, don't worry about it. I was actually relieved when you called because I had an unexpected client show up today who took up a good deal of my time this afternoon. We were making plans for an, oddly enough, anniversary party next month, and they wanted to have me handle the arrangements."

"That worked out great then. I just need to make sure I keep my eye on the time because I am teaching a class tonight. It's late, but still, I don't want to go in all frazzled, either."

Zara laughed. "I promise to keep you on schedule. Do you have any ideas in mind for what you want to wear to the party?"

I shook my head. "I have no idea. I just know that the pressure's on because Holden's expressed how much he appreciates my yoga wear and how he's really looking forward to seeing what I can do with something fancy."

"Alright, well I'm sure we'll figure something out for you. What I really want to know now is how it's even possible we're going to find you something to wear for a special occasion with Holden's family. When we talked last week, you were feeling pretty lousy about where things were between the two of you."

Even though Zara had gotten the time frame correct, it still felt like that had been a lifetime ago. Holden's change had been so abrupt and drastic that I could only just barely remember feeling so hopeless about the predicament I'd gotten myself into.

"Honestly, I have no idea," I answered truthfully. "It all came out of nowhere."

"What?" she asked.

I took in a deep breath and blew it out. "Your guess is as good as mine," I started. "He called me Friday afternoon, asked if I was free to go out on a date with him that night, and then spent that night and all day Saturday with me. I visited my grandma on Sunday at the assisted living facility, but when I got in bed Sunday night, Holden called me to check and see how things went with her. I don't know what caused the change in him, but I'm not complaining about it either."

"I think this is all really good news. Am I right to assume that he's giving you more now than just... how did you put it? Phenomenal sex, wasn't it?" Zara teased.

I couldn't help but laugh before I assured her, "He's still giving me that. I don't think I ever want him to stop giving me that. But yes, he's started giving me more than just that. It's not everything I'd ultimately want, but we are still very new. I can't expect he's going to spill all his deep, dark secrets after such a short time. So, I'm doing my best to do what his brother said and be patient with Holden."

From the corner of my eye, I could see Zara turn her head in my direction. "His brother told you to be patient with him?" she asked.

Nodding, I explained, "The night you and Lexi came to my first class at Reece's gym. After the class, he came in to talk to me about how everything went, but our conversation eventually went to Holden. I must have had the worry about our situation written all over my face because Reece easily guessed I was feeling uneasy about where things stood. He told me to be patient with Holden."

"Did he tell you why?" she wondered.

Shaking my head, I answered, "No. And as much as I want to know why, I'm glad he didn't. If there's something that's stopping Holden from completely giving in to what he feels for me, I'd rather know what that is from him. Besides, I wouldn't want to come between the two of them."

Zara shared my same sentiments when she said, "I wonder what it could be."

"Me too. But I don't want to force it out of him. I don't even want to let on that I know there's something he's dealing with. For now, considering I'm seeing positive changes between us, I'm working out the rest of the stuff I'm feeling through my practice. If things between us are supposed to get where I hope they'll go, I've got to just let go of what I can't control and surrender to fate. If it's meant to be, it'll be."

Zara didn't respond. And she was quiet for so long, I began to worry. In fact, her silence bothered me enough that I called, "Zara?"

"Yeah?"

"Where'd you go?"

There was a moment of hesitation before she remarked, "It's just… well, a long time ago, I found myself changing who I was for someone else. Thankfully, even though it was later than it should have been, that person is no longer in my life. It took me a long time to put myself back together. Luckily, I had Pierce there to support and encourage me every step of the way. I just don't want to see you end up in a place where you accept something that's less than what you want. Don't give up having the things you want in a relationship because someone else doesn't think you deserve to have them. I hesitate to say this because I know you guys are new, but I also think you need to know what your limits are. As long as you know that you should only accept what you want and can let go of something when it's no longer serving you, I think you'll be alright."

Maybe it was ironic that all I could do was smile when I heard Zara's words, but knowing where she'd likely heard the last of them made me happy. "Sounds like you've been taking one too many yoga classes," I teased.

She laughed and assured me, "Yeah, but the wisdom and healing I've found through it has been crucial. You've taught me a lot, Leni. If I have the chance to offer advice to you now, even if it's recycling something you've given me before, I'm going to do it."

It hit me then that I wouldn't regret forging a deeper connection with Zara. She was one of the sweetest and most genuine people I'd ever met, and I believed my life would be far more enriched with her in it.

As I turned into the Windsor Park Mall parking lot, I responded, "Thanks, Zara. I appreciate that. And you don't have to worry. I've already made a promise to myself that I wouldn't allow things to go back to where they were a week ago without some sort of explanation. If I feel Holden pulling away from me like that again, I won't hesitate to ask him about it. It's important enough to me to figure it out. And if he can't give me something to help me understand it, then I'll have a decision to make."

Having pulled into a spot, I turned off my car and looked at Zara. That's when I continued, "But for now, as long as things are like this and we're making steps to head in the right direction, I'll be patient with him on whatever is causing him to hesitate on some of the things I ultimately hope to have from him."

She smiled at me and agreed, "I think that's more than reasonable. And I really hope the two of you get to where you want to see this lead. You know I'm always here if you need to talk."

After all the support she'd shown me since everything happened with my studio, I truly believed her. "Yeah, I do," I insisted.

"Ready to go find something to drive your man crazy in front of his family where he won't be able to do anything about it?" she asked.

I shot her a blinding smile and nodded.

With that, we exited my car and went on a mission to find something that would *drive my man crazy*.

I'd just pulled into the parking lot outside Reece's gym.

Zara and I managed to have a productive trip to the Windsor Park Mall. Best of all, we did it in what could have easily been considered record timing. As a result, after thanking Zara and taking her back to her place, I had enough time to go home and get a bit more editing done before I needed to leave again to teach my class.

Turning off my car, I got out and grabbed my extra yoga mats from my trunk. I was hoping I would have been able to carry them along with the yoga blocks and straps I had in one shot, but I wasn't so lucky. Two of the mats fell out of my hands. Feeling defeated, I dumped everything back in the trunk and bent down to pick up the mats when I heard, "Leni!"

I looked up to see Connor coming my way.

"Hi, Connor," I returned.

"Do you need some help?" he asked.

"That'd be great if you don't mind."

He shook his head. "Not at all. Load me up," he ordered, holding out his arms.

I dumped a couple mats and yoga blocks in his arms and piled the rest up in my own. "Thank you for helping," I stated as we walked into the gym. "Are you just getting here?"

"No, I actually just finished and was heading out. But I saw you trying to juggle all of this and couldn't just hop in my car and drive away," he answered.

"This is late for you, no?"

"Yeah, but it's been like that all week this week," he

started. "There's been a lot going on at work, so I've been putting in quite a few late nights there."

That right there was one of the reasons I never regretted my decision not to stay at Ford Communications. I knew Connor liked his job, but I couldn't imagine it was his lifelong dream to always work as my father's assistant.

"Well, I hope all these late nights are paying off for you," I said just as we reached the front door.

Another gym-goer happened to be leaving when we made it there, so he held the door open for us. Connor and I both thanked him and continued moving toward the room I was teaching in tonight.

"I guess you could say that the long days are paying off in the sense that I don't think your father will ever get rid of me," Connor began. "The obvious upside of that is my job security, but there's just no room for growth either."

We walked into the room, and I immediately put the mats and blocks down. "You can set those anywhere," I instructed. After Connor put everything down next to where I'd placed what I carried in, I started unrolling the mats and setting up the room for class. But since I still had time before students would start arriving, I figured I'd talk with Connor. "Have you talked to my father about that?" I asked. "Does he know that you're unhappy where you are?"

He took a moment to consider my questions before he responded, "I like working for the company. I really do. I know I should just be thankful that I have a job that pays well, has great benefits, and paid vacation time. And I am. But I think your dad is so accustomed to having me there that he won't consider letting me take another position within the company. The only hope I had of seeking advancement within the company was when you were still there."

My shoulders fell as I looked at the man who'd become a good friend over the years we worked together. It was horrible to think that in following my heart and chasing my dreams, I'd prevented someone else from achieving their goals. "I'm so sorry, Connor," I apologized. "I truly never thought for a second that they'd ever consider someone other than you for that position."

He shook his head. "It's fine. It was a long time ago. I honestly don't believe it had anything to do with my qualifications for the position. Both your mom and dad knew I was more than capable of taking over that platform. I think it was more about your father not being able to deal with you leaving. He had lost control, and I think that forced him to find something he could stay in control of."

"That's not surprising," I mumbled.

"For those first few weeks after you walked out, I think he thought you were going to cave. But each day that went by without a call from you caused him to get more and more angry. It's done now, and I think he's moved past it, but he's holding on to a grudge for the sake of his reputation. At any rate, it is what it is now. There's nothing we can do about it at this point."

After I opened and set out another mat, I walked over to Connor. I put my hand around the back of his arm and gave him a squeeze on his tricep. "If you're unhappy, Connor, you should tell him. My father needs to learn that his feelings aren't the only ones that matter."

"I'm not sure it'll do any good," he debated.

"Why not?" I challenged. "Don't you think it'd be better for him to listen to the needs of his best employees so that he can keep hardworking individuals on staff? It shouldn't matter to him what position you're in; he should be thankful he's got an enthusiastic employee on the payroll who actually cares about his job."

Connor turned toward me and put a hand on my shoulder. "I'm not saying you're wrong, Leni. I'll think about it, and if I work up enough courage, maybe I'll talk to him. I'm just not sure that's how your father works."

"I'm sorry that—" I got out before the door opened and Reece walked in.

A funny look washed over his face as Connor took a few steps away from me.

"Hi, Reece," I greeted him. "Is everything okay?"

His eyes darted back and forth between Connor and me before he finally settled on me. "Yeah, I just wanted talk to you about something," he answered.

"I'm heading out anyway," Connor announced. "I'll talk to you later, Leni. Have a good class."

"Thanks, Connor. And good luck," I responded.

Connor stepped away and moved toward the door. Once he was out of the room, Reece asked, "You know him?"

I nodded. "Yeah, I've known Connor for years. He works for my parents. Years ago, he and I worked together on a project for their company. But I left the company a long time ago. He's still there."

Reece lifted his chin slowly in acknowledgment. "Right. Well, I just wanted to let you know that Holden managed to work a miracle and get us the approval we've been waiting on to finish the renovation project here."

"Wow, that's great news. He works quick, doesn't he? How did he manage that?" I asked.

Reece shook his head. "I honestly don't know. My brother is a brilliant man. I don't question his methods; I'm just grateful he has his ways."

I smiled.

Reece continued, "Anyway, the reason I'm coming to you with it is because I know you've been filming. I don't know what your filming schedule is like for the next few days, but it might get a little noisy in that room while they finish the last few details before the work for the pool is started."

"Oh, that's totally fine," I assured him. "The filming I did all day yesterday and earlier today were for a full course I'm working on launching for my students. I finished the filming this morning, so I'll be spending the next few days editing that content and coming in for these classes."

"Good. I was hoping we weren't going to mess with your schedule," he said.

"I appreciate the heads up."

Just then, the door opened, and a couple of my students filed in. I greeted them with a wave and a smile.

"I'll get out of your hair so you can get ready for your class. I guess I'll be seeing you this weekend," Reece noted.

I gave him a nod. "Yes, I'll be there."

Reece looked at me hard for a couple long seconds and muttered, "Fuck, I hope you're serious about him."

Before I had the chance to respond, Reece turned and walked away.

I stood there, dumbfounded by his words for several moments trying to process what he said and figure out what the heck it all meant. Unfortunately, I didn't have the chance to do that because the door opened again and Tanya walked in.

With that, I took in a deep cleansing breath I knew I was going to need to get through this class and moved to my mat.

CHAPTER 11

Leni

"Do you want me to come over for a little bit tonight?"

I'd just gotten out of my class and called Holden. I didn't know why, but something prompted me to reach out to him. I had a feeling my run-in with Reece followed by seeing Tanya walk into my class were part of the reason why.

"If you aren't busy, I'd love to see you," I answered.

"Give me about thirty minutes, and I'll be there."

"Alright, I'm heading home now. As soon as I get there, I'm going to hop in the shower," I shared. "I'll leave the door unlocked."

"Don't do that," he ordered. "Either lock it and I'll get in on my own or wait until I get there before you get in the shower. And, just saying, if you wait, I'll be more than happy to make it worth your while."

When he put it like that, I couldn't refuse. "I'll wait for you to get there," I decided.

"See you soon, sweetheart."

Once Holden and I disconnected, I quickly backed out of my parking spot and drove home. Ten minutes after I arrived at my house, Holden showed up. No sooner did he step inside, drop a bag on the floor at his feet, and lock the door behind him when he lifted me in his arms and carried me to the bathroom.

On the way there, he asked, "How was your day?"

He just barely had the chance to ask the question when I put my finger to his lips and pleaded, "No words right now."

Given the evening I'd had, I needed some time to just let my feelings for Holden consume me. For the first time, I didn't want any words or conversation. All I wanted was to surrender to him and whatever he wanted to do with me.

Holden's brows pulled together in confusion.

"Please," I begged.

He dipped his chin in acknowledgment and set me down on my feet when we entered the bathroom. He turned on the water and kept his eyes on me while we both stripped out of our clothes. While Holden pulled a condom out of the pocket of his jeans and set it on the windowsill that was just within arms' reach of the shower, I checked the water temperature and stepped inside under the spray.

Within seconds, Holden joined me.

And then we just continued to stare at one another while we showered. It wasn't until after we both washed our hair and our bodies that I gave in. I took the two steps toward Holden, removing the space between us, and pressed my body against his. He took that as his cue to enfold me in his arms and take the lead.

The next thing I knew, my legs were wrapped around Holden's waist, my hands were clasped behind his neck, and my back was against the wall. Holden's mouth was on mine, the velvety softness of his tongue gliding against mine. One of his arms was firmly planted around my waist while his other hand was cupping my breast.

This was what I needed.

Just the two of us, connecting like this, without any distractions.

Without any worries.

I moaned at the feel of his hand on me, his body pressed tight to mine, and his lips against my lips.

My head dropped back against the wall, separating our mouths, but Holden didn't miss a beat. He began trailing kisses down my throat, stopping occasionally to nip the skin with his teeth.

"Holden," I breathed, my voice a deep, guttural whisper.

Keeping one arm wrapped firmly around my waist, Holden pulled back just a touch, gazed down at my body, and lowered his mouth to my breast. As he licked and sucked, I began moving my hips in an attempt to find some friction between my legs.

Realizing what I needed, Holden quickly lowered my feet to the ground. His free hand immediately slid from my breast, down my belly, and right to my aching pussy. He gently played with me before he cupped me with his hand and slid a finger inside me.

My whole body tensed as my fingers gripped his shoulders.

And then it all changed.

Holden's molten eyes were fixed on mine, burning right through to my soul. The rhythm of his finger as it plunged inside me in the most ardent way. It was unremitting and completely consuming.

God, it was like magic.

My grip on his shoulders grew stronger with the continuous yet delightful torture. And it felt like mere seconds had passed when something else took over inside me and I had no choice but to surrender to Holden as he assailed my senses.

When my orgasm hit, my fingertips clutched him around the back of his neck and my body violently curled forward. I cried out, unable to do anything but hold on until it left me. And through it, Holden never let me go.

For the several long moments that immediately followed, Holden kept me held tight to his body. He gave me the time I needed to come down and be present again with him.

My forehead was planted in his chest when Holden loosened his grip around my waist and trailed his hand down over the curve of my ass. The hand that had been between my legs was in my hair as he tugged gently, forcing me to tilt my head back to look at him.

The minute my face was exposed, he captured my mouth. His tongue came out and explored my mouth as the grip he had on my ass grew tighter. He eventually pulled back and implored, "Let me give you more, Leni."

He took one look at my lazy expression before he reached outside the shower and grabbed the condom. After he rolled it on, he put a hand to my hip and urged me to turn around. I did as he silently asked and turned. Then, I placed my palms on the wall as Holden filled me from behind.

After two slow, deliberate thrusts, Holden lost control. From that point forward, he was relentless and determined. I listened and loved hearing how what we were doing was affecting him. Knowing I was responsible for that, knowing I'd made him wild like that, did something to me I couldn't begin to describe. Before I even realized it was happening, I felt another orgasm building low in my belly. Every muscle in my body contracted as I chased it. And when Holden's grunts grew louder, his fingers gripped my hips tighter, and his thrusts came harder, I found it.

Just as my second orgasm tore through my limbs making

me moan in pleasure, Holden buried his cock deep and came right along with me.

After our bodies were no longer connected and Holden had rid himself of the condom, we cleaned ourselves up and got out of the shower.

We still hadn't spoken any words.

But I could feel Holden watching me. I knew his mind was working, and I had no doubt he was going to want to make sure that I was okay.

Talking to him wasn't a problem for me, and in any other case, I'd share. I just wasn't exactly sure how to or even if I should bring up what his brother had said to me.

Holden and I toweled off. While he walked out of the room, presumably to get his bag with his clothes, I pulled on a pair of panties and a camisole.

Holden returned, slipped on a pair of boxer briefs, and moved toward me. The second I was within reach, he took my hand and led me to the bed.

Once we were there, both of us on our sides facing each other, he asked, "Are you okay?"

Nodding, I answered, "Yeah. It's just been a long couple of weeks, and there's been a lot on my mind."

I wasn't exactly lying. The truth was, my mind had been swirling with a million thoughts ever since the fire. And while the focus of my attention had shifted from my worry over the destruction of my place of business and how I'd continue to earn a living to the distance I'd felt from Holden and what exactly he wasn't sharing with me, I still wasn't completely at ease. It was just that this new situation with Reece added another layer of concern.

"Do you want to talk about it?" he questioned me.

Ultimately, I decided it was best not to bring up the

conversation I had with Reece. At least, not the last part of it anyway.

Sighing, I shared, "Tanya came to my yoga class tonight."

"I had a feeling that was going to happen," he started. "After we ran into her over the weekend, I had no doubt she was going to make it a priority to come to your class. She didn't give you a problem, did she?" he worried.

My arm, which had been draped over Holden's ribs, shifted slightly. I began running my fingers along the skin of his back as I replied, "No. She was fine, I guess. She just creeps me out a bit. But there wasn't anything specific that she did that was wrong. Typically, I love having new people in my classes, but there's just something about her that doesn't sit well with me."

I honestly didn't know why I felt this way with her. Holden had made it clear that he wasn't interested in Tanya despite her attempts to get him to notice her. I did not believe that what I was feeling was related to jealousy, but I couldn't exactly pinpoint what it was about her that made me feel so uneasy either.

"Tanya might be a bit of an annoyance, but I'm relatively certain she's harmless. I don't think you need to be worried about her doing anything to you," Holden stated.

"Okay," I replied.

"If that changes, though, make sure you let me know. And if it happens when I'm not there and makes you really uncomfortable, just let Reece know. He'll take care of it for you," he insisted.

"Thanks, Holden," I began. "Speaking of Reece… I heard you got everything squared away for him with the zoning approvals. That was great news."

Holden nodded and shared, "Yeah, I just had to go and

have a few words with the township about it. Once I did, they decided it was in their best interests not to delay it any longer."

My fingers stopped tracing over Holden's back as I tipped my chin up and looked at him. "Sounds like they either really like you and wanted to make you happy or you had some really good motivational words for them," I teased.

He let out a chuckle and guessed, "It's very likely the latter is the reason for the quick response and approval."

I tipped my head back and smiled at him.

After a bit of hesitation, Holden asked, "Are you sure there's nothing else bothering you? I can't imagine Tanya showing up is the only reason you were so different when I got here."

"Different?" I repeated.

Holden nodded and explained, "You didn't want to talk then. You've never really been like that, so I just assumed you'd had a bad day and needed to relieve some stress and tension."

"I'm sorry," I lamented.

"Why are you apologizing?"

"Well, that's kind of exactly how I was feeling, but I don't want you to think I was just using you for your body and an orgasm."

Holden squeezed my hip and laughed. "Leni, sweetheart, if that's the way you use me, I'm okay with it."

"You know what I mean," I maintained.

"Yeah, I do."

Following a beat of silence, I admitted, "It wasn't just about Tanya. I have some things I'm trying to work through right now. I've been using my meditation and yoga practice to clear my head and sort it all out. So far, it's mostly been working, but if I find myself stuck, I'll let you know."

"Are you sure?"

I shifted my body closer, sending Holden to his back. As I rested my head and my palm on his chest, his arm curled around my back and held me tight.

"I'm sure," I confirmed.

And I was.

I no longer had just my earlier conversation with Reece swirling in mind. There was something else much bigger that was suddenly taking up space. It was becoming clear to me what had happened with Holden in the shower. Understanding it, I knew I needed to hold back something. As hard as I knew that was going to be for me, I had no choice.

Holden hadn't yet opened up to me the way I'd hoped he would, and I was afraid of what might happen if I shared that my feelings for him were growing stronger.

So, I decided to keep them close to me for just a little bit longer. At least until I felt that I could surrender them to Holden, and he wouldn't break my heart.

"I bought a dress today," I shared after we'd laid there for a while just cuddling with each other.

"Yeah?"

"For your grandparents' party this coming weekend," I added as I lifted my cheek from his chest, planted my chin there, and looked at him. "Zara and I went shopping earlier today, and we managed to find the perfect dress. Or, at least, I hope you'll think it's the perfect dress."

He smirked and wondered, "What are the chances I can convince you to show it to me now?"

"Zero percent."

He cocked an eyebrow. "Really? There's nothing I can do to convince you? I could at least confirm that it's perfect for the occasion."

Grinning and biting my lip, I shook my head. Then,

because I was feeling good and excited about my dress, I teased, "But I promise you it'll be worth the wait. It's way better than the yoga outfits. And I trust my own judgment enough that I'm not worried about it being inappropriate."

Holden shared his pessimism. "I'm not convinced it's possible to top the yoga outfits. They complement your figure perfectly."

"Are you suggesting they'd be appropriate to wear for meeting your family?" I taunted him.

"If we were going to be at home, it wouldn't matter to me. But I get the feeling the restaurant might frown upon it."

That made me wonder. While I didn't disagree that my typical yoga wear wasn't exactly meant for wearing to a restaurant, I didn't agree with Holden about it not being a problem to wear when meeting his family, especially for the first time.

It made me think that he didn't seem to care what his family thought of me. And while I believe that could be good in some cases, I found it doubtful that Holden felt that way because of his undying devotion to me.

Was I disposable?

The thought made me visibly shudder. Holden noticed it and asked, "Are you okay?"

Thinking quick, I nodded, moved to sit up, and said, "I'm feeling a bit famished. I think I'm going to get a snack. Do you want anything?"

Holden eyed me in a way I knew he didn't believe me. Even still, he didn't call me on it. "I'm good," he assured me.

With that, I got up and walked out of the room toward the kitchen. On my way there, I tried to calm the twisting in my stomach. Maybe I should have shared my concerns with Holden. Maybe I should have told him that it worried me he didn't seem to care if his family liked me.

Normally, I didn't hold back. But something stopped me.

And I had a feeling it was the same thing that stopped me from sharing the words Reece had said to me with him.

Uncertainty.

Uncertainty about where he stood.

Worry that if I succumbed to what was in my heart and fell all in with him, he'd never reciprocate.

By the time I made it to the kitchen, I had to lean over the counter and take a few deep breaths. I'd just barely gotten two of them out when I felt Holden's body curl around mine. He slid his arms around my waist and brought his mouth to my ear.

"Sweetheart, talk to me," he begged.

I wish you'd talk to me, I thought.

I lifted myself up and took another deep breath. "Don't you care?" I blurted.

Immediately, tension flitted through Holden's body. It went from being mostly relaxed to completely rigid. And he made no attempt to answer my question.

Tears welled in my eyes.

"Why don't you care what they think?" I pressed.

That got me a response.

"Who?" he retorted.

I stepped out of his hold and turned to look at him. "Your family," I clarified.

"What do you mean?" he asked. "What makes you think I don't care what they think? And about what?"

"Me!" I cried. "You just said you wouldn't care if I showed up to meet them in a pair of yoga shorts and a sports bra if this party wasn't being held at a restaurant. Doesn't it matter to you if I make a good impression?"

Understanding dawned in Holden's features, and he

visibly relaxed. "Sweetheart, I said what I did because I know my family better than you do. They wouldn't be the slightest bit concerned with what you're wearing. There are so many other things that they'd be focusing on, not what you look like. When it comes to your looks, the only opinion I care about is my own."

Okay, so I hadn't expected that.

Holden continued, "My family will want to know what kind of person you are. They'll want to know that you are an upstanding member of society. Taking care of yourself and others is important to them. Knowing that it makes me happy to be around you is what they'll be most concerned with. Anything else, especially your clothes, is not of any concern to them."

"Oh," I murmured, diverting my eyes away from his.

He took a step toward me, brought his thumb and forefinger to my chin, and urged me to look at him. "How did we go from me being excited about seeing you in your dress to this?"

It was difficult to find my voice over the lump that had formed in my throat. Apparently, my grandma wasn't exactly right. It seemed my heart could still steer me in the wrong direction because I had just made a fool of myself.

Holden must have realized that I was struggling because he switched topics and asked, "Are you still hungry?"

I shook my head. "I never was," I admitted.

"You just needed to get away from me for a minute," he guessed.

Holden was entirely too perceptive. I shrugged because admitting that would have been horrible.

"Do you still need some time away from me?" he questioned.

Panic gripped me. "No," I answered immediately.

Holden shot me a beautiful smile and pulled me in for a hug.

I did all I could do.

I hugged him back.

CHAPTER 12

Leni

THE LAST TIME I FELT NERVES LIKE THIS, MY LIFE CHANGED forever. Part of that change was for the better, but there was a large part that just felt bad. It had been years since I felt like this, yet it was one of those things that I'd never forget. I remembered the fear I felt that day like it happened yesterday.

And because I didn't frequently find myself feeling fear like this, I had to wonder if there was a good reason for it. Years ago, my fear was justified. Because in the end, I lost my family. While I tried not to dwell on that, and I had no regrets for taking charge of my own life, it was hard not to think that perhaps I was having flashbacks of walking down the hall to my father's office all those years ago because I already knew how things were going to go today.

It was late Saturday afternoon, and I was preparing to go out with Holden to his grandparents' anniversary celebration.

Meeting the family was a huge step in any relationship, so of course it was only natural I was feeling anxious. But I had a feeling I was so twisted up inside about it because I still had the words Reece said to me earlier in the week playing over and over in my mind.

Fuck, I hope you're serious about him.

Combining that conversation with having the way he'd looked at me on three different occasions running through my brain was causing serious havoc inside me. There was still a small part of me that was wrestling with whether it was best to share it with Holden or keep it from him. Ultimately, I decided I didn't want to be responsible for any tension between the brothers who seemed to have such a close, loving relationship. So, I kept my mouth shut.

But it was more than frustrating to keep it to myself. Because those words made it seem like Reece thought I was playing a game with Holden when in fact I was the one who'd received the mixed messages.

To keep myself from going into a full-blown worry mode, I tried to look on the bright side. Overall, things with Holden had been much better this week than they were the previous week. We got together twice during the week, and the best part about it was that it wasn't just about sex. Obviously, sex was still a big part of it, but we had more than just that. It might not have been as much as I would have hoped for; however, it was far more than Holden had given me previously.

As much as I wanted more of him, I still felt like he was trying. I was going to be meeting his family today. That counted for a lot in my book. So, I made a silent compromise and promised myself I'd give him more time to open up on an emotional level. And considering he wasn't holding back from me completely, I believed he deserved to have that from me.

Holden was making strides in his relationship with me that proved that he'd gotten beyond whatever it was that kept him from really connecting with me beyond sex last week. And it was having that from him now that made me believe I needed to stop dwelling on the bad and focus on the good. The outside factors needed to no longer be a factor because they were negatively impacting my mindset, and I didn't need that kind of stress and worry.

So, I was going to try my hardest to let go of Reece's words and focus only on the things that Holden said or did. His actions and words were the only ones that should matter anyway. Deep down, I knew I was serious about Holden so Reece's words really shouldn't have affected me at all.

Obviously, I wanted to know what Holden's brother meant by them, but I wanted whatever that reason was to come from Holden himself. In the meantime, I knew where I stood. I knew where my heart was. And if Reece thought that I wasn't genuine, he would soon enough see that he was wrong. Only time would prove that to him that he'd made an incorrect assumption about me.

All that aside, I was still feeling worried at the prospect of meeting Holden's family. And even though he'd eased some of my fears about it by letting me know that they'd essentially reserve judgment until after they met me and got to know me, it only made things marginally better.

Realizing there was little I could do about their acceptance of me, I finished getting myself ready. I was wearing my dress I'd picked out just for Holden. Since he had such an appreciation for my legs, I went with something that was short, but not too short. It was a navy blue, fitted cocktail dress. The dress stopped just below mid-thigh, fit snug to my curves, and was a halter top. My shoulders were bare as was the majority of my back. It didn't dip too low in the back, which I didn't think would be appropriate for the occasion.

The skirt of the dress was solid, but from my neck down to about my belly button was a navy blue, stitched lace overlay. It dressed it up nicely, giving it an elegant look.

I hoped Holden would like it.

With near perfect timing, there was a knock at my front door.

The minute I opened the door, Holden gave me a once-over and muttered under his breath, "Fuck."

I gave him a coy smile and asked, "So, what do you think?"

Holden didn't respond immediately. Several long seconds passed before he replied, "Leni, you look amazing."

I spun around to give him the full view. Once I was facing him again, I questioned, "Is it better than the yoga outfit?"

"It's hard to say. At the very least, they're tied with each other. I like them both for very different reasons," he remarked.

I loved that answer.

"You look really nice, too," I declared after giving myself an opportunity to check him out.

Holden always looked nice, even when he was sweaty after a workout. But I could see that he'd put in that little extra effort tonight. It felt good because it made me believe he thought it was worth looking nice alongside me.

He stepped inside, brought a hand up to curl around the side of my neck, and pressed a kiss to my cheek. "Thanks, sweetheart."

I took a step closer to Holden so my body was just barely brushing up against his. With the two of us being that close together, he couldn't stop himself from giving me more than just that kiss on the cheek.

No.

If there was one thing Holden never held back on, it was this. Physical affection never seemed to be difficult for him. And I thought that was great because I believed physical affection was just as important in a relationship as the emotional connection. So, at the very least, while I waited for him to get comfortable enough with me on an emotional level, I had kisses like this to hold me over.

Holden and I did a fair amount of kissing and groping before separating from one another. "We've got to get out of here," Holden declared. He wasn't wrong. I believed wholeheartedly that if we didn't get ourselves out the door, and fast, we'd miss his grandparents' party completely.

"That's a good idea," I praised him.

A few minutes later, we were in his truck on the way to the party. Fifteen minutes after that, we'd arrived.

And that's when all my nerves came rushing back. But I didn't really have an opportunity to focus on them because Holden immediately exited his truck, rounded the front of it, and came over to meet me at my door. Then, he held my hand as he walked us to the entrance of the restaurant.

We were led down a long hallway to a set of double doors. Once there, Holden took one look at me and smiled before he pushed open the door. He ushered me inside ahead of him, but quickly took my hand and guided me farther into the room.

The two of us had arrived exactly on time. While I didn't know how big the guest list was, I had to assume based on how many people were already in the room that most of them had to have been there.

I barely had a chance to take in just how many people were in attendance when I heard someone call out, "Holden."

I shifted my gaze in the direction of the voice and saw a man who looked a lot like Reece heading our way with a beautiful woman on his arm.

When they made it to us, Holden didn't wait to introduce us. "Leni, this is my father, Troy, and my mom, Eva. Guys, this is Leni."

Troy and Eva both stood there silently a few seconds seeming a bit stunned. Eva was the first to snap out of it. She directed her attention to me, opened her arms, and threw them around me before pulling me in for a hug.

"It's so nice to meet you, Leni," she said.

"And you as well," I returned, hugging her back.

Holden's father came up to me after Eva stepped back. He greeted me with a kiss on the cheek. "Welcome," he started. "You look stunning, my dear."

I felt myself blush at the compliment. "Thank you," I replied. "It's lovely to meet you."

"Come, come," Eva urged. "I'll show you where we're sitting. You two can sit with us. Reece and his date are already here. We're all still waiting on the guests of honor to arrive. Your father spoke to your grandmother a few minutes ago, Holden, and she said they were still going to be another twenty minutes. So, we've got time to get acquainted."

Holden put his hand to the small of my back and guided me through the maze of tables and chairs as we followed his mother and father to where they were seated. I was doing my best to stay focused on where I was going, but I was so distracted by the number of tables.

Luckily, I managed to make it to the table without incident. Once there, Holden and I said hello to Reece and were introduced to his date, Sophie. She looked vaguely familiar, but I couldn't quite place her. Oddly enough, Reece didn't give me the strange look I'd been getting from him the last few times I'd been around him.

After one of the servers came around and asked for our drink order, Holden and I sat down. I instantly leaned into him and whispered in his ear, "When you said that this party was taking place at a restaurant, I assumed there were going to be a handful of people sitting in a couple of booths. I wasn't expecting this. There are a lot of people here."

Holden laughed. "I come from a large family. My dad's side is huge, so gatherings like this are typical for us. You don't have to worry, though. Everyone is super friendly."

I wasn't exactly worried; I just hadn't expected so many people.

"So, Leni," Troy called. "How did you and Holden meet?"

The instant he asked, I felt myself grow somber. I could remember talking with Holden not that long ago about his family. He told me that he and Reece were both very close with their father and Eva. Hearing Troy ask me how we met indicated to me that either they weren't as close as he made it seem, which I didn't believe was the case, or perhaps I just wasn't someone he felt was worth mentioning to them.

Doing my best to ignore the hurt in my heart, I explained, "My yoga studio was actually one of the businesses affected by the arsonist. It was completely torched, and Holden happened to be there after it happened. He was really wonderful that day, and he went above and beyond to help me out afterward. In fact, he talked to Reece about my situation, and now I've been working out of Reece's gym for the last couple weeks."

Troy and Eva both glanced at Holden and Reece with looks of approval. They were clearly proud of the men they'd raised. I couldn't say I blamed them.

"Don't give me that look," Reece warned his parents. "No doubt I did it for Leni and Holden initially, but it's been great for my business. You wouldn't believe how many people have asked that we offer yoga classes. Word has spread quick and I've seen an increase in my gym memberships."

"I'm one of them," Sophie chimed in.

That's when it dawned on me why Sophie looked

familiar. I'd seen her in one of my classes earlier in the week. Unfortunately, I hadn't had an opportunity to chat with her.

I gave her a friendly smile and stressed, "I hope you enjoyed the class you took and are planning to come back for more."

She turned her head in Reece's direction, smiled, and leaned into him as she confirmed, "Without a doubt."

I looked at the couple. While I didn't really know what Reece's dating life was like, I thought he and Sophie made a gorgeous couple. And she didn't hide the fact that she was totally smitten with Reece.

"You're a yoga instructor?" Eva asked, redirecting my attention.

Nodding, I clarified, "Yes, I actually have two separate sides to my business, though. Obviously, I had the studio to hold in-person classes. But I also used it to film courses for my online business."

"What do you mean?" she wondered.

"I've made a name for myself in the yoga community," I began. "As a result, I had a lot of people who were interested in taking classes with me; however, the expense of traveling here to take a couple classes over the course of a week just isn't practical. I found a way to bring my classes to anyone all over the world."

Her eyes widened as Troy gave me a nod of approval. "Would somebody need to have experience before taking one of your classes?" she asked.

I shook my head. "For some of them, you would. But a large portion of my classes are meant for all levels. Even when I do a class with more advanced poses and postures, I always try to offer modifications since not everyone is at the same level."

Eva grinned and looked to her husband. He advised, "You should try it."

It wasn't uncommon for me to have people interested in taking my classes, but I was curious why Troy was telling his wife that she should do it. Clearly, I'd been wearing my confusion on my face because he divulged, "Holden, Reece, Eva, and I are all very physically active people by nature. But my wife is on another level. She can't seem to keep herself still and is always looking for something else to do."

Eva held her hand up and interrupted, "It's not as bad as he makes it seem. From the time I was three, I was a dancer. I took every dance class known to man. Ever since, I've always craved movement. Troy just doesn't like to dance, so he gives me a hard time about it."

Just then, I stared into the eyes of my soul mate. I had absolutely zero doubt about this woman's ability to understand me in ways nobody else ever would, not even my own parents.

Eva continued, "That's why I insisted on getting the boys to dance with me."

My eyes widened. I directed my gaze to Holden, silently questioning him.

He gave me a nod and affirmed, "She isn't lying."

"You dance?" I asked.

"Not in the professional sense, and definitely not if I have a choice," he asserted.

I narrowed my eyes and turned my head slightly in Eva's direction. She warned, "Don't let him fool you. He always loved dancing with me as a kid. Both boys did, in fact. But Holden would seek me out to dance whereas Reece would wait for me to drag him into whatever room I had the music blaring in. Sadly, in more recent years, Holden's decided he's too cool to dance. I don't care, though. I'll still make him dance with me because he's just that good."

Unable to stop myself, and with a grin on my face, I blurted, "Will there be music here tonight?"

"Damn it," Holden muttered beside me as Eva slowly nodded her head and smiled deviously at me.

I turned my attention to Holden and proclaimed, "I want to see you dance with your mom, Holden Locke."

He shook his head in a way that I knew I was going to get what I wanted. And I couldn't wait.

From that point forward, all my nerves about meeting Holden's family flew out the window. They'd been warm and welcoming right from the start. And even after the guests of honor arrived and the party officially started, things only got better. There was a steady flow of conversation at our table throughout dinner. I learned a bit more about Holden's family, Reece never gave me any indication that he was doubting my loyalty to Holden, and I found a new friend in Sophie.

But the moment I'd been waiting for from the time I realized it was going to happen finally arrived. The music was on, dinner and dessert had been consumed, and folks were heading to the dance floor. Some had already made their way there.

Eva stood, fixed her eyes on Holden, and ordered, "Let's go."

I twisted my head and looked in his direction to find him looking at me. "Go ahead," I insisted. "I've been waiting all night to see this."

Holden got up out of his chair and acted as though someone was forcing him to do something he really didn't want to do. If it hadn't been for the small smile tugging at his lips, I might have believed he was genuinely unhappy about it.

By the time the pair had made it out to the dance floor,

I worried if they were going to turn around and come back to the table. The slow song that had been playing ended and Wham's *"Wake Me Up Before You Go-Go"* came on.

There was no way. No possible way Holden was going to dance to a song with this up-tempo beat. But to my utter shock and surprise, Holden put one hand around Eva's waist while the other held her hand.

Then, I fell in love. Officially.

Because Holden moved around the dancefloor spinning his stepmom while they both laughed and had what appeared to be the best time of anyone else that was out there with them.

I couldn't recall ever seeing him so happy before this very moment.

And it overwhelmed me.

I wanted that with him. I wanted him to laugh and smile like that with me.

Yep.

I couldn't deny it anymore. I loved Holden Locke.

Watching him with his mom, I felt something come over me. My eyes welled with tears. I didn't know if it was finally realizing what it was I'd felt days ago when Holden and I were in the shower together, if it was longing for a relationship with my parents like Holden had with his, or if it was something else entirely.

Before I could process that it was over, I saw Eva and Holden walking toward the table. The moment he was in front of me, Holden held his hand out to me.

"What?" I asked.

"Your turn," he declared.

"I… I can't do that, Holden. I love movement, and I love to dance. But I don't know how to dance like *that*."

He grinned and insisted, "You'll be fine. I promise. Just follow my lead."

I sat there, staring up at him completely dumbfounded. When I made no move to get up, Holden bent down, took me by the hand, and lifted me out of the chair. By the time we made it to the dancefloor, I was hoping a slow song would have come on, but I wasn't so lucky.

Bruno Mars' *"Runaway Baby"* had just started, and Holden was wasting no time.

"This is crazy," I maintained my stance.

Unfortunately, Holden wasn't having any of it. He moved us to the middle of the floor, held one of my hands, and slid his arm around my waist. Then, without any idea how it was happening, I was dancing in Holden's arms. He frequently spun me around and moved himself around me.

It was even more fun than I had when we went to the trapeze class. Every so often, Holden would pull me in close to him, smile brightly at me, and just look in my eyes. He didn't say anything. He communicated everything with those looks. And what he told me was that he was enjoying every minute of our dancing.

When the song ended, I assumed we'd head back to the table.

But I was wrong. The music rolled right into Clean Bandit and Jess Glynn's *"Rather Be."*

My eyes widened as I asked, "Another one?"

Holden simply nodded at me.

The ease with which he moved around the floor, guiding me, was magical. Deciding this was something I deserved to have, I let myself go completely and surrendered to Holden. The chorus hit, and I allowed him to hold me, spin me, twirl me, and move himself around my body on the dancefloor without an ounce of hesitation.

The minute I gave in to it, I couldn't wipe the smile off my face. I had told myself that Eva was my soulmate when I heard her say how much she craved movement, but now I knew I was wrong.

Because it was him.

Holden.

He was the one for me. Having this moment was so incredibly special, and I found myself thanking my lucky stars he'd come into my life.

But being so lost in the moment, having the best time of my life, I had lost all my inhibitions. So, when the last line of the chorus ended the song and Holden had pulled me close, I blurted, "I love you."

Holden was stunned.

In fact, he didn't say anything at all.

And that's when I realized I'd made a huge mistake.

CHAPTER 13

Holden

I LOVE YOU.

What was I thinking?

I stood there on the dancefloor with Leni in my arms, staring into her gorgeous eyes, as I let my shock consume me. I shouldn't have been surprised. I knew what I was doing. I knew if I didn't stop, this was bound to happen eventually.

I ignored the voice in my head.

Ever since I met Leni, I seemed to be doing the exact opposite of what that voice was telling me to do.

I tried so hard to stay away and keep things strictly physical like she had suggested in the beginning. I lasted barely a week before I couldn't take it anymore.

There was just something about her that I craved so much. But the day I picked up that phone and asked her out on a real date, I knew it was a mistake. Not because I didn't think she deserved to be treated right, but because I didn't think I'd ever be able to give her what she should have.

But now that she'd admitted her feelings for me, I didn't know what to do. And that worried me. Because it wasn't very often that I was ever in a position where I didn't have a game plan. Of course, I knew the reason I was stuck now had everything to do with the fact that I chose to ignore sound logic.

Apparently, either my shock and fear were too evident, or I waited too long to respond to Leni because she suddenly tensed in my arms. I felt the change in her body and knew I had to do something.

Unfortunately, I had no clue what that was.

"Leni..." I trailed off, my voice a hair over a whisper.

She took half a step back and stammered, "I'm... I'm so sorry."

Even though she took another step back, I didn't let her go. I couldn't. But I also knew I couldn't expect her to stay where she wasn't going to get back what she had to offer.

She struggled to pull out of my hold. "Please let me go," she pleaded, her eyes filling with tears.

"Where are you going to go?" I asked.

"Ladies' room," she choked.

Seeing her like that and hearing her strangled voice nearly broke me. It certainly threw me off balance enough that she was able to pull herself out of my arms. She didn't even look at me again before she took off in the direction of the restrooms.

Watching her walk away, it felt like there was a boulder lodged in my throat. I had known all along what could happen, but I ignored it. And in doing it, I knew I'd just hurt her.

No matter that I didn't think I could ever love Leni back, I never wanted to hurt her. Especially not like this.

I swallowed past the tightness in my throat and walked back to the table where my family was sitting. Once there, my eyes went to Reece's. He knew something had happened. And I got the distinct feeling his date did as well because she said, "Excuse me, I'm going to take a trip to the ladies' room."

"Take your time," Reece insisted.

Sophie got up and walked away.

I didn't have a chance to process all that was happening because my father called, "Son."

When I directed my attention to him, he smiled and declared, "She's amazing."

Fuck. They'd already fallen in love with her. This was not going to be good. In fact, I was mentally kicking myself for all the stupid decisions I'd made since I met her.

Eva chimed in, "I think she's wonderful, Holden. And I'm so happy you've finally decided to give yourself another chance at something special. It's clear that waiting and taking your time to really get involved with someone else again was the right thing to do."

"I've never seen you this happy before," my dad added. "And the way she looks at you... there's no doubting how much she really cares about you."

My mind was so consumed with the hurt I knew she was feeling that I couldn't seem to do anything but nod my head at them.

At that point, Reece stood and ordered, "Come grab a drink with me, Holden."

I was thankful for his interruption and walked away from the table with him. Because even if he was going to give me an earful, I knew he'd support me. I could talk to him about how I was feeling, and he'd give me solid advice. What he wouldn't do is feel disappointment over the loss of Leni like I already knew my parents would.

When we got to the bar, he ordered a drink while I just got myself a water. I didn't need my mind any more muddled than it already was.

I was leaning my back against the bar, looking back at the

table. Leni hadn't yet returned from the restroom and neither had Sophie.

"What happened?" Reece asked.

As I slowly shook my head, I stated, "She's going to get hurt." After a brief pause, I continued, "Worse than she already is."

"And why is that?" he wondered.

I looked at my brother and confessed, "Because she just admitted she fell in love with a man who will likely never be able to love her back like she deserves."

Something strange washed over Reece's face. As quickly as it was there, it was gone.

"Do you want to?" he asked.

I didn't honestly know the answer to that question. Shrugging, I answered, "All I know is I'm not looking to end up in a situation like I did with the last one. But at the same time, I never meant to hurt Leni like this either."

"Does she know about what happened with Kristen?"

"No," I replied.

"Maybe you should share that," he suggested. "If you're struggling to get somewhere you think you might want to be, I think the best thing you can do is talk to her about it."

I closed my eyes and turned my head away from him. When I opened my eyes again, I asked, "How well do you think that's going to go over? Sorry, sweetheart, my ex-fiancée did a number on me, and now I can't commit to you. But, hey, thanks for the mind-blowing sex."

"Listen, I'm not here to tell you what to do. You've got to figure out what's best for you. My only additional advice is that you are mindful of what you've been through. If you think Leni is someone special and you want to go after it, then that's what you've got to do. But if you have *any* doubts, don't hand your heart over to her and risk putting yourself in another place to be hurt again."

Shaking my head, I admitted, "I don't think I can do it, Reece. I know how I am. If I surrender to Leni, I'll go all in. And then she'll have the power to destroy me."

"Do you think she would do that to you?" he asked.

I took a minute to consider his question. Then, I replied, "I don't think she'd ever set out to do something like that intentionally. Then again, I never thought Kristen would have either. But I don't know if I can take that risk. Unfortunately, if I don't, I know I'm going to hurt her. And that's the last thing I'd ever want to do to her."

"Why?"

My brows pulled together. My brother knew me. He knew what kind of person I was. The fact that he was asking me why I wouldn't want to hurt Leni made no sense. "Are you serious, asking me a question like that?"

Reece nodded and explained, "You hooked up with other women after Kristen, and none of them caused you to look the way you do now. What makes Leni any different?"

I looked away from Reece, realizing he had a point I couldn't necessarily argue. And that's when I saw Leni and Sophie walking back to the table from the restroom. God, she was beautiful. Not just in the physical sense either. She lit up a room just by being in it. Her appreciation for everything around her and the fact that it was the littlest things that made her happy made her so special.

But even standing this far away, I knew she was hurt from putting herself out there and not getting what she had hoped for in return. And I hated that I was the one responsible.

"She's just not like other women," I admitted.

"She is if all you consider her to be is a great lay."

That wasn't how I saw her at all. She was the first woman since my ex that I cared about. Leni wasn't just a great lay. She was so much more.

But despite the fact that she meant something to me, I knew what my limits were. And I'd already crossed the boundaries I'd put in place. If I ignored what was happening now, I'd only end up hurting her more. That's when I knew I had a tough decision to make.

"She's more than that, Reece."

When he didn't respond, I looked at him. That's when he asked, "So, what are you going to do?"

I didn't want to say it, let alone do it. But Leni deserved to have someone who was going to love her back. So, there was only one option I had. "I have to be fair to her," I started. "When I take her home tonight, I have to end things."

I felt Reece's hand on my shoulder as I looked across the room and saw Leni sitting at the table with my parents and Sophie. She was doing her best to be happy, but I could see that she wasn't.

"Are you sure that's what you want?" Reece confirmed.

"It'll be better for her if I do it now," I assured him. "She can heal and move on."

Squeezing my shoulder, Reece noted, "That's telling me about her. I asked if that's what you want."

Sadly, I didn't have an answer for him. I simply shrugged and walked away.

When I made it back to the table, Leni glanced up at me before she looked away. Luckily, my parents didn't seem to notice and continued talking with both Leni and Sophie. I sat down next to her and began to dread what was ahead of me.

I was so distracted by it that I hadn't been paying much attention to the conversation at the table. That is, until Leni said, "Oh, um, my ride is here." She stood from her chair and moved to my parents, who also stood.

"Your ride?" I repeated.

Leni turned to look at me. "Yeah, I just figured I'd get a ride home since I'm not feeling well. I don't want you to have to leave the party because of me."

Leni was covering for me. She told them she wasn't feeling well, so she wouldn't have to break their hearts, too.

Leaning into my mom, Leni gave her a hug and a kiss on the cheek. "It was so nice to meet you. I hope I'll see you in one of my classes soon."

"You bet I'll be there. I'm so sorry you're not feeling well."

I watched as she moved to my father, gave him a hug, and said, "You're a very lucky man, Mr. Locke. You have such a beautiful family. Thank you for allowing me to be here to celebrate with all of you tonight."

"Anytime, dear. We loved having you. And honestly, you should make my son take you home so he can see to it that you make it there alright."

Before Leni had the chance to respond, I declared, "I will be."

Leni turned her head in my direction, and all I saw was anguish.

"Great," my dad said. "It makes me feel better that she's not riding home with a stranger. You take care, Leni. Hope you feel better and that we get to see you soon."

Leni gave him a nod, looked to Reece and Sophie, said goodbye, and walked toward me. When she did, she barely looked at me. The minute she made it to my side, I put my hand to the small of her back, felt her body tense, and guided her outside.

Once there, we saw the Uber driver was, in fact, there and ready to pick her up.

"You really don't have to leave, Holden," she started. "I can take—"

"No," I cut her off. "I don't care what happened in there. I brought you here; I'll see you home safely."

Leni pressed her lips together and didn't argue the point beyond that.

I opened the door for the Uber and let the driver know that we wouldn't be needing the service before Leni and I walked to my truck.

The drive back to Leni's place was silent. I knew what I had to say to her, but I felt she at least deserved to have me say it to her face and not the road.

But the minute I pulled my truck into her driveway, I saw she already had her fingers curled around the door handle. My reflexes were faster, so the second I parked and she started to open the door, I reached for her wrist.

Leni stopped moving and looked at me.

"Holden?"

"Wait," I urged her.

She hesitated a moment before letting go of the door. Before I could say anything, she spoke. And when she did, she was talking a hundred miles a minute. "I'm so sorry about tonight, Holden. I shouldn't have just blurted that out like that. I was caught up in the moment, and the words just flew from my mouth. I hope you know I'm not upset with you about how it all went down."

"Leni, sweetheart, you don't have to apologize," I assured her.

She held my eyes and waited for me to continue.

Taking in a deep breath, I saw her wince. She'd already

explained once before that she knew deep breathing usually meant something uncomfortable was coming. She wasn't wrong. "I should be the one apologizing to you," I started. "I'm sorry, but I'm just—"

"Not there yet," she cut me off.

I blinked in surprise.

Leni went on, "I understand. Trust me, nobody gets it better than I do. I mean, I won't lie and say it didn't sting a little when I said what I did to you at the party, but once I had some time to think about it, I understood. Most people don't move at the speed that I do when it comes to most things. I've always been the girl who goes after what she wants, and there's rarely anything holding me back. So, it's not surprising that when things changed between us in the beginning, I took that leap. I felt safe doing it. Because it's like my grandma said to me the other day. I've always just followed my heart. I did it when I decided to take charge of my own life, leave my parents' company, and do what made me happy. And while initially it might have seemed like things didn't go the right way, they eventually all worked out for the better."

I stared at her. This was getting worse and worse with each word she spoke. Unable to pull myself together fast enough, Leni continued, "I might move quick, but I'm a patient woman, Holden. Part of me already knew I'd get here before you. I'm okay with that. I like what we have, and I'd hate to see it end because you're worried that you aren't in the same place as me."

After a brief pause, Leni made it impossible for me to do what I needed to do.

"I trust my heart, Holden. And because of that, it seems like I'm always sprinting to the finish line. I can wait for you to meet me there."

How, after all of that, could I do it? How could I tell her that she shouldn't trust her heart when it came to me? Her convictions were strong, and I didn't have it in me to hurt her any more than I already had tonight.

So, I warned her instead. "It could be a really long road with me, Leni."

"That's okay," she assured me. "This is good between us. Honestly, this was one of the best nights of my life. I had so much fun dancing with you. I always have such a good time with you. So, to be honest, I don't mind slowing down and taking the scenic route if nights like tonight are what I'll get along the way."

She was killing me.

Or, I thought she was.

But then she brought her hand up to my face, pressed her palm to my cheek, and slaughtered me when she asked, "Please. Will you stay with me tonight?"

I hesitated at first but ultimately nodded.

After all of that, I couldn't say no to her.

CHAPTER 14

Holden

"I CAN SEE THINGS DIDN'T GO WELL LAST WEEKEND."

Oddly enough, that wasn't exactly true.

I looked at my brother as we stood out on his deck, and I hoped he'd be able to help me. I needed sound advice.

"That's the thing," I started. "I took Leni home, and we talked. I even spent the night with her. So, technically speaking, things did go well last weekend."

His brows shot up. "Well, it's clear they aren't going well now. What happened?"

Turning my head to the left, I stared off into the distance. I felt like such an ass. Leni deserved so much better than what I was giving her.

When I directed my attention back to my brother, I admitted, "I told Leni I didn't think I'd be able to get to the same place as her. She's all in, Reece. And she's such a good fucking woman that she's understanding of the fact that I'm not there with her. She's willing to wait for me."

"So, take your time and try," Reece suggested.

"I think it's wrong to do that," I argued.

"It's wrong to try?" he asked incredulously.

Shaking my head, I explained, "Of course not. But in this

case, I think it is. I'm not sure I can get there, and if that's the truth, she's wasting her time."

"You don't think you're worth it?"

I sighed. How could he not understand this?

"It's not about that," I told him.

"It absolutely is," Reece insisted.

When I didn't respond, he continued, "You've explained to her your reasons for holding back and not wanting to go there with her. If she understands that risk and is still willing to take the chance on you, that's her choice to make. If you don't give her and yourself that opportunity, you're just being foolish."

"I'm trying to be smart," I reasoned.

Reece moved to one of the chairs and sat down. "You think logic comes into play with love, Holden?" he asked. "You're probably the smartest man I know. There's no way you can actually believe that."

I was terrified of committing to a serious relationship with Leni, especially now knowing that she had such strong feelings for me, and my brother was sitting here talking to me about love.

"I don't want to hurt her," I declared. "I know what it feels like to love someone and to have them hurt you. That's the last thing I'd ever want to do to her."

"So, what are you going to do then? Have you seen her or talked to her since you took her home?" Reece questioned me.

I nodded. "I've seen her once since then, and we've communicated through phone calls and texts. But it's so hard, Reece. She gives me a hundred percent of herself, even when she knows I'm holding back. I'm purposely trying to distance myself to make it easier, and she just keeps giving."

"Distancing yourself to make what easier? And for who?"

"I'm trying to make it easier for her to end this. I figure if she has less and less of me, it won't hurt her as much when she doesn't have me at all. I don't know that my plan is working, though. Because when I'm with her, it's like I forget all the reasons I have not to continue pursuing something with her. But when I go home or when she's not around, I find myself wondering if I'm making a mistake. I'm scared shitless of giving my whole heart to her and having her stomp on it down the road. I don't think I'd ever recover from her."

Reece let out a laugh. I wanted to smack him for thinking there was anything funny about this. Before I could do that, he pressed, "Did you ever wonder why that might be?"

"Why do you think this is funny?" I shot back, ignoring his question.

He continued to laugh at me and said, "Holden, it's amazing that you can't understand what's going on here. I think you already know that you feel something more for this girl than you ever expected. I'm not going to tell you what it is because I know you're smart enough to eventually figure it out. But I hope for your sake you do that sooner rather than later. I'd hate to see you trash something that's worth it because you're afraid. Obviously, there are no guarantees about what will happen. But you need to decide if you ever want that reward. Seeing how she was with you last weekend, especially the way she looked at you when you were dancing with Mom, I have no doubts about how much she feels for you. Seeing you now, I know how much you feel for her. What I don't know is whether you'll wake up realize that she's someone worth taking this risk on the same way she's taking a risk on you?"

I looked away from him again, not sure what to do.

Coming to Reece's, I had hoped he'd tell me everything I wanted to hear. That I was doing the right thing—the smart thing—by pulling away from her. He was doing the exact opposite, and it was messing with my head.

Now, I stuck.

This was wrong. I knew it was wrong to keep stringing her along like this. But for some reason, I couldn't just end it. In a way, I guess I was hoping to take the easy way out. If I distanced myself from her, she'd get fed up and leave me. It would easier to cope with her being angry at me because the opposite was something I didn't want at all. I wasn't sure I could bring myself to look in her eyes and see the pain in them if I was the one who ended this.

"Fuck," I whispered as a vision of Leni popped into my mind.

A moment later, I felt Reece's hand on my shoulder. He gave me a squeeze there before he urged, "Don't let the people who disappointed you and caused you pain be the reason you hurt yourself even more."

That was just it.

"It's not me that I'm worried about hurting, Reece," I insisted. "It's her."

"That should tell you everything you need to know."

And with those parting words, my brother's hand left my shoulder. Seconds later, I heard the sliding door open and close as he left me on the deck with my thoughts.

Fifteen minutes later, I wasn't convinced he was right. Because I still had no idea what to do.

Leni

I was afraid I'd reached my limit.

Since I'd managed to make it to the day I promised my grandma I'd be coming to visit her without completely losing it, I knew I needed to use my time with her today wisely.

I needed her sound advice.

And I knew she wouldn't mind. She loved her time with me. While she always made every effort to bless me with her inappropriate comments throughout our visits, I knew she also enjoyed feeling like she had a purpose. Part of that purpose was imparting wisdom to help guide her granddaughter whenever said granddaughter was headed in the wrong direction.

On the drive over to the assisted living facility, I thought about everything that had happened over the last two weeks that followed the party for Holden's grandparents and brought me to this point of terror.

There was no shortage of activity in my days. Most of them had been filled with work. Between the few additional in-person classes I held and the new series I filmed for my online classes, I kept myself busy. When I wasn't actually doing yoga, it was likely that I was editing yoga videos.

But there were still some moments of downtime. And that was something I'd always hated because I knew how easy it was for me to think a lot during those moments. When I did, it always ended in me panicking about something I couldn't control.

Knowing what had been on my mind and the fact that it was precisely the kind of thing that could send my brain spiraling, I did use some of my free time to simply meditate. It was the easiest thing I could do to keep the bad thoughts from completely consuming me.

Working and meditating weren't something I could do nonstop, however.

So, there were times that I had no choice but to let my imagination run free. And when it did, I found myself beginning to fear that I'd made a really big mistake.

I was torn. Because a huge part of me did not regret for a moment that I'd told Holden I loved him. It was the truth, and I'd learned a long time ago that it wasn't worth it to hold the truth in, especially big ones like that. There was the other part of me that believed I might have ruined the progress Holden and I were making in our relationship, though.

Initially, I thought we were going to be okay. Holden spent the night of the party at my place, and for the most part, everything was great. We'd made love. Well, I did. Part of me believed that he was trying to communicate something to me then as well because when we were intimate that night, it was different. He took his time, never once rushing it, and was incredibly gentle. It was then I actually believed I'd done the right thing by telling him how I felt about him. Because he made me feel like even though he wasn't ready to say the words back to me, he had somehow found another way to share his feelings.

Following our lovemaking that night, Holden even spent some time talking to me. We talked about a couple different things, but mostly I wanted to know more about his knack for dancing. He shared openly and honestly with me about it.

When I fell asleep that night, I didn't do it with the feeling of a gaping hole in my belly like I'd felt when I'd initially blurted my feelings to him and got nothing in response. Naturally, when we woke the next morning and Holden left after having breakfast with me, I didn't think twice about it.

But then it changed.

Things started happening that made me begin to worry.

It wasn't nearly as bad as that first week where Holden only showed up to have sex and leave without anything in between, but it definitely wasn't what it had been between us. I didn't want to admit it, but deep down I had a feeling he was pulling away from me.

And none of it made sense to me.

Which is precisely the reason why I was excited to finally pull into the lot outside the place my grandmother lived. No matter what, I knew she wouldn't let me leave here until I made sense of it all or until she helped me come up with a plan to figure it all out.

I parked my car, grabbed the cookies I'd baked for her yesterday, and made my way to the front door. Walking in, I saw Pauline looking bright and cheerful, ready to greet me.

"Hi, Leni. How are you?"

"I'm doing well, Pauline. How's Grandma been?" I asked.

Pauline smiled and assured me, "She keeps us on our toes, that's for sure!"

I jerked my head toward the double doors that led down the hall to her room and asked, "Is it okay if I head back?"

With a nod, Pauline confirmed, "Absolutely. I'll buzz you in."

"Thanks."

I walked through the doors and down the hall to see my favorite woman in the world. When I got there, I knocked on her door and popped my head inside keeping my eyes closed. "Is it safe to come in?" I jokingly asked.

"Oh, knock off your nonsense and get in here," she ordered.

I stepped into the room, closed the door behind me, and

walked toward her. After giving her a kiss on the cheek, I pointed out, "You have to admit that it's not really nonsense. I mean, you're the craziest one living here. I never know what I'll find when I walk into this room."

"I'm not crazy," she retorted. "I just like to grab life by the balls. What fun would it be to just sit around waiting for stuff to happen?"

I couldn't help but laugh. Only my grandmother would talk about grabbing life by the balls. But that's precisely why I loved her so much. She had no filter, and she didn't care if you liked it or not.

Holding the container up between us, I announced, "I baked cookies."

"Are they any good?" she asked. "I know how you always seem to put things in the oven and then forget about them."

"I don't forget about them, per se. I just get busy doing other things."

"Nearly every time you've burnt something, my darling girl, it's because you were standing upside down," she reminded me.

She wasn't lying.

I wasn't exactly a bad cook, but I wasn't great either. I knew enough to get me by and didn't typically venture outside of what I knew I could handle. But on certain occasions, like coming for a visit with her, I'd try to do something special. Unfortunately, it didn't always turn out the way I hoped. Thankfully, I'd recently learned the art of setting a timer when I put things in the oven. It had helped tremendously with cutting down on the number of failed baking attempts.

Ignoring her reminder of my culinary flops, I opened the container and held it out to her. She took two cookies and ordered, "Alright, Leni. Lay it on me."

"What? What are you talking about?" I asked.

"I always know when you have something on your mind that you need to talk about because you bake for me. I think it's your way of letting me know you need me."

Wow. That was kind of creepy. Until she mentioned it, I hadn't realized that what she said was true. But thinking back over the years, that's precisely what I did. If I was coming in just to catch her up on things in my life, I brought myself alone. But when something was really weighing on me, I brought treats.

When I didn't immediately respond, my grandma surmised, "It's about the boy, isn't it?"

"Grandma, I keep telling you that he's not a boy."

"And like I said before," she started. "Until he proves otherwise, he is. So, what did he do?"

Taking in a deep breath, I held it, prepared myself, and blew it out. Then, I said, "Nothing specifically. And I think that's what the problem is."

"I don't understand."

"Two weeks ago, I told him I loved him," I began. "He didn't say it back, but we talked about it, and I thought he just needed more time. I was okay with all that because what he was giving me up to that point was more than enough for me. In fact, the things he did do showed me he cared in a way that words probably never would."

Grandma's face softened as she chimed in, "Actions speak louder than words, my darling girl. Have his actions shown you something else now?"

I nodded, feeling myself get emotional. "The night I told him how I felt was great between us, obviously after we talked about where he stood with things. But ever since he left my house the next morning, I feel like he's grown more and more distant."

"In what way?" she asked.

"In the way that I don't really see him much," I replied. "We both work hard, and I've been extremely busy the last two weeks. But I still would have set aside the time to see him. I still had the time to see him. We manage to connect on the phone, but that's been about the extent of it. I've seen him once in the last two weeks. And because I'm craving that time with him so much, I even put in the extra effort and reached out to him to ask him if he had time to get together with me."

"Did he?"

I shook my head. "He wasn't able to meet me that day. Apparently, there is a case he's been working on that's been taking up some of his time at work. I understand that completely, but he has had stuff at work before that never resulted in him not finding any time to see me. I just know in my heart that it's something else."

My grandmother, as she always did when she felt I needed her love and support, took my hand in hers. "And what do you think it is?" she questioned me.

I shrugged. "I honestly don't know. Him pulling away from me doesn't make sense at all. At least, not if everything else he's done and said was true. We talked and he said it would probably be a long road for him to get to where I am. I explained that I could be patient because what we had was enough for me. Given where I knew his head was, I've been trying to not push him for anything. I merely just want time with him that isn't just about connecting with him physically, but also on an emotional level. I don't have any intentions to pressure him about anything specific; I just want whatever he's capable of giving."

Sadness washed over me as I took a moment to recall how much things had changed. When I spoke again, I admitted,

"Sadly, I don't think he's in a place anymore where he's capable of giving me anything. And I think that's why I feel like I've reached that place where I have to make a decision."

My grandma squeezed my hand and recalled, "Didn't you say his brother told you to be patient with him?"

I nodded. "Yes. And even though I've never mentioned to Holden that his brother shared that with me, I made it clear to him two weeks ago that I am content to give him the time he needs as long as he's giving me those little bits and pieces he has along the way. Unfortunately, I'm not getting any of that."

"Well, have you talked to Holden about this?" she pressed.

Shaking my head, I mumbled, "No."

"You need to," she ordered. "And don't wait. If you want to give him the benefit of the doubt, you can. But it's unfair of him to string you along like this. It's quite childish, in my honest opinion. If he doesn't want to be with you, he needs to be truthful and tell you. And if he does want to be with you, you need to stop hiding what you need and communicate that to him."

I felt myself grow somber as my eyes dropped to my lap and my heart physically hurt in my chest.

"Why do you seem so sad?" she wondered.

As a tear rolled down my cheek, I said, "I thought my heart wouldn't lead me astray. I guess I'm just trying to figure out why when it seems like the things I want the most, people walk away from me. I already know it, Grandma. I already know he's going to walk away. And it's the moments like this that make me hate the fact that I always listen to my heart. Because when I do, I risk getting hurt this bad."

The next thing I knew, my grandma pulled me in for a hug. When she did, I let go of everything I hadn't been able to with my practice and meditation over the last few weeks.

As bad as it hurt, I knew I was exactly where I needed to be… in the arms of a woman who'd never turn her back on me no matter what.

Hours later, when I was finally home and had put off doing what I knew I needed to do for long enough, I found Holden's name on my phone and touched the screen. Two rings later, he answered, "Hey, Leni."

"Holden," I murmured, already doing my best to fight the tears threatening to fall.

I instantly heard the panic in his voice when he worried, "Are you alright?"

"No," I answered honestly.

"Where are you?"

"Home," I replied. "And I really need to see you. Is there any way we can get together today?"

A moment of silence passed before he responded, "Yeah. I can come over now if that works for you."

Now. He was going to come here now. And all that meant was that I was mere minutes away from doing one of the hardest things I knew I'd ever do.

"That works," I confirmed.

Another beat of silence before he returned, "See you soon, sweetheart."

I choked back a sob just long enough to disconnect the call. As soon as I did, I let go of the tears I hadn't shed in my grandmother's arms.

Sadly, when there was a knock at my door twenty minutes later, I still hadn't stopped.

CHAPTER 15

Leni

I OPENED MY FRONT DOOR AND COULD JUST BARELY SEE THE WORRY on Holden's face through the blurriness in my eyes.

"Leni, what happened?" he asked, stepping inside and closing the door behind him. He immediately wrapped his arms around me and pulled me in for a hug.

For a long time, I didn't say anything. I just held on tight to him and breathed in the scent of him. When too much time had passed without a response, Holden urged, "Sweetheart, you've got to talk to me. Are you okay? Is it your grandma?"

I finally stepped out of his hold and moved to the couch. Holden followed and sat down beside me.

There were so many things I wanted to say, and so much I simply wanted to avoid. But my grandmother was right. If I didn't communicate what I was feeling with Holden, I couldn't expect him to try and make any changes that would get us back on track. Unfortunately, I already knew that this wasn't going to go the way I hoped it would. Perhaps my goal was for us to get back on track, but I had a feeling Holden wasn't even close to wanting that with me.

Knowing that, unsure of where to start, I blurted, "Do you want to be with me?"

Holden slowly lowered his gaze and closed his eyes as he sighed.

There was my confirmation. Without him even speaking a single word, I immediately knew what his answer was. Even still, I felt I deserved an answer. After all that we had, I deserved at least that much.

"I need you to give me the truth, Holden," I pleaded. "I know I told you I'm a patient woman, and I really am. But I also told you that I needed just that little bit of something along the way. You're not giving me anything right now."

"I know," he replied. "I'm sorry."

"I'm not going to push you for more than you can give, Holden, but you can't expect me to stick around when there's nothing."

"It was selfish of me. I should have told you right from the start where things stood for me. It was unfair of me to keep it from you."

My eyes searched his face. "Whatever it is, I'd rather know now than to continue hoping for something that's not in the cards for me."

Holden placed his hand on my thigh, gave me a squeeze, and assured me in a soft voice, "It's in the cards for you, sweetheart. I just don't think it's in the cards for me."

Disappointment moved through me. Even already knowing this was where this conversation was going to end up, the feeling of it was so much worse than I expected. "So, I guess that answers my question. You don't want to be with me."

"Leni, I'm sorry," he lamented. "I know I've said that already, but I'm not sure what else to say. You've got to know that it's not you."

I wasn't sure I believed that. This whole thing didn't make much sense to me at all. He was so hesitant in the beginning with us, not really wanting to start anything. Ultimately, though, he seemed to move beyond whatever was holding him back relatively quickly. And once he gave me just a touch of who he really was, I thought he was the most amazing man I'd ever met.

"Over the last two weeks, I've been purposely trying to keep my distance," he shared.

My lips parted in shock. He intentionally set out to do this to me. "What?" I whispered in disbelief. "Why?"

A moment later, I knew I wasn't going to like what he said because he took in a deep breath. "I did it because I needed us to get to this point, and I guess I was hoping that if you had some time apart from me, it would hurt you less. It was wrong of me to do that to you, but I couldn't bring myself to just come out and tell you. I know it might not seem that way, but in all of this, the last thing I ever wanted to do was hurt you."

"Is it something I did?" I wondered.

Holden didn't hesitate to respond. "Absolutely not. Leni, if there is one thing you take from this conversation, please let it be this. No matter what, I need you to know that this has nothing to do with how I feel about you. I think you are an incredibly special woman. I care about you a lot, but I'm not sure I can commit to you in the way you probably would like and in the way I know you deserve."

My heart was breaking with every word he said. "Why?" I asked.

"Because a few years ago, I was engaged to a woman I loved who broke my heart in the worst way possible," he revealed.

Oh my god.

Holden had been engaged.

"Her name is Kristen. We were together for two years before I proposed. Eight months into our engagement, she went on a work trip. She worked for a fashion magazine and had to go out to some exotic location for a shoot. She was there for two weeks. And another two weeks after she returned, things ended between us. I happened to be at her place when she received a package delivery. She ended up opening that package right in front of me."

I felt like I was sitting on the edge of my seat just waiting to hear what this woman did to him.

Holden didn't make me wait. He said, "Kristen didn't recognize the sender and had assumed it was a wedding gift from someone who wasn't going to be able to make it to the actual wedding. As it turned out, it was a framed picture of her from the trip with a note attached. The note all but thanked her for the wonderful time on the trip. When I asked her what it was about, she told me that she'd been having an affair with her co-worker, who is one of the photographers, for the previous three months."

I gasped. "Please tell me you're kidding."

He shook his head.

That was horrible. I felt awful for him and took a minute to consider everything he'd just shared. It suddenly all became clear to me why he'd been so wishy-washy with me. Hot one minute, cold the next.

It all boiled down to one thing, though.

This handsome, caring, and incredible man was simply insecure. It hardly seemed possible that someone like him could ever feel anything but confident; yet, somehow this woman had done that to him.

But no matter what she did, Holden couldn't go the rest of his life without finding someone who was going to make him happy.

So, I asked, "What do you want?"

His brows pulled together in confusion. "What do you mean?" he retorted.

"In your life," I began. "What do you want to have in your life?"

He shrugged. "I know what you're getting at, Leni, but it's not that simple for me. I'm not sure I can take that risk again."

"What risk?" I asked. "Finding happiness? You don't think you deserve to have that in your life?"

His features softened, and he held my eyes for the longest time. "It's not about that for me," he began. "I'm just not cut out for opening myself up to the possibility of that kind of hurt again. Not only did it happen once to me already, but I saw it with my father. When my biological mother left him, he was shattered. And it took him a really long time to move past that."

"And I bet it was the love of a good woman who helped heal him," I guessed. "There's no way that Eva isn't a big part of why your father is as happy as he was the day I met him. He might have been hurt, but he didn't just give up on giving himself what he deserved."

I was feeling such a mix of emotions over all of this. Anger at what Holden's ex did to him. Frustration that he was just throwing in the towel on finding a healthy relationship again. And sadness. Sadness because even if he believed before now that he could get hurt again, it upset me to think he thought I could do that to him.

"If nothing else, I would have thought you knew what kind of person I am," I said perplexed. "I don't understand."

"Leni, I told you this isn't about how I feel about you or what I think of you," he insisted.

"But it is," I challenged. "You had something terrible happen. I'm sorry that you had to go through that. With your mom leaving and with your ex. But the fact that you won't take a chance on me tells me you think I'm the kind of person who'd do that to you."

The minute the words left my mouth, something changed in Holden's face. It was almost like what I'd said made him reconsider his entire stance on this whole thing. As quickly as it was there, it was gone.

"Why did you even start this thing with me?" I asked. But suddenly feeling my anger creep back up again, I held my hand up. "Actually, don't answer that. I already know. It was my fault because I offered you a no-strings-attached physical relationship. You were just taking what I was offering."

Holden's hand immediately came up and wrapped around the side of my neck. "Don't you dare try to insinuate that you were just available pussy to me, Leni," he ordered. "That's not what you were at all."

He was angry about what I'd said, and I knew that anger was genuine. But it didn't matter anymore. So, as my eyes welled with tears, I rasped, "Well, right now it sure feels that way."

The tension coursing through Holden's body was palpable. Every single muscle and body part was rigid and stiff. Except for his thumb. His thumb that was gently stroking over the skin at the front of my throat.

Then, he spoke and the sound of his broken, husky voice nearly killed me. "How could you think that?"

"I didn't always," I assured him. "That first week, I did. I didn't blame you then because I was the one who offered a no-strings-attached affair when deep down I knew I couldn't handle it. But just as I made the decision to talk to you about it and either end things or tell you I'd need something more, you called me up and asked me out on a real date. And it was the best first date I'd ever had. From that point forward, I knew you were holding yourself back, but I saw you trying to build something with me. I felt like I mattered to you. I thought my heart would be safe with you, and that's why I allowed myself to fall in love."

Holden watched as a single tear left the corner of my eye and streamed down my cheek. When it fell from my jawline, he tried to comfort me. "Since her, you are the first woman I've truly cared about. You're the only woman I've had to fight myself not to come back and see time and time again. I never meant to hurt you, and it kills me now to know that I did."

It wasn't much consolation. On one level, it was hard not to believe that he was genuine in his apology. The part of me that could have faith that he was being honest was the part that refused to let go of the good that I had with him. But the other part of me was the scorned woman. And that's the part that made trusting his words difficult. Because if he truly cared, why was he willing to walk away?

"So, this is it then?" I deadpanned.

Holden's shoulders fell, and his body relaxed. But he didn't respond.

"Can I ask you one question?" I asked.

He jerked his chin down in response.

"What is your life going to be without any passion in it? How could you not want someone to love?" I questioned him. "Someone that would love you back."

"Leni..." He trailed off.

"It might be safe for you to live your life like this, but what's the point? We're not talking about someone preferring to be on their own. You were *engaged*. You don't just decide you aren't someone who wants that in your life. This is about being scared to take a risk. About never being able to surrender to what you feel because you're worried you'll get hurt. Do you know where I'd be right now if I hadn't followed my heart? Sure, I'd have my parents in my life but at what cost? I gave in to what my heart was telling me I needed to do, and I don't regret that for a single second. If I'd have just listened to the sound logic, I'd be working at Ford Communications doing something I hated instead of loving what I do every single day. Never taking a risk isn't about being smart, Holden. It's not living. And it absolutely breaks my heart that you, a man who from the very little that I've seen has so much to offer to a relationship, would allow one person to take that away from you."

I shook my head feeling utterly disappointed before I ended, "What a waste of all that you are."

Several minutes passed without either of us saying a word. It dawned on me that I'd pretty much dominated the conversation. Now, I wasn't saying anything, and Holden still had nothing to say to me.

Deciding it was time to put us both out of our misery, I declared, "Well, I guess that's it. I've got nothing left to say, so I'll just say thanks for coming here so that I could get some closure on this."

Holden's pained expression came to mine. "Leni, sweetheart, I'm so sorry."

My throat was so tight it hurt when I rasped, "Please don't call me that anymore."

Defeat came over him. I felt bad for doing that to him, but he hurt me. I was still feeling really raw.

Nodding, he stood from the couch and moved to my front door. I followed behind him as the pit in my belly grew with each step. When he made it to the door, he stopped and look back at me one last time.

I felt so consumed with heartbreak, I couldn't even begin to react quick enough to stop him when he curled a hand behind my head and pressed a kiss to my forehead.

"Take care of yourself, Leni," he whispered when he pulled back.

With that, he turned and walked out.

And when the door closed behind him, I realized something. Grandma was wrong. Following my heart wasn't always the best choice.

CHAPTER 16

Leni

IT HAD BEEN A LONG THREE WEEKS.

In that time, I'd done what I could to try and heal myself. The truth was, I knew Holden wasn't going to be easy to get over. As much as I hated that he wasn't up front with me about where he was emotionally from the beginning, I had to be honest. He was genuinely a really great guy.

And the moments I had with him that were truly special made it even harder to get over him. Because of that, I'd done what I had to do to minimize my chances of seeing him. Since my studio was still under construction, I had no choice but to continue to work out of Reece's gym. Luckily for me, Reece hadn't made any attempt to approach me since Holden and I broke things off. I wasn't sure if he knew what happened or if I'd been so good about getting myself out of there immediately following my classes that he never had the opportunity to approach me.

Either way, I didn't care. I was relieved that I hadn't needed to have that conversation.

To help myself heal from the heartbreak, I spent a few extra days with my grandma and gave myself more time on my mat at home. I only went to Reece's gym when I was scheduled to teach an actual class. Beyond that, I knew I'd just need some time.

So, until I managed to fully recover from my broken heart, I did my best to get up each day and find something with which to occupy my mind. And I knew that as long as I continued to do that, over time the pain would lessen and the wounds would heal.

For the time being, though, I had to push through the moments that were always a bit nerve-wracking. Like now. I had just pulled into the parking lot at Reece's gym. It was late afternoon, and I was actually scheduled to teach two back-to-back classes. As was always the case, I was looking forward to having the extra time on the mat. But if I was being completely honest, there was the part of me that was dreading being here for the extended period of time. There was just too much opportunity for something to go wrong...like running into Holden.

As I walked through the front door, I quickly gave a nod and a wave to the employee at the front desk. I kept my eyes focused on my destination, which was the room my class was being held in.

Once I made it there, I let out a sigh of relief. I got to work on setting up the space in preparation of my class that was expected to start within the next fifteen minutes. It was no surprise that my classes lately had a heavy emphasis on heart openers. That was precisely what today's classes were going to be as well. I needed to just find all the ways I could to open my heart and air it out. To let the dust of my failed relationship settle somewhere that I could finally find a way to sweep it away.

As I'd opened up the last of the mats and adjusted the

lighting in the room, the door opened. I expected to look up and find my students walking in. Instead, it was Reece.

It seemed my lucky streak was about to end.

Reece shot me a friendly smile and greeted me, "Hey, Leni."

I swallowed hard before I returned a solid, "Hi, Reece."

I wanted to do my best to appear strong and unaffected. It wasn't that I was embarrassed by my emotions or feelings, but I didn't think it was wise to reveal it all to Reece either.

Reece stopped walking a few feet in front of me but didn't say anything.

Starting to worry, I asked, "Is everything alright?"

Just then, the door opened and two students walked in. A look of frustration came over Reece.

"Before you leave today, would you mind stopping in my office?" he asked. "I just want to talk to you about something before you go."

I nodded. "Sure."

With that, he turned and started to walk away. But because I cared too much and was concerned, I called, "Reece?"

Reece stopped and turned around. "Yeah?"

"Is everything okay?" I asked, hoping he understood the meaning in my question.

After a brief pause, he confirmed, "Yes."

I lifted my chin in acknowledgment and did my best to rid myself of the worries I had before class started.

Just two classes and I'd be able to see what Reece wanted to discuss with me.

For the next few minutes, I sat on my mat at the front of the room. I watched and waved as my students arrived but tried to focus on my breathing at the same time. The sooner I got myself into a regular breathing pattern, the sooner I'd be able to calm my nerves.

With a minute left before I was going to start my class, the door opened again and another student walked in.

Tanya.

Ugh.

The day was just getting better and better.

Ever since the first time she'd shown up to one of my classes, she made the effort to come to one weekly. Obviously, it was great for my business to have a returning student, but something about her just rubbed me the wrong way. And now it was even worse because I couldn't even say that I had Holden.

Funny enough, it was like I'd become Tanya. The girl who wants the guy that wants nothing to do with her. Of course, my brand of Tanya didn't come with the creepy aspect that the original did.

When she came in, her eyes came to mine and she shot me a devious smile. I didn't know what it meant, and I really didn't care. I just knew I did not like her at all.

A few more students trickled in behind Tanya, and everyone found a place to practice. Once my students were settled on their mats, I told them we'd be starting our practice in sukhasana, a seated yoga posture very often used for meditation. That was how I planned to get my mind right for the rest of the class.

A few minutes into that posture, I managed to clear my head of the last-minute disruptions. From that point forward through the remainder of the class, I focused only on opening my heart and releasing the hurt from it.

When class ended, my students began to file out of the room. I gave myself a thirty-minute window between the end of this class and the start of the next when I scheduled it. Realizing I had some time to take care of it now, I decided

I'd quickly clean all the mats so I could run out and talk to Reece. I figured it was best for me to do it before the next class because depending on what it was, I might be able to reap the benefits of my class afterward.

I moved to my bag, snatched up my yoga mat cleaner and towel, and turned to tackle the project. No sooner did I do that when I heard, "Leni?"

I knew that voice.

And it was one I did not want to hear.

I turned around and returned, "Yes, Tanya?"

"Um, I just wanted to say that I really enjoyed today's class," she said.

I smiled and returned, "I'm happy to hear that."

"Yeah, I actually talked to Reece. He said that your studio had been affected by the arsonist, but that once it's rebuilt, you'll still be staying on here part-time. I'm happy about that because I'm finding that I've been benefiting from the classes."

While I had spoken to Reece about staying on after I was back in my own studio, that was before everything went down with Holden and me. Now that Holden and I were no longer together, I wasn't sure it was the best idea for me to continue teaching at his brother's facility. It hit me then that perhaps that was what Reece wanted to talk to me about. Maybe he wanted me to stop immediately.

Ignoring that as best I could and not wanting to give Tanya any indication of what was going on in my personal life, I replied, "That's great. A lot of people find that as they continue to practice, there's a lot more benefit beyond just the physical. I'm sure if you stick with it, you'll find yourself reaping those additional rewards, too."

"I'm sure I will, too, because I'm already noticing them," she remarked.

Silence stretched between us for a moment, and I could tell she was hesitating with something. Eventually, she just came out with it. "I haven't seen Holden coming in with you recently. Is everything okay?"

I knew it.

I knew from the moment she walked through the door earlier today that there was something else on her agenda. The look on her face when she first showed up was not the friendly one she tried to make it appear to be. It was all evil.

"Everything is great," I returned, doing my best to seem cheerful. There was no way I was going to say anything that would allow her to gloat about where Holden and I stood.

She looked perplexed and doubted, "Really? That's wonderful if that's the case. I was worried that something had happened when I realized I hadn't seen the two of you coming in together anymore."

Sneaky and conniving. The two best words I could use to describe Tanya.

"Oh, yeah," I started. "Just conflicting schedules and both of us working a lot."

Tanya gave me a look that told me she didn't believe me, but I honestly didn't care.

"That's great. Well, I'll let you get back to work then. I guess I'll see you next week," she ended.

I gave her a nod before she turned and moved toward the door.

Doing my best to rid myself of the conversation with Tanya, I got back to work on the mats. As soon as I finished, I went in search of Reece.

On my way to Reece's office, I saw Connor.

"Hey, Connor," I greeted as I walked by and waved.

Connor looked up at me, and I immediately noticed

something wasn't right. I stopped in my tracks and moved back toward him.

"Is everything okay?" I asked.

Connor nodded, but contradicted that when he explained, "I thought about what you said, and I took your advice."

My eyes widened in surprise. "You told my dad you weren't happy?"

"Yeah."

"That's great. What did he say?" I wondered.

Connor shrugged and shared, "He is not even remotely interested in considering having me in another position within the company."

My shoulders fell. "I'm sorry. I guess I should have been smarter than to think it would be easy to convince him."

"Yeah, tell me about it. You would think after what happened with you, he would have a different outlook on situations like this, especially when he claims that he values me as an employee."

I shook my head. "It's so disappointing. I'm truly sorry to hear that it didn't go well. What are you going to do?"

Connor smirked and offered, "It wasn't all bad. I mean, as a consolation prize he did give me a pretty hefty raise."

Grinning, I teased, "Well, there you go. Always looking on the bright side."

"I try," he insisted.

I glanced up at the clock on the wall and lamented, "I'm sorry to cut this short. I have another class starting soon, and I need to stop in and talk to Reece quick. We can catch up later if you're still around."

"No problem. I'll probably be out of here before you finish, but I'll definitely see you soon, I'm sure."

"Sounds great. Take care, Connor."

"You too, Leni."

With that, I turned and continued my trek to Reece's office. When I made it there, I found his door was open. I knocked on the jamb, and his head came up.

"I figured since I have some time before my next class that I'd stop in now to see you," I explained the reason I was there so early.

"Oh, that's great. Thanks. Come in and have a seat," he urged.

I did as he asked. Once I was sitting across from him, he explained, "I just wanted to make sure everything was okay. I've only seen you coming in for the classes. I always thought your filming was an ongoing thing."

"It is," I confirmed. "But I decided to take a break from it for a little bit. I have enough content to hold me over for a little while, so it's not an issue for me to set it aside when I need to."

"Need?" he repeated.

I sighed. "Truthfully, I'm trying not to be here as much as I was previously. I'm only coming in to teach the classes because I've made the commitment. If it weren't for those classes, I wouldn't be here at all. I don't know what, if anything, you know about the situation between Holden and me, but—" I got out before he cut me off.

"I know."

I gave him a nod. "Well, then I guess you can understand that I'm trying to avoid running into him here. I'm not exactly ready for that."

"He's not coming in, Leni," Reece declared.

"I'm sorry?"

"Holden told me that he wasn't going to be in for a while," he started. "He knows that you're here, trying to work, and he doesn't want to make it more difficult for you. Until your studio is back up and running, he wanted to give you the respect he felt you deserved. Once you're back in your own space, he'll start coming back in here. And he'll do it at a time that you aren't scheduled to teach a class."

My lips parted in shock. Holden was purposely staying away so he didn't create an uncomfortable or awkward situation for me. Or, that's what he wanted Reece to believe.

In any other situation, I might think that his gesture was sweet. I might believe he was being a good man who wanted to make an uncomfortable situation less awkward. To anybody else, Holden would appear to be the good guy. Deep down, I didn't believe he was a bad guy.

But this was Holden.

And experience told me this wasn't him being a stand-up guy. This was just more of the same from him. He was hiding again.

"And here I've been thinking I was getting lucky every time I showed up and he wasn't here."

"Do you really think it's luck?" Reece asked.

When my confusion at his question became evident, he clarified, "My brother cared about you. More than I think either of you realizes."

"Reece, it's not that simple."

"I told you that you'd need to be patient with him. I told you that if you could give that to him, you'd never regret what he'd give you in return."

My nose began to sting at everything he was saying. Of course, I knew part of what he was saying was true because I'd seen what Holden was capable of giving. The problem was that he stopped giving anything. As my breaths grew shallow, I forced out, "I don't doubt that for a minute because I witnessed first-hand just how good Holden can give when he wants to give. But with all due respect, Reece, you need to understand that Holden stopped giving. And I can be patient. I was patient. For a long time. But if he doesn't want to work for this at all, I can't do it alone."

"So, that's it? You both just give up?"

What was he not understanding about this?

"I don't know what you're looking for me to say. I tried. I really did. But like I already told you, I couldn't do it alone. Holden knew what he was doing and even admitted he was purposely pushing me away. I love him, and I could have waited. But I wouldn't do it with zero effort from him. And in the end, if I was only going to end up with half of him and his heart, I'm sorry, but I deserve better than that."

Reece was clearly frustrated, but he took a moment and finally decided, "You're right. I'm sorry. I shouldn't have gotten involved. It's just that... well, he's my brother and I know how big of a mistake he's making."

"It's okay," I assured him. "I understand you wanting to look out for him."

"Yeah, but I should have just let it go like I did the night of the anniversary party," he maintained.

Tilting my head to the side, I asked, "What do you mean?"

Reece cautiously advised, "You'll probably hate me for this, so I'll apologize in advance. I'm sorry. But with everything Holden went through with his ex, I felt it was my job to make sure he didn't end up in a similar situation with you. You were the first woman he had a relationship with that was more than just a hookup. So, when I saw you here being friendly with the guy you used to work with, I wondered if it was something Holden should be worried about. I never said anything to him about my concerns, though. And when I saw you with my brother at the party, I knew then how much you cared about him. Even now, I've known for weeks that things ended between the two of you, and I can still see how much it's hurting you."

While it finally made sense to me why Reece had been looking at me funny for so long, I narrowed my eyes wondering how he could make assumptions about how I was feeling now.

As if reading my thoughts, he added, "I know you're hurting because you've got the same look on your face that Holden has had on his since the night of the anniversary party."

He needed to stop talking to me about this. I did not need to know how Holden was handling anything. If he was truly upset about where things were between us, only he could change them.

"I won't keep you, Leni," Reece said, snapping me out of my thoughts. "I know you have another class starting shortly. I just wanted to make you aware that Holden's purposely staying away so he can give you, and presumably himself, the space you need."

With a nod, I responded, "Thanks, Reece. I appreciate it."

At that, I stood and moved to the door. Once there, Reece called my name.

I looked back and asked, "Yeah?"

"Maybe it's not my place to say it, but I think you should know that he does love you. Unfortunately, he's too afraid to admit it."

My breath caught in my throat. I parted my lips and whispered, "Excuse me."

Then I ran out of his office.

CHAPTER 17

Leni

"THANK YOU SO MUCH FOR OFFERING TO HELP," I said as I threw my arms around Zara and gave her a hug.

"Oh, it's no problem at all," she insisted. "Besides, not only am I glad that you are going to be close by again, I'm also happy you're at least a little further removed from that situation."

Zara was talking about me being at Reece's gym.

It was only a week ago when I ran out of Reece's office after he told me that he knew Holden loved me. When I made it back to the room to try and pull myself together before my students showed up and class started, Zara was already there.

Instantly, she knew something was wrong. I told her everything that happened in Reece's office but didn't get the chance to fill her in on everything that had happened to bring an end to Holden and me.

Regardless, she knew I was hurting and mentioned that she'd seen significant progress being made on the studio. As soon as she said it, I knew I needed to reach out to my landlord to see how much longer it was going to be.

That night, when I got home, I called him up and learned that the major parts of the rebuild had just been completed, but that the cosmetic stuff needed to be taken care of. The minute he said that, I asked if I'd be able to bring a couple friends and do the painting and any extras myself. It took a little convincing, but he ultimately agreed, asking that I give him a few days before taking over.

Now, I was here in my studio for the first time since that dreadful day a few months ago. So much had happened since then, making it feel like I'd lived a lifetime waiting for the rebuild to be completed.

"Yeah," I agreed with Zara. "I think it's going to be much better for me in the long run to be back in my own space. Obviously, it'll be nice to go back to Reece's gym occasionally to see some of those students who won't make the drive out here, but it feels good to be coming back."

"Well, we're going to work our butts off to get you set up as quickly as possible. In fact, Pierce should be here shortly with one of his co-workers."

My body instantly tensed, and Zara noticed.

"Don't worry. It's not Holden," she assured me. "I specifically told Pierce that if he wanted to bring one of the guys from work, we'd love the help, but he was forbidden from even mentioning it to Holden."

I let out a sigh of relief and mumbled, "Even if he knew, it's a sure bet he wouldn't have shown up anyway."

"Oh, you never know," she started. "It's possible he—"

Before she could finish the door opened and Pierce walked in with another guy. He was a handsome man, a bit taller and bulkier than Holden, but he seemed just as physically fit.

"Hey, beautiful," Pierce greeted Zara. After giving her a kiss, he looked at me and greeted, "Morning, Leni."

"Good morning, Pierce," I returned.

He looked to his left, held out his hand, and said, "Leni, this is Tyson Reed. Tyson, this is Lennox Ford, but she goes by Leni."

"It's nice to meet you," I remarked. "And thank you so much for allowing Pierce to drag you over here to help. I really appreciate it."

"It's no problem. I grew up doing construction, so painting some walls, hanging some shelves, and putting up a bunch of mirrors will be no sweat," Tyson assured me.

"Okay, well we should get to work," Zara declared. "The faster we get this done, the sooner I can walk to yoga class instead of needing to drive."

"The boss has spoken," Pierce teased. "How about Tyson and I get started on hanging these mirrors while the two of you start on the paint?"

I looked at Zara, shrugged, and agreed, "That works for me."

After I showed Pierce and Tyson where the mirrors were and where they needed to be hung, we all got to work. While the boys worked in the room at the back of the studio, Zara and I started out in my reception area. I had no plans for it to look like an official reception area, but I did need a space where I could greet new students, or where my current students could lounge and just hang out.

Once we'd pulled out all the supplies and filled up our trays with paint, we got to work. For the next couple of hours, we worked in the big open space at the front of my studio. Throughout, Zara and I talked about a bunch of inconsequential things. In addition, I'd also learned from her that she'd been battling some feelings of resentment and betrayal she'd felt at the hands of her family. Forgiveness had been something she was struggling with, and she was finding that yoga was helping her tremendously with it. Hearing stuff like that always made me feel good about what I chose to do with my life.

Ultimately, our conversation shifted into talks of relationships. It went there naturally with Zara talking about Pierce, but it eventually came to me.

"So, if you're not up for talking about it, that's totally fine, but what's the story with you and Holden?" Zara asked. "I thought you guys were making great strides toward a deeper connection."

"We were," I confirmed. "But then I told him I loved him, and it all went downhill."

Zara was so shocked, I could feel her neck snap as she turned toward me. I stopped rolling paint on the wall and looked at her.

"What?" I asked because the look on her face was so alarming.

"Are you serious?"

Nodding, I said, "Yeah. After we had the chance to talk about it the night of the anniversary party for his grandparents, it all seemed okay. But once he left my place the next morning, things changed. I saw him less and less. And he didn't call nearly as often. Even though I attempted to get together with him one day, he declined the invite. It was like no matter what he'd said or shown me before then, nothing was the same."

"I don't understand. Why?"

I rolled my eyes before I started applying more paint to the wall. Then, I shared, "I had the same reaction." After a brief pause, I explained, "He's had some things happen that make him afraid of taking the risk with me. I understand it, but it doesn't make it any easier. Nor does it explain why he would ever give me the impression that there was ever anything more between us than just sex."

As I dipped my roller back into the tray of paint, Zara wondered, "Did you ever ask him why he went and gave you all the bells and whistles if sex was all it was supposed to be?"

Even though there was nothing funny about the answer to that question, I let out a laugh and responded, "I hinted at it, and he got really angry at me. He claims that it wasn't just about sex and that he legitimately cared about me. The thing is, he never should have given me anything beyond a physical relationship if he knew there was no way he'd ever work for a real relationship and want to fully commit at some point. That's what upsets me the most. I fell in love with a man who showed me somebody truly amazing. And it was all just… honestly, I don't even understand what the point of it was."

"Maybe he did have feelings for you," Zara suggested.

"Well, you know the whole reason I'm here now painting these walls instead of at Reece's gym. According to him, Holden does love me and is just afraid to admit it. I'm just not so sure I should believe that because it doesn't make sense that anyone wouldn't want to be with the person they love."

"Believe it," Tyson interrupted our conversation.

Zara and I both turned around to see the guys standing there.

That's when Tyson went on, "It's not my business, and I didn't mean to eavesdrop, but we finished with the mirrors and thought we'd see what else you need hung or lifted before we join in on the painting. And from what I just heard you say, you should know that Reece isn't lying."

Perhaps to everyone else it was great news to know that Holden loved me. Maybe they thought it helped me to know that he felt something deep for me. The truth was, I didn't think it was helping. And I wasn't sure they could make statements like that unless they'd heard those words from Holden himself.

"Not to be rude, but has Holden actually told you this and confirmed it?" I asked.

Walking farther into the room toward me, Tyson shook his head. "No, but evidence would suggest it's the truth."

"Evidence?" I repeated.

Nodding, Tyson added, "We're private investigators, babe. It's our job to pick up on the subtleties that might go unnoticed by others."

My eyes shifted to Pierce. He jerked his head to Tyson and insisted, "He's not wrong."

"About which part?" I mumbled.

"All of it."

With my mind swirling with a bunch of emotions I couldn't even begin to dream of sorting out when I had my studio to finish painting, Zara came to my rescue. She knew, just like any good woman would, that neither Pierce nor Tyson offered any real proof of their claims.

"What evidence do you have that suggests Holden loves her?" she asked. "Because from what I just learned, I'm not sure that's the case." After a brief pause, she directed her attention at Pierce and scolded him, "And you told me a few months ago that Holden was a great guy that Leni would be lucky to have in her life. I'm having a hard time seeing anything special about how he's treated her."

"Beautiful, I think if you talk to Leni about the good she had with Holden, you'll see that I wasn't lying," Pierce started. "But we all have our own things we've got to work through. I know you understand that. And that's the case with Holden, too."

Tyson added, "Holden hasn't shared anything with us about the status of things between the two of you. Obviously, all the guys know what happened to your studio and how he reacted to it, so we've gotten on his case since then. But he doesn't share anything about your relationship."

"There is no relationship," I corrected him.

"Maybe not now," Tyson retorted. "And my guess is that there hasn't been one for a good three or four weeks now, am I right?"

My brows pulled together. "I thought you said that Holden hasn't shared anything."

Tyson grinned, making him look impossibly handsome. He wasn't Holden or anything, but the man was still a catch. "He hasn't," Tyson confirmed. "But that doesn't mean we can't figure out what's going on based on his mood. He comes in and does a great job at whatever is on his plate for the day, but beyond that, he's not his usual self. The man is just as torn up over you as you are over him. I swear, sometimes I look at him and wonder if he's actually slept decently over the last couple weeks."

I took in a deep breath and blew it out. This broke my heart. I shouldn't have been standing here feeling bad for Holden, but for some reason I did. Maybe it was the words his co-workers were sharing with me. Maybe it was because I missed him. But there was something about standing in my newly rebuilt studio that made me feel a bit overwhelmed.

In an instant, my mind flashed back to the day I thought I would die when this place went up in flames. I remembered standing outside feeling relief that I could continue to breathe in the fresh air, but also being devastated that I'd lost something I'd worked so hard and given up so much to have.

As awful as that was, it didn't take long for me to see the

positive side of it. The biggest blessing to come out of it all was meeting Holden. The compassion he showed me was like nothing I'd ever experienced before, especially from a stranger. And he quickly became so much more than just a nice guy doing something for a woman who was down on her luck.

He wormed his way into my heart, showing me all the things that I'm sure Pierce was referring to when he told Zara I'd be lucky to have Holden in my life. Once I let him in, I got those little nuggets of gold that proved just how special he was.

And in remembering all of that, I looked at Holden's friends and asked, "Do either of you dance?"

"No," they replied in unison.

"Do any of the guys you work with dance?"

Confusion washed over them as they looked at each other. "Just Dom. He's crazy and always the life of the party. Other than him, nobody at the firm dances."

"Holden does," I deadpanned.

Pierce and Tyson were legitimately surprised. They had no idea. And knowing he'd given me that, something these men didn't know about him, I lost it.

"Fuck," I whispered, as my eyes filled with tears.

Then, even though it wasn't overly dramatic or anything, I cried. Tears spilled down my cheeks as I stared off into space.

Tyson, being the closest to me, pulled me into his arms. After a few minutes passed, with one hand moving up and down my arm, he asked, "Is he any good?"

"What?"

"Locke. With his dancing. Is he any good?"

I closed my eyes, smiled, and whispered my reply, "The best I've ever seen."

Tyson shook his head and laughed. "Never thought that man would have any moves," he teased.

"Oh, he's got moves," I assured him.

They all laughed, which made me laugh. I hadn't intended to put that kind of information out there, but I was caught up in the moment. And in the end, it made me feel better to get some of it out.

Before we got back to work, Tyson gave me a squeeze and offered, "We can't make you any promises about where his head is and if he'll come around. But I know one thing's for sure. He can't keep functioning like he is now. So, if that gives you a reason to hope, run with it. And if you'd rather not hope, then at least you can feel better knowing he's feeling just as miserable as you are right now."

I wasn't sure I was in the mindset currently where it was beneficial for me to have hope. Sure, it would have been nice, but I had a feeling it would only lead to more disappointment down the road. And I had to be realistic. There was nothing wrong with dreaming and following my heart, but there was also a point where I had to listen to logic and protect myself.

So, for the time being, I'd find comfort in the fact that Holden was feeling just as miserable as I was.

I looked up at Tyson and said, "Thanks. It helps to know that."

"No problem. Are you good now?"

I gave him a nod before he let me go.

Then, Pierce chimed in and asked, "What's next?"

I gave out instructions on what I needed done next and the boys got to it while Zara and I got back to painting.

And it was then that I finally started to feel a small part of myself beginning to heal.

CHAPTER 18

Leni

IT WAS FINALLY FRIDAY NIGHT. AND IT WAS LATE.

Normally, the day of the week didn't really play a factor in the way I felt, but this had been a long and exhausting week for me.

I spent most of my free time during the week working at my studio. While Zara had enlisted the help of Pierce and Tyson last weekend, they weren't able to come and help out during the week when they were at work. Luckily, Zara did come over in the evenings after she closed her shop for the night to help me out.

I'd just finished my last live yoga class at Reece's gym for the next two weeks. Given the week I'd had, feeling as exhausted as I did, I decided to make tonight's class a restorative one. At the start of class I told my students that I thought this was the best way to unwind and recover after a long, stressful week, and they all seemed excited about taking a class that would offer some restorative benefits.

Now that class had just ended, I was planning to clean up my mats and take most of them back with me since I'd need them at my studio. Then, I was going home so I could get to bed early. I wanted to put in a full day at the studio tomorrow and figured it was best to do it after I'd ensured I had a decent night's rest.

As my students began filing out of the room, I got to work on the mats. I decided to just roll them up and get them in my car. I'd deal with cleaning them before they were used again.

"Leni?"

I turned around to see Tanya, who hadn't yet stopped coming to my classes, standing there.

"Yeah?" I returned as I continued to roll up the mats.

"I saw that you aren't going to be holding another class here for a few weeks," she started. "Are you not teaching at all for the next two weeks, or is your studio finally rebuilt?"

"My studio has been rebuilt, but I'm putting some of the final cosmetic touches on it right now. I'm taking the time next week to finish it up and will start hosting classes the week after."

"Oh, okay. Um, would it be alright if I came to classes there as well once you are up and running again?" she asked as she joined in and started rolling up the mats with me.

I could not read this woman. Sometimes, she seemed like a decent human being, but other times she just came across as sneaky. I never really knew what I was getting with her, and it kind of creeped me out.

Even still, I recalled Holden's words and believed she was mostly harmless. So, I answered, "Yeah, that's totally fine."

"Great! Where exactly is your studio?"

"Do you know where Tasha's Café is? It's on the corner of Pine," I said.

"Yes, I do. I've been to Tasha's a few times."

Nodding, I explained, "I'm on Pine at the opposite end of the block, next to Harvey's Tool Box."

She smiled, rolled up another mat, and declared, "I know

exactly where that is. Do you have a website where I can check out the class times?"

"Yes, but I probably won't have those sorted out until sometime next week," I answered before giving her my website and rolling up my last mat. "Just check it out around this time a week from now."

"That's perfect. Thanks so much."

"No problem."

"Did you need any help with the mats?" she asked.

I shook my head and insisted, "Thanks, but I think I'm alright."

She hesitated a moment, but finally said, "Okay. Then, I guess I'll see you soon at your new studio."

Smiling at her, I replied, "Sounds great. Thanks for helping me roll these up."

With that, Tanya turned and walked out. I went to my bag, pulled out Holden's zip-up hoodie that I still had and slipped it on. It was much colder outside, but I still had the heat in my body from the class. Once I'd gathered up my things and packed them into my bag, I loaded the mats up into my arms. Then, I walked out.

I stepped outside into the cold and instantly felt grateful that I had zipped up Holden's hoodie. It was significantly colder out than when I had arrived. When I made it to my car, I opened the trunk and dumped the mats inside. No sooner did I close it when someone came up behind me and put me in a chokehold.

Seconds later, everything went black.

Holden

What a waste of all that you are.

For weeks now, I'd heard Leni's voice repeating those words to over and over. And when I heard them, I could hear her disappointment. More than anything else, knowing that Leni was disappointed in me was like pure torture.

Because when I recalled her saying those words along with all the other things she said to me, it took everything inside me not to go back to her. Somehow, I'd managed to stick to my guns and keep myself away.

But today, I was finally admitting defeat. I couldn't do it any longer. I had to surrender. Sleep and my appetite had eluded me. My parents were devastated when they heard I'd ended things between Leni and me. And while he didn't ever do anything but offer his undying support, I knew Reece was disappointed in me, too.

Unless I found a way to completely focus on my work-related tasks, no other thoughts consumed my mind. It was only ever her.

All I'd done for the last several weeks was miss her. When the pain of not being able to see her or talk to her had grown to be too much to handle, I had to admit the truth to myself. I didn't just care about Leni. I loved her. If I didn't, it wouldn't have hurt this bad.

Any doubts that I had about it flew out the window when I realized that no matter how much time passed, the pain never lessened. When things ended with Kristen, it didn't feel this bad for this long. That's when I knew that it had been Leni the whole time. She was the one for me. She was the reason why things never worked out with Kristen.

But now that it had been weeks since I'd last seen her, I didn't know what to do to make it right. I didn't even know if I still could. For all I knew, she could have moved on already. The thought of it made me sick.

I was still at work.

I could have left hours ago, but this had become my new normal after Leni. Going home meant that I was stuck alone with my thoughts. At least if I was at work, I could find something to do to occupy my mind a bit. It didn't always work, and sometimes I even found myself struggling to keep my focus, but it was better than being in bed wishing she was there with me.

The only plan I could come up with was to just go to her and hope she'd be willing to see me. Just as I was about to get up and round my desk to leave my office, Tyson's frame filled the doorway.

"Everything okay?" I asked him.

"I'm good, brother," he replied. "The better question would be… is everything okay with you?"

I didn't respond. I simply gave him a look that told him I wasn't in any mood for him to give me grief. Tyson ignored my look, walked in, and sat himself down in the chair on the opposite side of my desk.

"What's going on?" I wondered.

He cocked an eyebrow. "You tell me."

The guys didn't know anything about my relationship with Leni. All they knew was that I'd overreacted when I caught the guy who'd been setting the fires and was responsible for nearly killing Leni. They took that overreaction to mean that I felt something for her. I didn't necessarily deny it, but I also didn't give them anything to indicate that they'd gotten it right either.

When I didn't reply to Tyson, he pointed out, "Look, man, I know you probably think I have no right to be here telling you anything about this, but somebody's got to do it. This isn't you. For weeks now, you've been getting here early and leaving late. I understand dedication to the job when there's something to investigate. But that's not what's happening here."

"I'm a grown man, Tyson. I think I can make my own rules up about how I spend my time, especially when what I'm doing isn't affecting anyone else."

"I'm not saying you can't. But if you're a grown man as you put it, why don't you be one and own up to your feelings?"

My eyes narrowed at him as I shot back, "Excuse me?"

Before Tyson could respond, Gunner appeared in the doorway. He didn't hesitate to join in the conversation. "It looks like Tyson has finally said something," he surmised.

What the hell was going on?

Confusion washed over me. "Is there something going on that I'm unaware of?" I asked.

"You mean other than the fact that you feel something deep for this girl and you won't admit it?" Tyson challenged.

I stared back at him and said nothing.

He kept going. "Your silence says it all," he started. "We've all seen it, and I'm sick of watching you sit around and do nothing about it. That girl loves you."

"How do you know anything about what she feels?" I asked.

"Because she broke down crying in my arms nearly a week ago," he offered.

My whole body tensed. "What?"

Tyson grinned. "She's cute," he taunted me. "I can see why you fell for her the minute you laid eyes on her. And then knowing she does yoga. I bet that girl is *real* flexible. That's got to be a lot of fun."

"You better stop fucking talking about her like that," I warned him. "Tell me why you were with her and how she ended up crying in your arms."

"That's a lot of emotion for someone you claim to not have any feelings for," he goaded me.

I looked to Gunner. "Hayes, man, you need to talk some sense into him," I advised him. "Otherwise, you're going to be breaking up a fight in about five seconds."

"Tyson," Gunner called. When Tyson looked to him, Gunner urged, "Just tell him."

"What?" Tyson threw his hands up. "It's not like I'm saying something that is different than what everyone else in the office is thinking. I see a man I respect, a man we *all* respect and care about, throwing away something really fucking good. For someone who's so smart, this nonsense is just that. Nonsense. Holden, brother, you live your life using logic and sound reasoning. You can't possibly tell me that it's anything but illogical for you to think that you won't be able to have a healthy, loving relationship again. That's just not possible. Especially not when the girl I met is the girl you've got that shot with."

He paused a moment while I took in everything he'd said. None of what he said was wrong. Obviously, he didn't know that I'd already admitted to myself that I loved her and that I was planning to do whatever I had to do to get her back.

As a result, he continued, "Her studio is mostly renovated. Pierce's woman was all about helping your woman get her place looking nice again. So, Pierce asked me if I'd go over with him and help out with some of the heavy lifting."

"Why was she crying?" I asked again, my jaw clenched.

Tyson shrugged and answered, "I don't know, honestly. One minute she was talking about you dancing, and the next minute she was crying her eyes out."

This was just wonderful.

"Dancing?" Gunner repeated.

"Apparently," Tyson replied before bringing his attention to me. "Didn't know you had that in you, Locke."

I just shook my head at him.

"I'm going to go and talk to her," I announced.

I watched as their eyes widened in shock. "Just like that?" Tyson asked. "You mean all I had to do was come in here and say all that? Fuck. We could have ended this madness weeks ago."

I shook my head. "No, asshole. I decided about ten minutes before you came in here that I'm no longer interested in trying to fight this anymore. I can't think about anything but her right now. So, I'm going to go to her place and see if she still wants to try and work this out."

My co-workers, who were my closest friends, grinned at me. Tyson added, "She will."

Just then, we heard the buzzing coming from our front door. Entrance into the Cunningham Security office was impossible without either having the code or being buzzed in. It was late, well after our normal business hours, so not only was Deb, our receptionist, already gone for the day, but the three of us immediately grew alert as well. This was not a common occurrence.

Being the closest, Gunner was the first one to move out of my office. Tyson followed him, and I was out right behind him.

Before Tyson and I made it out to the front, I already heard Gunner opening the door. A woman was frantic. Once we joined them, her eyes left Gunner's and came to mine.

"Holden, I'm so sorry."

My body tensed. "What's wrong, Tanya?"

Tears were spilling down her cheeks as she whispered, "It's Leni."

The second I heard her name, my stomach dropped.

CHAPTER 19

Holden

"Tell me what happened," I ordered.

"Her class had just ended," Tanya began. "Ever since the first class I took of hers, I haven't missed one. I almost didn't go tonight, but I'm so glad I did."

"Tanya," I called.

Her eyes shot to mine.

"Focus," I instructed her. This was not the time for her to be reminiscing.

She shook her head, ridding herself of the mindless thoughts and focused. "Right. I'm sorry. Anyway, after class ended, I asked her about the location for her new studio so that I could come and take classes there. We talked for a few minutes, and then I left. I walked out to my car, but I got a phone call on the way, so I hopped in and took the call as I waited for my car to warm up. While I was sitting there talking, I saw Leni walk out with the yoga mats toward her car. She got them in her trunk and then…" She trailed off.

"Then what?" I pressed.

She closed her eyes, her whole body showing signs of her defeated mindset. "He came up behind her and put his arm around her neck. It only took seconds for her to go unconscious."

Fuck.

Fuck.

"Did you see who it was?" Tyson asked.

Tanya nodded and said, "I don't know his name, but he goes to the gym. I've seen her talk to him a few times before."

I wracked my brain trying to think of everyone I'd ever seen Leni talking to at the gym. She was so friendly and welcoming to everybody that it could have been any number of people.

"Is it someone who takes her classes?"

Tanya shook her head. "No."

"Can you describe him to Reece?" I asked.

Tanya nodded.

I pulled out my phone and called Reece.

"Hey, Holden. What's up?" he greeted me after two rings.

"Someone from your gym put Leni in a chokehold until she passed out and kidnapped her from the parking lot outside your gym," I returned, barely taking a breath until I got it all out.

"What?"

"Tanya just showed up at my office. She watched it happen and can describe the guy to you. I need you to tell me if you know who it is," I explained.

"Of course," he agreed.

I put the phone on speaker and Tanya immediately rattled off the description of the guy she saw take Leni.

"Connor," Reece stated. He was so matter-of-fact about it.

"Who?" I asked.

"Connor," he repeated. "He's the guy she once told me she used to work with. Apparently, he works for her parents."

Right then, I knew who he was. I'd met him the first day I brought Leni to Reece's gym. But it didn't make any sense that the guy would kidnap his employer's daughter, even if they were estranged.

"Why would he take her?" I wondered aloud.

After a beat of silence, Reece said, "I have no idea."

"Why did you hesitate?" I asked.

"It's nothing," he tried reassuring me.

I wasn't buying it.

"It's her life, Reece. Even if you think it's nothing, it's not. Just tell me," I ordered.

He blew out an audible breath. "I don't know. The guy creeped me out. I walked into the room Leni was setting up for a class one day, and I saw him with his hands on her."

Rage boiled up inside of me. "What do you mean he had his hands on her? And you didn't tell me?"

"It was weeks ago," he started. "And at the time all I could think was that I hoped you hadn't gotten involved in another situation with a woman who was just like Kristen."

"Reece!" I barked.

"What?"

"Explain what you mean about him having his hands on her?" I demanded.

"They were standing close. She had her hand on his arm, and he was touching her shoulders. That's it. Knowing what I know of her now, I think it was completely innocent on her behalf. I'm not so sure about him, though."

I took in a deep breath and announced, "Alright, I've got to go. Thanks for the help."

"Let me know what else I can do," he insisted.

I disconnected with Reece, looked at Tanya, and asked, "Did you see what happened after Leni was unconscious?"

"Yes. He put her in the back of his car and took off. I tried following them but got stuck at a traffic light and lost them."

"Okay, can you give the description of the vehicle along with the direction it was headed until you lost it to Gunner?" I asked.

"Sure."

I gave her a nod and directed my attention to Gunner. "I need to get on a computer," I started. "After you get that information from her, I need you to check the surveillance footage from the parking lot. See if there's anything there we can work with that'll help us find her."

Gunner jerked his chin in understanding.

I walked away from the front reception area and moved back to my office. When I got there, I pulled up a search database and tried to find anything I could on this guy Connor. I did at least know that he worked for Leni's parents at Ford Communications. I was hoping that would give me something with which to work.

"What are you thinking?" Tyson asked as he followed me in.

"I don't know yet," I admitted. "But it doesn't make sense that he'd go after the daughter of the people who employed him, unless…"

"Unless what?"

"Unless they're paying him to do it," I concluded.

Realization dawned in Tyson's face. "Who are these people?"

"The founders and owners of Ford Communications," I shared.

"You want me to take him or them?" he offered his help.

My eyes narrowed as I felt the rage boiling up inside me. "I've got him," I seethed.

With that, Tyson left me alone in my office to head to his so he could get to work on Leni's parents. I sat in my chair and got started.

As I began my search, it took everything I had not to want to kick myself for my foolishness. If I hadn't been such an idiot, Leni would never have been in this position. If something happened to her, I'd only have myself to blame.

And she might not ever know the truth about how I felt about her.

Leni

It was dark, cold, and I couldn't move.

Of all the things in the world I could experience, the inability to move my body would be the one that that would cause me to panic.

Throw me in a burning building, and I'll be alright as long as I can move. Move and breathe.

But restraining me and restricting my movements was a surefire way to make me anxious. Especially when I was rendered immobile in what felt like a lot of water.

I blinked my eyes open. It took me a minute to figure out where I was.

Reece's gym. In the area that was being renovated. The work on the pool had been recently completed, but Reece hadn't had it filled yet.

However, for some reason, it was now filled up to my chest. I was sitting down, bound to a chair. A chair that, no matter how much I tried to wiggle and squirm, would not move. It was then I realized that the chair had been bolted to the floor of the pool.

"Ah, you've decided to join me again," I heard a familiar voice say.

I turned my head to the left, looked up, and saw Connor sitting on the edge of the pool. His feet were dangling over the side, the water just grazing his ankles.

"Connor," I started, still feeling a bit out of it. "What's going on? What are you doing?"

"We could have been so good together," he stated.

Blinking my eyes in surprise, I asked, "What?"

Connor looked off to the side, not at anything in particular. It was like he was just contemplating something. He didn't look back at me when he said, "But you had to go and ruin everything."

"Connor, please," I begged. "Please just remove these restraints, and we can go somewhere to talk about this."

I hated the fact that I sounded scared, but I couldn't hide it either. There was a menacing edge to his voice. The tone of it slid through me in an uncomfortable way that sent chills down my spine.

I didn't actually think he would have listened to me, but I knew I couldn't just sit and wait for him to do whatever he planned to do to me.

Sadly, I didn't have to wait much longer for him to show me what that was. Because without another word, he stood and moved toward the wall. That's when I noticed the hoses that ran from the spouts at the wall to the pool.

Connor turned the water on.

Suddenly, I couldn't breathe. I was going to drown. The thought terrified me.

"Connor," I yelled out. "Why are you doing this?"

He walked away from the wall and moved closer to the edge of the pool. "Because you had to be selfish," he accused me. "You couldn't just be happy that you were being handed everything on a silver platter. No. Lennox Ford had to prove she could go after what she really wanted in life. And in the process, she didn't care who else was affected by it."

"I had no idea my father would ever think of putting anyone else in that position," I insisted. "You were the smart and obvious choice. I never meant to do anything that would have hurt you, Connor. I swear that to you."

"Your word means nothing," he countered. "Why, Leni? Why couldn't you just be happy with all they were giving you? Don't you know how successful we could have been together? Don't you realize how much money we could have made?"

"Of course, I do. But money isn't everything," I claimed.

"Yes it is," he shot back. "Do you think I'd be here right now risking everything if it weren't about the money?"

As the water level slowly began to rise, I knew I had to try a different approach. I had to get him to calm down.

"Yes, Connor, I do. Because right now you're doing exactly what I did. Maybe you're going about it in a completely different way, which I might add is not going to be good for you in the long run, but you still have the same thing driving you that I did."

He jerked back at my words as his face was awash with confusion.

"Passion," I stated. "You have a drive to be a successful man. Yeah, the money is great, but you know it's not everything. Because my father just gave you a raise when you expressed your desire to grow within the company. If this were about money, getting that raise would have been enough. So, you know, Connor, that this is about something so much deeper than that. This is about you wanting to use the skills and talents you have to become someone. You want your hard work recognized."

I thought I was getting somewhere because the anger was

gone from his face. But it only lasted a few fleeting seconds. Apparently, trying to praise him wasn't going to work either.

I decided to try a different tactic. "But you're a coward," I declared.

"Fuck you!" he exploded.

"What? Did I strike a nerve?" I asked. I honestly believed I had nothing left to lose at this point. I mean, if I was going to die, I was going to make sure Connor knew exactly what I thought of him now.

"Fuck you, Leni!"

"No, Connor. Fuck *you*! You're a coward," I spat. "You didn't get what you wanted, so you this is how you handle it? Instead of being lazy and feeling bad for yourself about the position you're in, maybe you should have gone after what you wanted. If it wasn't going to happen at Ford, it could have happened somewhere else. The problem is, you don't believe in yourself. You gave up. Maybe I won't make it out of here alive, but you know what? At least I can die knowing that I didn't take the easy way out. I didn't surrender. I knew what I wanted in life, and I went after it. And you know what? I got it. All you'll be from now on is a coward. And a murderer."

Connor clearly didn't like hearing what I had to say. He gave me one last smirk and admitted, "Maybe you're right. But while I'm that, you'll be dead."

With that, he turned and walked out, leaving me in a pool with water at my throat and steadily rising.

I sat there staring at the door he walked through for about ten seconds before I started to panic. I struggled and pulled against the restraints, feeling them tear into my skin.

"Help!!!" I screamed. "Help me!!"

I knew it was late and nobody was out there, but it made me feel better to scream. Because at the rate the pool was filling, I knew I didn't have much time left. I wanted to use my lungs for as long as I could. So, I took deep breaths and continued to scream.

And even though I didn't know how much time had passed, I knew it hadn't been very long when the water came up and I took in my final deep breath.

CHAPTER 20

Holden

Fifteen minutes earlier

There were no words to describe just how useless I felt. I had no idea where Leni was or if she was okay. I knew that I could have driven all over town looking for her, but I'd be wasting time if I didn't at least have a good idea of where she might be.

It felt like so much time had passed since Tanya showed up telling me that Leni had been kidnapped. And all I could do was try to stay focused on figuring out where Connor would have taken her. If I couldn't keep it together, I knew my chances of finding Leni were going to diminish. So, I did my best to keep my emotions out of it and treat it just like any other case.

But deep down, I knew that wasn't what was happening.

Just then, movement in my office caused me to look up from my computer.

"I'm going to check out the parents' place and their business," Gunner announced as he walked into my office. "Tanya gave me a description of the vehicle Leni was taken in. I checked the outside surveillance and confirmed everything went down just as Tanya said. Tyson mentioned that you're concerned her parents might be involved. He's still digging. I'm going to see if I can locate that vehicle."

I was about to respond to Gunner and let him know that I'd reach out as soon as we heard anything, but before I could, my phone rang. Looking down at the display, I saw Reece's name.

"Reece," I answered after the first ring.

"Are you at your office?" he asked, but he was clearly out of breath.

My body tensed as I stood. "Yeah, why?"

"Then you're closer to her than I am," he explained. "She's at the gym. He took her back to the gym."

I grabbed my keys and started moving as I relayed the information to Gunner. He told Tyson as I continued to run to the front door. Tyson was beside me in a flash. "You're with me," he ordered.

As soon as we got inside Tyson's truck, I asked, "How sure are you? How do you know?"

Reece explained, "After you called, I got on the computer here at Sophie's place and checked the surveillance footage. I went back through and looked at it from the time she arrived at the gym just before her class began. After I'd gone through all of it and realized there wasn't much I'd be able to give you, I closed the screen with the recorded footage. That's when I saw the live stream."

"Is she okay?" I asked.

I waited for Reece to respond, but one never came.

"Reece!" I shouted.

"She's in the pool, Holden," he sighed. "And she's anchored to something. I can't tell what because the water is so high. I don't fucking know how he filled it so fast, but he did. And she's nearly out of time."

Damn it.

"What is he doing?" I asked.

"There's nobody else there with her now," Reece returned. "I can go back and check the footage later, but I figured it was best to get there before it was too late for her."

"I've got to go."

"I'm ten minutes behind you," he returned. "I'll call the police and get an ambulance on the way."

After I disconnected the call with my brother, I sat there staring out the window. I could have yelled at Tyson to drive faster, but he was already breaking the law by driving at a speed that was well above the speed limit. There was no way he'd be able to get us there any quicker than he was already trying to.

She's nearly out of time.

Leni.

My girl.

Alone.

And nearly out of time.

"Holden, brother, talk to me," Tyson urged.

I shook my head back and forth as I remarked, "She's going to drown. He put her in the pool and she's going to drown."

In the next instant, I heard the engine RPMs increase as Tyson pressed the gas pedal, and with a voice full of determination, he promised, "No she's not. We're going to get her."

Panic and dread filled me. There was no way this could happen. She couldn't die not knowing that I loved her. And the thought that she might gripped me with such a crippling fear.

Minutes later, Tyson pulled up right in front of Reece's gym. He didn't even have the chance to throw the truck in park when I was already out and heading for the door. I used my key, opened it up, and raced through the gym with Tyson on my heels. We made it to door at the back of the gym that led to the newly renovated addition. Opening that door, we quickly moved through the space to get to the door that led into the pool area. I flung it wide open and went in to rescue mode the minute I saw where she was.

Tyson and I raced along the side of the pool to the opposite end where she was completely submerged in the water. We both jumped in, and I immediately went under to see how we could free her. Seeing her for the first time in weeks like this, her lifeless body attached to a chair, caused something stir inside me. It threatened to take over, but I knew I couldn't lose it now.

Seeing how she was restrained, I resurfaced and yelled to Tyson, "Zip ties. We've got to cut her free."

I didn't wait for Tyson to respond because I knew he'd have, just like I did, a knife in his pocket. And I had every confidence that he'd do exactly what I'd ordered him to do so we could get Leni free and out of the water.

As soon as I went back under the water again, I worked on freeing her left wrist and ankle. And even though I wasn't paying attention to Tyson, I knew he was doing the same exact thing on her right. The minute I had my side free, I glanced over and saw Tyson indicating she was free on his side. We immediately stood and lifted her.

I held on to Leni, keeping her head above the water while Tyson heaved his body out. The second he was out, he turned and took Leni from my arms. While I lifted myself out of the pool, Tyson laid her down on her back and listened for her breathing and checked for a pulse.

"She's got nothing," he said.

I didn't waste any time. I unzipped the hoodie she was

wearing, belatedly realizing it was the one I'd put on her the day of the fire at her studio, and immediately began performing CPR.

It felt like time was slowly ticking by as I did chest compressions and breathed air back into her body.

"Come on, sweetheart," I begged, continuing to pump.

I no longer even sounded like myself. The fear I felt, evidenced by the growing pit in my stomach and the boulder lodged in my throat, was beginning to take over. There was no more controlling it.

Moving my hands from her chest, I pinched her nose with my thumb and forefinger and gave her two breaths. I listened. Nothing.

"Come on, Leni. Breathe!"

Tyson took over the next round of chest compressions. I tried to breathe life back into her body again.

Nothing.

By the time Tyson reached the halfway point of the third round of compressions, we heard a cough and a gurgle.

"Roll her, roll her," I directed Tyson. As we shifted her to her side, I encouraged her, "That's it, Leni. Get it out, and come back to me, sweetheart."

The relief I felt was so immense. Never have I ever felt so scared in my entire life and hearing her fight to breathe was simply overwhelming.

I continued to hold her head in my hands as she vomited up the water she'd ingested. Tyson kept his hands on her body, making sure she didn't roll to her back again.

That's when the door into the room swung open. My back was to it, but Tyson announced, "It's Reece."

"Is she out? Is she okay?" Reece yelled, running over to us.

Tyson answered Reece as I lowered my head and looked

at Leni. "You're okay, sweetheart," I whispered. "I've got you. You're going to be okay."

Leni was struggling, but she was breathing on her own. I never thought I'd be so relieved to see her in such a state.

While anyone who looked at me might think that my face was wet from being in the pool, it really was just a cover for the fact that I couldn't stop tears from leaking from my eyes. In a matter of moments, the awful choice I made to let this woman slip through my fingers and walk out of her life hit me full force.

She could have died. A second time.

If that wasn't enough to show me that life was short and precious, nothing would be. As I looked into her eyes, all I knew was that this whole thing reaffirmed the choice I made when I was sitting in my office before Tanya showed up.

Leni was meant to be in my life. She was the one for me. And the minute she got through this mess, with me by her side, I had every intention of making things right between us again.

Leni

My eyes fluttered open.

When I took in the scene around me, it all came back.

I nearly died because Connor tried to drown me. I couldn't even begin to think about where he was or if anyone knew he was the reason I had been so close to death. All I cared about was that I was lucky enough for the second time in my life to survive something that many people might not have lived through.

I had been held overnight for observation.

And while I had been mostly confined to the bed for the last several hours, I wasn't restrained to it. My wrists and ankles were bandaged up from where the restraints had dug into my skin as I struggled against them. I was finding that my breathing was getting better. When I first arrived at the hospital, I was having quite a bit of trouble taking in full, deep breaths. But as they administered the oxygen, it started to improve.

I glanced at the side of my bed and saw the back of Holden's head. He'd spent the night with me, refusing to leave my side, even after the hospital personnel told him he couldn't stay.

Chaos had been swirling around me from the minute the paramedics arrived at Reece's gym. I still had no idea how Holden knew that I was even kidnapped, let alone where to find me.

Now, for the first time since being rescued, I was able to take advantage of the silence and think about the things that had been lingering at the back of my mind.

Mostly, that meant Holden.

I tried to talk to him last night, but he insisted that I get some rest, assuring me he wasn't going to go anywhere.

But it was morning, and I had rested all I was going to rest knowing that Holden was sitting right here.

I knew where things stood between us, but I still felt compelled to touch him. So, I lifted my hand and cupped the back of his head.

Almost instantly, Holden stirred and lifted his gaze to mine. There was something in his eyes that I hadn't seen before from him. I immediately pulled my hand back and gave him a worried look.

"Are you okay?" he asked.

I gave him a slight nod but didn't say anything.

For several long seconds, neither of us said anything. We continued to stare at one another. And while I had no idea what was going through his head, I was feeling so consumed by the fact that it was the first time I was seeing him in weeks. Or, at least, the first time I was seeing him where I could actually breathe and talk.

I eventually broke the silence and said softly, "Thank you for rescuing me last night."

Devastation washed over him. "Leni, sweetheart, you never should have been in that position. You don't need to thank me. I should be apologizing to you."

"For what?"

He held my gaze quietly before he replied, "For not admitting how I truly felt about you weeks ago. I'm so sorry."

"How you truly felt?" I repeated.

His voice was so gentle when he spoke. "I love you. I love you so much, and you almost died before I had the chance to tell you."

My eyes widened. "What?"

"You were right," he admitted. "I was too afraid to surrender to my feelings because I was worried about getting hurt. But for weeks, I endured pain so severe without you in my life, I finally got to the point I couldn't stand it anymore. And the moment I realized it, the day I decide I'm going to go and make things right with you, I find out you were kidnapped."

He paused a moment, looking down and shaking his head in disgust.

"I'll never forgive myself for what happened to you," he rasped. "Seeing you like that yesterday... terrified that you wouldn't survive. God, Leni, I'm so sorry for what I did to us. I sorry for what I did to you."

I took his hand in mine. "Holden, what happened yesterday isn't your fault," I insisted. "I can appreciate where you're coming from, but you're not to blame for what Connor did."

"If I hadn't walked away from you, I probably would have been there at the gym with you last night. You wouldn't have been alone, and he wouldn't have had that chance to grab you."

It was so like Holden to take it all on his shoulders. I hated that for him, and I knew if I didn't find a way to get him to see otherwise, he'd never let it go. "If it hadn't been last night, it would have been another night," I began. "Connor was on a mission. And I have a feeling that if you had been there with me last night, he would have found another way to get to me."

"You're not going to erase the guilt I feel, Leni," Holden stated. "It's there, and a big part of me believes it's what I deserve after treating you the way that I did. I never should have played with your emotions like that. I'm sorry, sweetheart. I hope you can forgive me."

I couldn't handle this. I needed to lighten the mood because this was not the Holden I wanted to be around.

I sighed, "Well, there's really only one way you can make it up to me."

He didn't hesitate to respond, "Anything you want."

Smiling, I shared, "Once I break out of this joint, you can take me dancing."

Holden let out a huff of laughter and closed his eyes. When he opened them again, he asked, "Can I kiss you?"

I cocked an eyebrow. "You're asking?"

He shrugged. "I screwed up. I'm not going to make any assumptions."

"You had your mouth on mine last night," I reminded him.

"I was trying to save your life."

I lifted my hand to his face and stroked my thumb along his lips. My eyes watched it move until I got to the opposite side, looked in his eyes, and urged, "Kiss me."

Holden wasted no time. He stood, sat on the edge of the bed, and leaned in to kiss me. The moment his lips touched mine, I whimpered. It felt like a fairytale come true having him back. When he pulled back, he said, "Thank you."

"For what?"

"Being gracious enough to forgive me and give me a second chance," he responded.

I grinned and explained, "I love you."

"I love you, too."

Then, he kissed me again.

When he pulled back a second time, I shared, "I have a question."

"Okay."

"How did you know I was even kidnapped?"

He shook his head. "You're not going to believe this."

My brows pulled together.

"Tanya came to the Cunningham Security office. She was frantic."

"Really?" I asked, my shock evident.

Holden nodded. "Yeah, apparently after your class she went to her car and took a phone call. That's when she saw you come out and then Connor taking you. In fact, he put you in his car and drove away with you. Tanya followed him, but ultimately lost you when she got stuck behind someone at a traffic light."

"Wow," I marveled. "Maybe the yoga classes really are helping her."

Holden shrugged. "I told you she's harmless."

"She's not just harmless, Holden. She's the reason you had the chance to save me and that I'm alive right now," I reasoned.

"Yeah," he agreed.

"Are the police going to find Connor?" I asked.

"If they don't, we will," he promised.

"Okay. I don't want to talk about this anymore right now. Will you just climb in this bed and hold me for a little while until a nurse comes in and scolds you?"

Holden laughed.

But then he climbed in the bed, curled me into his arms, and held me. When the nurse came in a few minutes later, she didn't say a word.

Holden gave me a squeeze and pressed a kiss to my forehead.

Then, we fell back asleep for a little while.

CHAPTER 21

Leni

It had been three weeks since Holden saved my life.

Three weeks that I'd had him back.

And it was amazing.

From the moment we left the hospital, Holden had given me everything. Not material things. Just him. Everything that I loved about him was finally, completely mine.

He no longer just gave me bits and pieces of himself when it was convenient for him. It was all of it, all the time.

Admittedly, I was skeptical. But Holden worked hard to prove himself to me.

I talked to him every day. And it wasn't just over the phone. For the first week after I left the hospital, he didn't even go into work. He stayed with me, never once leaving my side.

Physically speaking, I was back to feeling a hundred percent. The first few days after my whole ordeal, I took it easy and didn't do much. Even though I'd been gung-ho about getting my studio all finished up before, now I didn't mind taking my time. Given everything I'd just been through, I decided to give myself a little extra time before going back to work.

The whole incident had taught me that it was okay to take a step back and slow down. I loved movement, and I thoroughly enjoyed what I did, but I didn't always have to be moving. When my body and my mind craved it, I could give it extra. But when my heart wanted time with Holden, it wasn't a problem for me to indulge in that either.

So, I put an announcement up on my website letting students know that I'd be delaying the re-opening of the studio for at least another week.

On the attempted murder front, things had finally settled. Before I left the hospital, I had a visit from the police. They came in to question me about Connor, so that I could give them all the details of what had happened. I shared all that I knew, and they were able to confirm everything with the surveillance footage from the gym. Three days after he tried to kill me, Connor was picked up at a motel in Montana. Apparently, the Windsor Police Department put out an APB on Connor, and a motel manager in Montana who had seen him on the news called the police when he walked through the door looking for a place to spend the night.

And now, it was just a few days before Christmas, and I was finally doing something I'd been wanting to do for months. Since getting out of the hospital, I'd been over to visit my grandmother. I told her about what happened, and she was understandably distraught. I promised her I was okay, and she was relieved to hear that Connor had been caught.

Of course, in all of it, she had to take the time to express her displeasure with my parents as well—my father for his reluctance to meet anyone else's needs but his own, and my mother for standing by my father when she knew he was doing something wrong. I couldn't say I blamed my grandmother.

When the first week following the situation had passed, I had officially realized that things were final between my parents and me. They made absolutely no attempt to reach out and make sure that I was okay. And there was zero chance that they were unaware of what Connor had done. The police had gone to their place of business to confirm what, if any, evidence he'd left behind there as well. So, my parents knew. They just didn't care.

But I was ignoring all of that today. Because I was finally taking Holden with me to visit my grandmother. I wanted her to meet him, and the minute I'd expressed this to Holden, he said, "Whenever you want me to go and meet her, I'll go."

So, I talked to her and explained I wanted her to meet him. At first, she was hesitant. I knew it was because she was secretly still very annoyed with him for breaking my heart. I explained to him at least twice already that I had no doubts she would give him a hard time or do her best to make him feel uncomfortable. It was just her way. But if he survived it, she'd let it go.

I had stayed at Holden's house last night and brought a bag with me. We'd actually been doing that a lot. Ever since we'd reconciled, Holden and I hadn't spent a night apart. I think part of him needed to have me close to him for a while, and since I loved being with him, I never complained.

When he walked back into the bedroom after going downstairs to grab coffee for the both of us, he found me still in his bed. Smiling at me, he set the mugs down on the nightstand and slid under the blankets with me.

He wasted no time in slipping his arms around me and tugging my body toward his. "Missed you," he said with his face buried in my neck.

"You only went downstairs," I noted.

He shrugged. "I still missed you."

I gave him a hug in return.

"Are you planning to spend all day in bed today or are

you going to get up and get ready so I can finally meet your grandma?" Holden asked.

"I'll get up," I assured him. "I just wanted a few extra minutes to cuddle under the blankets with you."

"Just a few?" he asked. "I can do that for you."

Then, Holden did just that by scooting himself even closer to me than he already was. This was him giving me everything. It was about extra cuddles in the morning when I needed them.

A couple hours later, after Holden and I cuddled and had breakfast, we walked through the front door of the assisted living facility.

"Leni!" Pauline greeted me. "You brought someone with you."

"I did," I confirmed. "Pauline, this is my boyfriend, Holden. Holden, meet Pauline."

"It's so lovely to meet you," Pauline gushed as she held out her hand.

Holden smiled, took her hand in his, and replied, "Likewise."

Pauline kept a good grip on Holden's hand as she leaned in and whispered, "Don't let Grandma get to you. She loves her girl here, so she's going to go tough on you to start. Deep down, we all know she's really excited to meet you."

Holden gave her a nod before Pauline let his hand go and buzzed us through the door. We walked down the hall to my grandma's room. Since her door was closed, I tapped on it before cracking it open.

"Come in," she called out.

I walked in ahead of Holden with a huge smile on my face. Grandma took one look at me and returned that smile, but it faded the minute she slid her eyes to the man standing behind me.

I ignored her attempt to be menacing and walked her way. Kissing her on the cheek, I greeted, "Hi, Grandma."

She gave me a squeeze and returned, "Hello, my darling girl."

I stood and held my hand out to Holden. "Grandma, this is Holden. He's the man I've been telling you about for months now."

"Hmm," she grumbled as she assessed him.

"Mrs. Ford," Holden started as he stepped toward her and took her hand in his. After pressing a kiss to the back of her hand, he said, "It's a pleasure to meet you."

"You could have met me a lot sooner," she scolded him.

I bit my lip, worried about how he'd handle it.

Holden took one look at me, regret flashed in his eyes, and he admitted, "I know. I was such a fool to risk losing Leni."

"Well, as long as you know that," she countered.

Just then, my attention was pulled away to the television. The commercials had just ended, and her favorite talk show was back on. Seeing it, I realized my mistake. I should have planned for us to visit her later in the day. Now, I wouldn't be surprised if Holden never wanted to be around her again.

"Grandma, please tell me you aren't going to be watching this today," I pleaded.

"Of course, I am. Why wouldn't I?"

I shifted my eyes to Holden and said, "Because I brought Holden here today to meet you. I thought you two could get to know one another."

"Well, if he really wants to get to know me, I should be myself, shouldn't I?" she challenged. "Besides, they've been showing previews for this one all week. I've been dying to see it."

"But—" I got out before Holden put his hand to the small of my back and cut me off.

"It's okay, sweetheart," he insisted. "We can watch with her if that's what she wants. In fact, my grandmother watches the same one, and I haven't seen it in a long time."

I jerked my head back in surprise as Holden looked at my grandma and asked, "Can I sit with you?"

She gave him an incredulous look but nodded.

I joined the two of them on the couch, Holden sandwiched between the two Ford girls, and wondered if Holden really had watched the show previously with his own grandmother or if he was simply saying it to impress and win mine over.

As the host began speaking, my grandma explained, "This guy has got himself in quite the situation. He and his girlfriend have been together for years and have discussed marriage, but he hasn't yet proposed. Today, he's going to reveal the reason why."

Holden seemed curious and asked, "Do you know what the reason is?"

Grandma nodded and shared, "He's already married."

I gasped as Holden marveled, "Wow, this ought to be interesting."

"And highly entertaining," Grandma chimed in, her excitement palpable.

"And heartbreaking," I added.

Holden glanced at me, threw his arm around me, and curled me into his chest. "I'm not married," he said softly before giving me a kiss on the top of my head.

I pressed my palm to his chest and tried to push away. "I know that. But you can't hold me like this in front of her, Holden. That's not nice," I hissed.

"Why? If she and I are getting to know each other, I should be myself. And I'm a guy who likes to hold you when we watch television."

"We don't ever watch television," I pointed out.

"We do when we visit your grandma," he replied with a grin.

My eyes slid to hers. She had been watching us, but the second I focused my attention on her, she turned away. Then, I couldn't help but notice the small smile tugging at her lips.

I knew she'd like him.

We spent the next hour watching a talk show with my favorite woman. When it finished, she turned off the television and moved to get up.

"Where are you going?" I asked.

"To get your Christmas present," she answered.

"Now?" I replied. "I'm going to come here on Christmas Day to visit you."

She shook her head. "Aren't you and Holden spending the holiday together?" she questioned.

I nodded.

"Okay, well, I assume you'll need to see his family, too. You don't have to worry about coming here that day. It'll be a lot and you won't be able to enjoy the day if you're driving all over town."

She broke my heart. To think that she'd give up seeing me on Christmas simply because she wanted me to thoroughly enjoy the holiday was more than I could bear. My eyes welled with tears.

Holden jumped in and offered, "Why don't Leni and I come by on Christmas morning to pick you up?"

"Pick me up?" she repeated as my body tensed.

Holden nodded and explained, "Yeah. Then, you can come and spend the whole day with Leni, me, and my family."

I looked up at the man who still had his arm wrapped around me and whispered, "Holden."

He glanced down at me and smiled before turning his attention back to my grandma. "What do you think?" he pressed. "Are you up for breaking out of here for a day?"

Her eyes came to mine. "My darling girl, you've got yourself one fine young man, didn't you?"

I grinned and reminded her, "I told you he wasn't just a boy."

"And I told you that until he proved himself, he would always be a boy," she shot back, not missing a beat. Looking to Holden, she accepted his invitation. "I'd very much like to blow this joint for a day and spend it not only with my beautiful granddaughter, but also the people that I hope will be there for her long after I'm gone."

A tear slid down my cheek. "Grandma..." I trailed off.

"Come here," she ordered quietly.

I stood and went to her.

Then, she engulfed me in her arms and whispered in my ear, "He's perfect, Leni. I love him for you, and I hope he always makes you happy."

Knowing Holden had her approval meant the world to me.

"You know what," Holden interrupted us. "Why don't you two ladies do me the honor of allowing me to take you both out for lunch today?"

"Boy, am I glad I had Melissa come over yesterday to set my hair for me. Now, at least there will be a few more people who will get to see it."

I laughed. "It does look fabulous," I noted.

"I'd love a lunch date," she answered Holden. "If you'll just give me a minute to get myself ready, we can go."

"Take your time," Holden insisted.

With that, she turned and moved to her bathroom. Once

she closed the door, I turned around and found Holden standing. I walked back to him, threw my arms around his neck, and kissed him. When I pulled back, I breathed, "I love you so much."

He gave me another kiss before he returned, "I love you, too."

Ten minutes later, we broke my grandma out of the assisted living facility for the afternoon. She had the best time.

I was warm and toasty in my bed, Holden spooning me.

It was Christmas morning.

Holden's hand was dipping dangerously close to the forbidden fruit.

"I know you're awake," he said lazily.

I smiled and pushed my bottom into his lap. He groaned, but that didn't stop him from sending his hand lower.

As I fell to my back, Holden shifted to give me space. I parted my thighs and gave him full access. He wasted no time in slipping his fingers into my panties and right through the wetness.

The minute he slipped a finger inside, I moaned and lifted my hips, seeking more. He'd only just touched me, but I was beyond ready for anything else he had to offer.

Holden's head had been propped up in the hand that wasn't between my legs, but once my breasts were exposed to him, he wasted no time in dropping his mouth to them. He licked and sucked and teased while his hand continued to work me between my legs.

Using the arm that was closest to him, I reached down and

gripped his length in my hand. I gave a firm squeeze before I started stroking him. Holden groaned and broke the suction he had on my breasts.

Moving his mouth up toward mine, he continued to plunge his fingers into me.

"Holden," I panted.

He smiled against my lips and whispered, "I love you, Leni."

It was a good thing I was in bed. I'd been hearing those words frequently from Holden ever since he'd saved my life about a month ago. And every time he said them, I still couldn't believe I was hearing them.

I whimpered and knew the reason for it was because of not only what Holden was doing to my body, but also what he'd done to my heart when he said those words.

"More, babe," I begged.

Holden didn't deny me.

He never did.

Pulling his fingers from my body, he urged, "Roll to your belly, sweetheart."

It took some effort because I was dealing with the loss of his hand between my legs. I finally managed to start moving as Holden reached over to the nightstand for a condom. And by the time I made it to my belly, I started to push up onto my hands and knees.

"No," he said.

My body froze. "No?" I repeated.

"Stay on your belly," he insisted.

I slid back down until I was lying flat on the bed. Then, I felt Holden's knees press into the bed on either side of my legs. A hand went to the bed at my side while the fingertips of the other traced gently down the skin of my back.

Holden's fingers made it to my lower back, but they didn't stop there. They moved down over the curve of my ass where he squeezed one cheek and then the other. When his hand moved to my hip and lifted it just a touch, he shifted his body forward and slid right into me.

I moaned at the sensation. "Holden," I cried, arching my back.

The moment I did that, Holden growled and went deeper. Initially, he moved slow, draping his torso over my back and kissing my shoulders. But each thrust of his hips into my backside sent me over the moon.

It was utter bliss.

My legs were pressed tight together, making the intrusion of his cock all the more delightful. Holden shoved a hand between my body and the mattress and slipped it down until he found my clit. I arched my back a bit more, sending my ass back into Holden.

He pulled his torso back, brought his free hand to my hip, and picked up his pace. Thrusting relentlessly while he continued to work my clit, Holden had me struggling to catch my breath.

"Babe," I gasped, feeling myself on the verge.

"Are you close, Leni?" he grunted.

"Yes, Holden. Please. Come with me," I begged.

A few thrusts later, we both cried out and came together. It was beautiful.

Holden collapsed on my body but kept the weight in his legs and his arms so he wouldn't crush me. He pressed a few gentle kisses to the heated skin on my shoulder before he said, "I'll be right back."

"Okay," I sighed, feeling happy and sated.

Then, I felt the loss of him between my legs as he pulled out and moved to the bathroom.

"Merry Christmas, sweetheart," Holden whispered when he returned to the bedroom.

"Merry Christmas," I returned. "Is it time for presents?"

He laughed as he fell to his back. "We can do presents," he agreed. "Let me give you one of yours first."

I perked up at the mention of more than one present and said, "Works for me."

Holden pulled on a pair of sweats as I watched. After, he grinned at me and pointed across the room. My eyes shifted away from him to the opposite side of the room. There was a big red bow on a piece of furniture I hadn't seen before in Holden's bedroom.

I sat up in the bed, looked back at Holden, and asked, "What is that?"

Confusion washed over his face. "You don't know?"

"It looks like some kind of fancy chair," I replied.

His brows pulled together as he hit me with the oddest response. "But you do yoga."

I cocked an eyebrow in question because that didn't tell me anything. "What does yoga have to do with anything?" I wondered looking back at the chair.

It looked like a rather luxurious chaise that curved like the letter 'S' tipped over. I stood and walked over to it. Then, I took a seat. It was even more comfortable than it looked, and the fabric was super soft.

When I looked up at Holden, he looked completely confused. "What?"

"This isn't a special yoga chair?" he asked.

I raised my brows and shook my head. "No."

"That's what it was labeled as," he insisted. "I saw it and realized you didn't have one at your house or the studio. I thought it was something you'd like."

"I do like it," I assured him. "But it doesn't have anything to do with yoga."

"Are you sure?"

I let out a laugh. "I've been doing this for quite a few years, Holden. I'm sure. Did it come with any paperwork?"

He shrugged. "I never looked at anything else in the box. Hang on."

I watched as Holden left the room. He was clearly upset about this, and I didn't think there was any reason to be. It was a gorgeous piece and it was super comfortable. I loved it.

Holden returned a few minutes later and had a look of horror on his face.

"What's wrong?" I asked, my body tensing as I swung my legs to the side and stood up to walk toward him.

He instantly curled his arm around my naked body, pulling me to his side. "Leni, sweetheart, I swear to you this was marketed as a yoga chair. I thought it was something new and different."

"Okay. I believe you. Why do you look so upset? I really love it," I assured him again.

He closed his eyes and held them shut tight as he took in a deep breath. When he opened them up and looked at me, he admitted, "It's a sex chair."

My eyes widened. "What?!"

"I swear I had no idea," he insisted. "I promise you."

I burst out laughing, burying my face in his chest. My body shook with the force of my laughter. When I managed to get it under control, I asked, "Are you serious?"

Still looking horrified, he held up a booklet and said, "There's a whole book filled with positions you can try."

I snatched the book out of his hands and started flipping through it. "Wow," I marveled as I walked back toward the chair. "This is amazing."

Draping my still naked body over it, resting on my front, I said, "I think this one looks fun."

"Leni?" Holden called my name, snapping me out of it.

I dropped the booklet from in front of my face. "Yeah?"

"You're not upset about it?"

My poor guy. He looked completely terrified. "No, Holden, I'm not. I liked it before we even knew what it was really designed for. Now, I love it even more."

Moving toward me slowly, he confirmed, "You're sure? I feel awful."

"Don't. This is great for the both of us. Look," I said, holding up the pamphlet. "Some of these positions are supposed to increase the intensity of my orgasm. Why would I be mad about that?"

Holden gave me a squeeze and mumbled, "I'm glad I have another gift for you. I can't believe I did this."

"Stop," I ordered, leaning toward him. After pressing a kiss to his lips, I promised, "I love this, Holden. And I can't wait for us to use it."

"Can I give you your other gift?" he asked.

I shook my head. "Not until I give you yours."

He sighed. "Fine."

"Kiss me first," I demanded.

Holden kissed me.

It lasted a long time. When we separated, I asked, "Feeling better?"

He gave me a nod and a smile.

"Okay, my turn," I declared. I walked over to the bed and pulled an envelope out of the nightstand beside it. Once I handed it to him, he did not hesitate to tear into it. I loved that his enthusiasm matched my own. Inside was a heartfelt Christmas card that had a smaller envelope inside of it. After he read the card and expressed how much the words moved him by kissing me again, he picked up the smaller envelope and opened it. Inside was a small card, about the size of a postcard, that was a voucher for a year of dance lessons.

His eyes came to mine.

"It says these are for me and a partner," he noted. "Are you going as my dance partner?"

"If you want me to be," I replied. "And I'll just say that I really hope that's what you want."

He smiled, and I instantly knew just how much he liked the gift. Given that I really didn't have the opportunity to talk to him about his dancing when I first learned how good he was at it, I asked, "Why do you hide the fact that you enjoy dancing?"

He shrugged. "I wouldn't say I hide it," he debated.

"Tyson and Pierce were shocked to find out that not only do you do it, but that you also do it well," I pointed out. "I just don't understand why you wouldn't say anything about it. You aren't embarrassed by it, are you?"

He shook his head. "Not at all. It's just not the kind of thing that comes up when I'm at work. And, quite frankly, I really haven't done it much in the last ten years or so. It was something special I had with Eva. I guess I had gotten to a point there, probably in my early twenties, when I would have been embarrassed if the guys knew. But it doesn't bother me now. I like what I like, and I do what makes me happy."

"I love that you love it," I assured him. "The first time I saw you dance, I was mesmerized. I'd never seen you look like that before. So happy and carefree. And when you took me out on the dancefloor with you, I remember feeling exactly the way you looked. I want to have that between us. Plus, I figured that by getting you the year, you'd have to stick around for at least that long."

His features softened. He promised, "I'm not going anywhere."

I didn't reply. I simply leaned forward and kissed him.

When our mouths parted, he declared, "Alright, the second part of your gift should at least give you an indication that I'm serious and have no plans to go anywhere."

"Okay?"

"I want us to move in together, Leni," he started. "I don't know if you're attached to your house, but if you're not, I thought we could move into my place for the short-term. When we're ready to take the next step, we can get a new place."

"Do you not like my place?" I asked.

"I do. Honestly, it really wouldn't matter to me if we stayed at your place. But since mine has the extra space, I thought it would be better."

"Why? Do you think that if we live together you'll suddenly realize I'm crazy and you'll need to sneak off to your finished basement or guest bedroom to get away from me?" I teased.

He shook his head and got serious. "Not at all. But I think the extra space would be nice for your grandmother."

"What?" I gasped.

"Leni, sweetheart, you love her. And it's clear you're the light of her life. Why would you want to limit yourselves to a visit with one another to a couple hours a few days out of the month. That woman has so much to offer the world, and she's stuck there."

"You... you would... you want me and my grandmother to move into your house?"

"Yeah. If that's what you want."

I knew it. I knew long before I ever shared it with him that

Holden was a special man. I already thanked my lucky stars every day that we managed to work through our differences. Because not having a man like Holden in my life would have been an absolute shame.

Overcome with emotion, I launched myself into his arms and burst into tears. "You are the best man I've ever met," I cried.

Holden kept his arms around me and just gave me a gentle squeeze in response. He held me a long time until I finally got myself together.

When I did, he asked, "Is that a yes?"

"Yes. Of course, it's a yes."

He grinned. "Good. How about we get moving this morning so we can go pick her up and give her the news?"

"I love you, Holden."

"Not as much as I love you, Leni."

I decided not to fight him on it. I figured I'd just have to find other ways to prove how much he meant to me.

So, I leaned in, gave him another kiss, and promised him many rewards for later that evening.

Then, we got ourselves ready and went to get my grandma.

And that night, Holden and I celebrated the end of our first Christmas together by breaking in my gift. It had been the best Christmas I'd had in a really long time.

EPILOGUE

Holden
8 Months Later

"WHERE IS SHE?"

I looked down at Leni's grandmother and waited for an answer to my question.

"I want to see it first," she demanded.

I let out a laugh. I should have known she'd figure it out and demand to see it. It wasn't like she hadn't warned me when I asked her about this a few months ago.

My legs moved and carried me the few feet from where I was standing in the doorway to the living room to where Audrey was sitting on the couch watching her favorite show.

I slipped my hand into my pocket, pulled out the velvet-covered box, and handed it over to her.

There was no stopping the smile that spread across her face. She took the box, opened it up, and gave me a nod of approval.

"It's perfect for her," she declared.

"Thank you," I returned. "And thank you for giving me your approval to do this. You mean the world to her, and I think she'll appreciate the fact that I came to you first to ask."

Audrey handed the box back to me, but her face grew somber.

"It devastated me when my son turned his back on his daughter," she began. "She's my only grandchild, and I love her more than I could ever tell you. When her parents took a stand to no longer be in her life, I made it my responsibility to always be there for her. Of course, I would have always been there for her regardless. But the fact that she had nobody else troubled me. I'm honored to welcome you to the family, and I can breathe a sigh of relief that she's going to have someone here who loves her at least as much as I do long after I'm gone."

"You've got a lot of years left in you," I assured her.

She huffed. "I know that. But I was still worried about Leni. I didn't want to leave this Earth without knowing she was going to be taken care of. I know she can handle herself, but I don't want her to be alone. You're taking on a huge responsibility, Holden. I expect you'll give her the world."

"Without a doubt," I promised.

Audrey held my eyes for several long moments. Finally, she said, "She's out in the pool."

I gave her a dip of my chin and stood.

"Good luck," she wished as I walked toward the French doors that led out to the deck of our home.

Leni and I started looking for places a few months ago. When we found this one and I saw the look on her face, I knew it was the one for us. We moved ourselves and her grandmother from my townhouse to our home only a month ago.

But it had been the best month of my life.

And I was grateful that I finally figured out how to get out of my own way. Because Leni made my life so much better. I often recalled the words she said to me about my father when things were turning sour between us.

I bet it was the love of a good woman who helped heal him.

That's precisely what it had been for me.

Her love.

I'd never known anyone like her, and that's precisely why I was now doing this. I wanted to make this official between us.

Surprisingly, despite my bad experience with an engagement before, I had no concerns about doing this with Leni. I knew she was the one for me. What I felt for her was unlike anything I ever felt for anyone else.

I made it to the doors, looked back at Audrey, and said, "Thanks."

Then, I walked outside onto the deck.

I stood there for a brief moment looking out at Leni in the pool. After her ordeal with her former co-worker trying to drown her, I worried how she'd handle being in a pool again. Thankfully, she didn't seem to have any lingering anxiety about it because she'd been swimming in our pool every day since we moved.

As I walked down the steps and toward the woman of my dreams, I watched her swim to the edge of the pool. She pressed her palms flat to the edge of it and hoisted herself up; however, she didn't exit the pool as I expected.

Instead, the next thing I knew, she was upside down right on the edge of the pool. She held the posture for a few moments before her legs began to move slowly. I watched in awe as she created multiple shapes with her gorgeous body.

Never.

I'd never get tired of watching her move.

And the control she had over her body was beyond impressive.

Leni lowered her feet down, essentially folding her body in half, but held her feet just a few inches off the ground. The strength and flexibility she had always amazed me. When she finally put her feet on the ground, she still hadn't noticed me.

She moved her arms and legs around, almost as though she were dancing in slow motion. And not even a minute later, she folded herself in half again, put her palms on the ground, and pressed up into another handstand. This time, she took her legs out wide before pulling her feet together above her head. She stayed like that for a few moments before lowering herself back down and into the pool.

Fuck.

I loved her.

I could watch her do this all day, every day.

And I'd never tire of it.

Leni resurfaced, pushed her hair back, and wiped the water from her face. That's when she finally noticed me.

Her face lit up, and that one look pierced me right through the heart. I don't know how I ever thought I could live without her. I had been a fool.

A lucky one considering she allowed me back into her life.

But a fool, nonetheless.

"Hey, you," she greeted me.

"Hey sweetheart," I returned, smiling down at her. "Are you planning to swim for a while yet?"

She shook her head.

"No, I just wanted to get some time in the water today," she began as she came to the edge of the pool again. "I figured the best time to do it would be when my grandma was watching her ridiculous show."

Leni lifted herself out of the water and walked over to me. Then, she gave me a kiss. When she pulled back, I decided not to wait.

"I love you," I blurted.

Beaming at me, she returned, "I love you, too."

"I want to spend the rest of my life with you, Leni."

Instantly, her body froze. "What?" she rasped.

Keeping one of my hands on hers, I reached the other one into my pocket before I dropped down to one knee.

"I love you more than I know what to do with," I started. "And I want to make things official between us, sweetheart. Will you marry me?"

Tears fell from her eyes as she bobbed her head up and down. "Yes, Holden. I'll marry you."

I took the ring from the box, slid it on her finger, and stood. Still wet from her swim, Leni jumped into my arms and wrapped her legs around my waist.

"I love you so much," she cried, nuzzling her face in my neck.

I held her tight and stroked my hand up and down her back. "Kiss me," I urged her.

Leni kissed my neck before she lifted her head and brought her mouth to mine. After we kissed a long time, we managed to tear ourselves away from one another.

"Thank you," I whispered.

Tipping her head to the side, she asked, "For what?"

After a moment of hesitation, I answered, "For proving to me that it was okay to surrender to what I felt for you. For being the woman that you are and showing me that you'll always protect my heart."

More tears fell from her eyes.

"I promise I'll protect yours just the same, Leni."

She held my eyes briefly before sliding her arms tight around my shoulders and burying her face in my neck again.

"You are the best thing that's ever happened to me," I shared.

"I feel the same way about you," she rasped.

I gave her a squeeze and simply held her while she pulled herself together. When she did, she asked, "Can we celebrate?"

"I planned on it. What did you have in mind?"

She swallowed hard, looked up at the house, and back at me. "I want to tell my grandma first. Then, I want to go out dancing with you."

"Anything you want, sweetheart."

"That's what I want," she confirmed.

With that, I gave her another kiss before I turned and carried her to the house. Once we got there, she went in and told her grandmother the good news. Then, we got ready to go out dancing.

And after I made love to her that night and had her beautiful body tucked tight to mine, I didn't immediately fall asleep. I took a moment to think about the woman I was holding in my arms. Leni changed my life in a way I never dreamed was possible. For that, I owed her a debt of gratitude. I'd spend the rest of my life working to make sure she never felt that it was a mistake to surrender to her heart and fall in love with me.

Need more Holden and Leni? I've written a bonus epilogue for their story. You can download your FREE copy here.

www.authorakevans.com/surrender-bonus-scene

ACKNOWLEDGEMENTS

To my husband, Jeff—Surrendering my heart to you was the best decision I ever made. Thank you for never making me regret it. I love you.

To my boys, J&J—You are always exactly where you are meant to be in your life. No matter what obstacles you face or where your heart takes you, Daddy and I will always be there to support you through it. I love you.

To my loyal readers—Thank you never seems like enough. I'm not sure I'll ever have the words to tell you just how much it means to me that you continue to read my stories. I love each and every one of you.

To S.H., S.B., & E.M.—You're like the dream team. I'm grateful for all three of you. Thank you, thank you, thank you.

To the bloggers—Thank you for all that you do. You don't get nearly enough credit for what you do to help authors get their books into the hands of readers. I appreciate you all so much.

CONNECT WITH A.K. EVANS

To stay connected with A.K. Evans and receive all the first looks at upcoming releases, latest news, or to simply follow along on her journey, be sure to add or follow her on social media. You can also get the scoop by signing up for the monthly newsletter, which includes a giveaway every month.

Newsletter: http://eepurl.com/dmeo6z

Website: www.authorakevans.com

Facebook: www.facebook.com/authorAKEvans

Facebook Reader Group: www.facebook.com/groups/1285069088272037

Instagram: www.instagram.com/authorakevans

Twitter: twitter.com/AuthorAKEvans

Goodreads Author Page: www.goodreads.com/user/show/64525877-a-k-evans

Subscribe on YouTube: http://bit.ly2w01yb7

Twitter: twitter.com/AuthorAKEvans

OTHER BOOKS BY A.K. EVANS

The Everything Series
Everything I Need
Everything I Have
Everything I Want
Everything I Love

The Cunningham Security Series

Obsessed
Overcome
Desperate
Solitude
Burned
Unworthy
Surrender
Betrayed (Coming February 11, 2020)
Revived (Coming June 16, 2020)

Road Trip Romance

Tip the Scales
Play the Part (Coming December 10, 2019)
One Wrong Turn (Coming early 2020)

ABOUT A.K. EVANS

A.K. Evans is a married mother of two boys residing in a small town in northeastern Pennsylvania, where she graduated from Lafayette College in 2004 with two degrees (one in English and one in Economics & Business). Following a brief stint in the insurance and financial services industry, Evans realized the career was not for her and went on to manage her husband's performance automotive business. She even drove the shop's race cars! Looking for more personal fulfillment after eleven years in the automotive industry, Andrea decided to pursue her dream of becoming a writer.

While Andrea continues to help administratively with her husband's businesses, she spends most of her time writing and homeschooling her two boys. When she finds scraps of spare time, Evans enjoys reading, doing yoga, watching NY Rangers hockey, dancing, and vacationing with her family. Andrea, her husband, and her children are currently working on taking road trips to visit all 50 states (though, Alaska and Hawaii might require flights).